Seasons of Fate

Seasons of Fate

A NOVEL

ANITA GILBERT

© 2023 Anita Gilbert

Published by Columbia Road Management, LLC
All rights reserved.

ISBN   PAPERBACK 979-8-9880494-0-1
       EBOOK 979-8-9880494-1-8

*This book is dedicated to my favorite person in the world.
To the final love of my life.
To my inspiration…
This book is dedicated to my son, Tayon.
I love you more…*

And to my sisters (shishies): Sancha, Carla, and Shannon.

"If we had not winter, the spring would not be so pleasant; if we did not sometimes taste of adversity, prosperity would not be so welcome."

—ANNE BRADSTREET

WINTER – 2014

Lake Como, Italy

Naya

17 Years Old

It was the time of night when it seemed the whole world was asleep. The Christmas lights on the window outside sparkled and the snow disappeared as it fell from the sky and met the water on the lake. Naya pulled the purple blanket with pink stripes up under her chin. It was her mom's, and she took it everywhere with her, just as her mom had when she was younger. Naya strained to read the words on the last page of the book with just the light of the fire in the living room. Everyone went to sleep hours earlier and her Aunt Zoey had turned off the light in the kitchen, thinking Naya was asleep. The house was so quiet that she could hear the flames as they moved and crackled in the small brick fireplace. Fire always reminded her of that day—the day her parents died.

Naya could also hear the light snores of her cousin, Taye, as he slept at the other end of the couch. His cold feet touched the back of her knee as he flipped over slowly. He insisted on sleeping with her no matter what. They didn't see each other often but she loved him. He was more than a cousin to her in so many ways. She watched him, amazed at how hard he slept, but then realized that he hadn't yet gone through the loss that she had. There was nothing to keep him up at night. Taye was five years old. He looked just like her and she imagined him as an adult. He would be handsome and tall like his dad… like her dad. Naya hoped that Taye would have an easier life than she did. She hoped he would have an easier life than his mom and dad. She smiled thinking about how she got there, sleeping on a small couch in the house in Italy that she called home. As she watched her cousin's eyes flicker softly in his sleep, she was thankful for the family that fate had brought her to be with on this Christmas night. The house was full of people that loved her. She was the luckiest, unlucky girl alive. She probably shouldn't even be alive if she was honest with herself. As she looked at Taye, with his innocent face glowing in the firelight and curly dark hair messy from sleep, Naya wondered if she had ever slept that peacefully in her 17 years of life.

Finally, she closed the book and turned it over to look at the picture of her dad on the back. With the words on the pages in her dad's book, every question she had was answered and she understood why they had waited so long to let her read it. In his book, Matt had tried to make sense of every single loss, but sometimes, he concluded, loss just isn't fair. That was something they could agree on. They also agreed on the fact that sometimes, with unexpected loss comes unexpected love. And though she had many questions throughout her young but challenging life, one question she never had was if she believed in fate.

CHAPTER 1

FALL – 1996

Zoey

The hair on my arms stood as I pedaled my blue and white 10-speed bike down the quiet country road in Idaho toward home. It was Sunday night and the chill in the air reminded me that summer had officially come to an end. I was probably one mile from the horse farm off Columbia Road that I grew up in along with my sisters, parents, and countless thoroughbred racehorses. We also had a dog, Mia, who would be standing at the end of the dirt lane waiting to greet me.

I wouldn't know it then, but this Sunday night was the last of my bike rides with my high school sweetheart, Matt. The summer before our junior year was also the last few months of either of our childhoods. We had no idea that the next few months would require us to each long for our peaceful summer bike rides, where all we had to worry about were the mosquitos and getting home before dark. On that crisp September night, little did we know that, soon, there would be so much more to worry about.

The summer of 1996, Matt and I met a few times a week at the end of my lane and would pedal for hours on the quiet country roads. Some nights, he would bring his CD player and we would take turns listening to his favorite album, *The Score* by The Fugees, as we rode, stopping as it skipped at almost every turn. Occasionally, we would pedal to the small theater in town and watch a movie. We would stop at Super C Corner Store and lock our bikes up and I would shove a box of Junior Mints in my bra before we walked the two blocks to the theater. Matt's best friend worked there and laughed at us when we passed him, trying not to look guilty as we smuggled in the treats.

On this night, Matt didn't pedal home with me to my dirt lane on Columbia Road. Tonight, Matt couldn't stay out late as his mother told him he had to get home. As I pedaled slowly, I thought of how much he had changed. He had just gotten back from a two-week trip to Italy with his family and it seemed like I was the last thing on his mind since the day he returned. I thought of how distant he was becoming, and I wondered if my first love was even real. I felt a lump in my throat and my stomach sank every time I was around him. When I watched music videos with my sisters on Saturday nights, I thought of him. Every song and movie made me think of him. He had been my boyfriend since 8th grade when he moved to my small middle school from another town. We had spent three summers riding our bikes together on the country roads, racing against the sunset, and more often than not, sneaking past our parents because we lost the race.

I pulled up to my mailbox and Mia slowly stood from where she laid in the middle of the dirt lane. The moon was bright, and I could see the expression on her face as if she was reminding me that I was late. I looked at her and wondered what her voice would sound like if she could talk. I smiled and got off my bike. She turned and led the way, and we walked the quarter of a mile home as the stars began to peak into the sky. My mind was racing. I looked up and saw a shooting star and took a deep breath.

I laid my bike on the grass and pet Mia on the top of her head. The soft sound of Tracy Chapman's guitar seeped through the screen door from the CD player in the kitchen. The melodic sound of the water fountain on the front porch sounded like a part of her song. My mom's laughter filled the air as I passed her and my dad, each drinking a glass of wine on the front patio. After all these years, they were still in love. I smiled and my dad nodded at me and smiled back. Mia ran over to my mom, stretched, and rolled over on her back. As my mom looked down, I rushed past them to the front door. I didn't want to talk. Luckily, my twin sister, Jasmine, had her headphones on and was laying on her bed when I opened the door to our bedroom. Her eyes were closed, and I could hear the music seeping through her headset. When I shut the door, she opened her eyes and looked at me. She could tell I didn't want to talk and nodded her head and rolled over. Mia scratched on the other side of the door, so I opened it to let her in. She climbed into my bed as I plopped down on my back, staring at the pictures of Matt and I taped to my walls.

The next day, I woke up and it was the beginning of the second week of my junior year at Kuna High School. Jasmine finally emerged from the bathroom we shared, giving me just enough time to strive for a record in getting ready for school. Steam filled the hallway as she whisked past me with a towel wrapped on her head. She opened her eyes wide at me and crossed them just as she passed. Our birthday was two weeks away. I was seven minutes older than Jasmine and she was the type of twin sister to call me her "older" sister when we would finally reach the age that we were not so proud to admit we had reached.

Jasmine was pretty with blonde hair that fell to the middle of her back. She had striking green eyes just like our mom and had the face shape of my dad with high cheekbones and long, lean legs that seemed to be tanned all year long for some reason I could never figure out. She was a straight-A student who tried harder than anyone knew. To those watching, Jasmine was effortlessly perfect, but I knew how hard she worked. The older we got, the more we needed each other. This year was the year I would slowly begin to realize this fact. Before the fall of 1996, everything felt so easy. It was then that everything changed.

"Zoey, you should really try to look a little less like a 10-year-old boy." Jasmine lingered just outside the bathroom to watch me secure my daily ponytail. She was twisting her neck and shaking her head while she looked me up and down with a smile. I had washed my face clean and couldn't recall the last time I wore makeup. I caught a glimpse of her in the mirror and pulled open the top drawer, looking for her mascara. She was right. I should do what I could to look more like her and less like our 10-year-old neighbor, Jimmy, who peed his pants well into elementary school. I had natural beauty but nothing on the level of either of my sisters.

My older sister, Erin, was also pretty much flawless with thick lips and porcelain skin. Erin and her best friend, Sophie, had breezed through Kuna High School years earlier, leaving behind many broken hearts and a legacy neither Jasmine nor myself ever attempted to live up to. Erin and Sophie left out of our small town the first chance they got and were sophomores at Arizona State University. Erin was the most sophisticated person I had ever met, and Sophie was like another sister for all three of us. It was almost as if Erin had found her twin in Sophie. All those facts never really changed the older we got.

I often couldn't help but think I got the short end of the stick. That day, if the freckled face looking back at me in the mirror with the tight ponytail and light green eyes could talk, she would have said to knock it off and be happy with who she was. It took me years to listen to that voice.

"Matt is never going to want to touch your boobs if you look like Leonardo DiCaprio in *What's Eating Gilbert Grape*." She was laughing at herself and winked at me while I struggled to tighten my hair. I tried to hide my smile as I opened her mascara. My favorite movie and my favorite actor had been used against me by my own twin sister. Jasmine wasn't just a pretty face.

"We are juniors now and I know you have more in your closet than this old Oregon Track Hoodie."

"Yes. I do have more clothes in my closet. I just choose comfort over style." I looked at myself closely in the mirror. I was no Jasmine or Erin, but I was no Arnie Grape. I might not have been the prettiest sister, but I surely wasn't ugly. I was tall with straight teeth. I had my mom's green eyes like Jasmine, but they weren't the same color of green that stopped someone on the street like hers were. I had avoided pimples my entire teenage life but didn't have the porcelain skin that Erin had. I did have the cutest boyfriend in the school, so I didn't really feel a need to change how I looked. But Jasmine was right… a little mascara wouldn't hurt.

"Alright, Tyra Banks. Do you need me to twirl for you now or after I put my boring black leggings on?" I said as I blinked rapidly, trying to adjust to my mascara-clad eyelashes. *Weightless, my ass.*

Jasmine smiled at me. She knew she at least had competition in who was the funny twin. She turned swiftly, making sure her long hair hit me in the face, and laughed as she walked down the hall to the bedroom we shared. "Leaving in 10, dummy!" she yelled just before she slammed the door closed. I immediately heard Jasmine singing "Creep" by TLC at the top of her lungs behind the closed door. I smiled as I listened to my sister sing. She and I had a relationship that I couldn't explain to others. We were best friends, mortal enemies, each other's biggest competition, and each other's loudest cheerleaders all at the same time. Our relationship was so simple that it was complicated. It took me years to realize what both of my sisters meant to me, but I knew even then that I could never put it into words.

Jasmine and I pulled up to Kuna High School in our shared 1980 Audi that had been my mom's car for as long as I could recall. Jasmine slammed the passenger side door, said, "Bye, bitch!" and left me alone in the driver seat. I watched as she sauntered away from me through the parking lot and onto the sidewalk in front of the school. She was looking down and didn't realize everyone she passed turned their heads in awe. Beautiful Jasmine Jordan had arrived at Kuna High School. I shook my head and smiled as she held the front door of our school open for the only kid I had ever known in a wheelchair. His name was Kevin, and for as long as I could remember, Kevin couldn't walk. She nodded at him and waved her arm into the open door as though she was urging him to enter Disneyland instead of his high school where I was sure he was picked on every day. Her eyes lingered on Kevin for just a moment as he wheeled himself through the door. He turned back and she smiled as if to say she was sorry for appearing perfect to the boy who couldn't walk. Kevin turned his head and smiled back. I wondered if this was the best part of Kevin's day as I watched them from across the parking lot. The pair disappeared into the school.

I turned and could see Matt pulling his backpack from the backseat of his blue Jeep Cherokee just a few feet away. The radio station was playing the beginning of my favorite song, "Candy Rain" by Soul for Real. I listened as the song asked if I had ever loved someone so much that I thought I might die.

Yes, I do love someone that much, I thought as I watched Matt catch a glimpse of me in my car, staring at him. He smiled slightly but looked sad or mad… or a combination of both. I had been meaning to ask him what was wrong lately. I felt an uneasy drop in my stomach as I watched the boy I loved from the driver side seat. His eyes were heavy, and he looked like he had just woken up from a restless sleep. My heart felt the first pangs of true love that summer, but today, I was living the lyrics of the song playing on the radio. I was worried. Something was wrong. High school was hard—it wasn't the actual schoolwork that was hard, but pretty much everything else. Matt made his way to my car, opened the passenger side door, and sat down.

"Hi," I said quietly, wishing he would touch my hand or kiss me on the cheek like he had just a few weeks ago. Whitney Houston's voice singing "Exhale (Shoop Shoop)" from the *Waiting to Exhale Soundtrack* took over the radio as I leaned in to turn the volume down.

Whitney was right that when words are unspoken, hearts get broken. I wondered if Jasmine was also right. Why would Matt want to be with someone like me who wore a ponytail every day and the same black leggings to school? He could have anyone he wanted and maybe he had finally realized it.

"Hi. Listen, Zoey…" he trailed off and his eyes darted to watch a football fly through the parking lot from one meathead wearing a football jersey to another. The meatheads had stopped their game of pass just a few minutes earlier to watch Jasmine walk across the parking lot like a bunch of dogs in heat. It didn't seem possible that these kids were the same age as Matt. He seemed years older than the two boys that were now wrestling in the parking lot over a ball. One of them stood up quickly and flipped his long brown hair out of his eyes. He saw us in the car and immediately made a kissing sound in our direction. Matt nodded at him and smiled. The boy was suddenly thrust forward and tackled from behind, his long hair whipping through the air. Matt lowered and shook his head. I thought I saw a small smile. Nothing like some dumb jocks to lighten the mood.

"Zoey. On my trip, there was a lot… I should have told you right away, but I didn't really know what to say or how I felt yet."

Whitney's angelic voice rose.

Here it comes…

Maybe he wasn't going to be my last first kiss. Maybe Matt would move away to a big cosmopolitan city without me. He would drive home from college with another girl and someone else would kiss him on his cheek each morning before work. Maybe I wasn't going to see him sip coffee while I packed our kids' lunches after all. He still had time to find a different high school sweetheart. He surely realized he shouldn't be wasting his time with me. I took in a deep breath and clasped my hands together in my lap. There was no use making them available for him to hold. Whitney's voice made me think of the last movie we watched alone in his basement, *The Bodyguard*, which also happened to be the movie we watched on our first date a few years earlier. My dad dropped us off at the movie theater in the middle of the day. We were in 8th grade and had to sneak into the movie because we failed to realize it was rated R. That was the day I had my first kiss. As we watched the movie for the second time together just a few weeks earlier in his basement, he had his arm around my shoulders and was holding my hand. His long thumb was rubbing my skin softly. It was a feeling I loved that sent chills up my arms and brought back those flutters in my stomach I had become used to.

In my car, as I looked down at my hands clasped together, I felt like I was losing him. Everything had changed after his trip. I listened closer to the words in the song on the radio—maybe this was the point when I would exhale. I let out a deep breath and waited. Maybe these flutters in my stomach were preparing me for this. I had felt them all summer, so I had to be ready for this, right? He was going to break up with me. Matt looked deep into my eyes.

"My mom has cancer, Zoey. She has breast cancer. She is going to die." Tears started to stream down his face once the words spilled out of his mouth. His green eyes were glassy and the boy who seemed to have it all together was now crumpled up in the passenger seat of my mom's 1980 Audi, sobbing. I had just seen her right before the trip to Italy and she seemed fine. They were a perfect family with two perfect kids, and they couldn't be losing their matriarch. It all happened too fast.

Suddenly, nothing else mattered. Hearing Matt stumble through those words that day was the first time of many times in my life I realized that, in an instant, it can all be gone. The people you love can be taken away in the blink of an eye. Matt started to gasp for air and the tears were now furiously coming down his cheeks. I couldn't think of what to say. Selfishly, I was relieved to hear his news was not a breakup, but this… this was devastating. He wasn't going to break my heart that day. He was dealing with his own broken heart, and I had no idea what to do or say.

As Matt sobbed in the passenger seat, I envisioned my own mom and how she lost her mother at the age of 17—the age Matt would be in just a few months. It changed my mom forever when her mother died. The night before Valentine's Day, the year my mom turned 17, my grandmother kissed her children goodnight for the last time. In a large brick house in a suburb outside of Philadelphia, my grandmother said her last, "I love you," to my mom. She retreated to her room with my grandfather, went to sleep, and never woke up. She was 42 years old and died immediately of a heart attack in the middle of the night. Needless to say, my parents do not celebrate Valentine's Day.

I looked at Matt and suddenly saw my 10-year-old neighbor, Jimmy—the kid who peed his pants in school. He was a mess and needed me to say something and comfort him. The trip to Italy had changed Matt. I wasn't losing him, he was losing himself, and what felt like his childhood. I felt a sense of guilt wave over my body as I sat there watching him cry. I had been obsessing over his changed behavior and he was dealing with this without me.

Matt and I sat in my car in the parking lot until the lunch bell rang. We never missed class, but today, nothing mattered. I never figured out the right words to say but realized he didn't need my words; he just needed my company. Matt needed time to sort out his thoughts—in my car in the Kuna High School parking lot on the second Monday of our junior year. I took that time to sort out my own thoughts too as we sat in silence. I really did love this boy. I didn't want to lose him when we graduated from this shitty school and finally stepped outside of the town. I knew I loved him, although we had never said those words to each other. I had never said those words to anyone besides my parents and my sisters. I felt something for him that terrified me and gave me butterflies and hope all at once.

I thought about my relationship with Jasmine during those hours of silence. Of how we depended on each other and how I felt the same way about Matt as I felt about her—that I couldn't live without either of them. That was the terrifying part because there was a chance I would have to live without Matt, or my sisters, or my mom and dad one day. After hours of silence, Matt reached into his backpack that was stuffed between his large high-top Jordans. He pulled out a crumpled sheet of paper and handed it to me.

"Zoey, I love you. I am sorry I have been distant. In whatever capacity, I want you in my life." Matt put his hand on my cheek and then around the back of my neck and pulled me close to him. His other hand was gripping my thigh hard. I realized I was grasping the crumpled sheet of paper so hard that my hand started to throb. I relaxed and released the paper that fell to the ground below the steering wheel and clasped my hands around him. I melted into his kiss for what felt like hours but was only a few minutes. I felt his hot tears on his cheeks as we kissed. I never wanted to leave that car. It was a kiss full of passion I hadn't felt yet in my young life. My heart dropped when he pulled his lips away from mine. I looked down at the paper as he opened the car door and walked away across the small parking lot of our high school without another word. He swung open the same doors Jasmine and Kevin had entered earlier and disappeared into a blur of students. As the doors closed behind him, I opened the paper and began to read.

Matt's mom died two months later. She left behind Matt, his little brother, Brandon, their golden retriever, Bandit, and his heartbroken dad, Dan. I spent most of those two months trying to comfort him and watching him grow further and further into maturity away from the childish kids at our school. He stopped laughing at the meatheads when they tried to joke with him. Life wasn't a joke anymore when your mom was dying of cancer. I couldn't help but feel it was a matter of time before he would outgrow me. I would stay in Matt's life, but it would be in a way that I had never imagined.

Matt's mother's funeral was on a cloudy Tuesday in November at the only non-denominational church in our town. The leaves had all fallen from the trees and we were yet to welcome our first snowfall of that year, which was unusual for Idaho in the late fall. I borrowed one of Jasmine's black dresses and Mia watched us from the window as we piled into my dad's truck. Jasmine and I sat in silence as we drove to the church with our parents.

At his mother's funeral, Matt pulled a crumpled piece of paper out of his pocket and stood in front of a room full of family and friends with his familiar tears streaming down his cheeks. I sat in the front row, looking up at the boy I loved as he read a poem I thought he had written for me two months earlier. The words on that crumpled piece of paper were for her.

Together
Together they sat looking down on the waves, smiling in spite of themselves
Above the trees and the sea, they had nothing but time, as the wind circled through the clouds.
And the sun never set but the pink in the sky gave way to the dark of the night
So, the waves grew still and she smiled again and held him one last moment in time.
Then she left his side and he cried and he cried and he saw her never again.
Until, at last, together they sat when the night gave way to the light
And in his dream were the trees and the sea and she held him again as they smiled in spite of themselves…

I realized that day that Matt would eventually stop loving me. I had come to understand that first true love is just that—a first of more to come. He would never stop loving his mom and losing her would change him forever.

I wiped the tears from my cheeks and smiled sadly at Matt as he folded the paper and put it back in his pocket, his eyes glassy from a sea of tears. Jasmine grabbed my hand and pulled it into her lap. I vowed to continue loving this boy until he stopped doing the same. I took a deep breath and exhaled.

CHAPTER 2

SUMMER – 1996

Matt

It was the summer before his junior year, and Italy was the most breathtaking place Matt had ever been to. Although he hadn't traveled much, he had seen some beautiful places in his 16 years of life so far. He was in the country for only four days, yet his mother had already whisked him, his dad, and his brother from Rome to Montepulciano where they would stay for the next night. She didn't want to miss anything on this trip, as though she felt they were running out of time.

Matt was anxious to explore the medieval city he had been reading about for the months leading up to this trip. He was more anxious for the following day, when they would travel to the Cinque Terre—five villages on the northern coast of Italy that he spent the most amount of time researching.

Matt was not your typical teenage boy who played Mario Brothers and had burping contests with his friends. He was the type of boy to spend the months leading up to an international vacation studying the culture, language, and geography of the destination. He was different and he knew it.

The summer had been a romantic one with his girlfriend, Zoey. He knew he was falling in love with the girl that lived just a short bike ride away… but something was missing. Although he did enjoy the time they spent together in June and July, he had been counting down the days until August and this trip. He was finally out of the small town and felt more like himself in this exotic European country than ever before. He was not meant to live a life in a small, conservative town full of farmers and homemakers. Matt wanted to explore the world and learn about other cultures and people. He wanted to do that all with Zoey and hoped that this trip would confirm how he felt about her. He missed his girlfriend more than he thought he would and something about the rolling hills and cobblestone streets in Italy made him long for her in a way he hadn't longed for anything before. He knew he loved her, but he didn't know what it was he was still longing for in their relationship.

Matt walked out onto the deck of the small apartment his family was renting for the night. He wondered how much the rent was for this beautiful view and knew not to ask. His dad was the most frugal person he knew, and he had heard his parents arguing about the cost of the trip a few weeks earlier. His mom had somehow convinced his dad to splurge.

"You only live once!" He recalled her saying to his dad in the kitchen when they were on the phone making reservations for this very night.

The sky seemed twice as big as it did in his hometown. From his front yard in Idaho, he could almost see Zoey's house. That night, on a small deck overlooking the Tuscan Hills in Montepulciano, Italy, Matt felt like he could see forever. He sat down on the rickety chair and leaned forward to rest his chin on his arms that laid across the rusty railing. The sun was going down and he could hear his mom and dad's music playing in the living room of the apartment, even with the door closed between them. He turned just in time to see his dad reach out his hand to his mom and pull her close. They were dancing. His dad's other hand was resting on the small of his mother's back. They were almost the same height and had started to look like each other the older they got.

Matt knew he was lucky to have parents that seemed to still be in love. He wasn't the type of teenage boy to be grossed out by his parents dancing in the living room during a rare European vacation. In fact, it made him smile and envision himself one day dancing with his own wife in the hills of Italy. Matt strained to hear the words of the happy music that made his parents dance, but the words were drowned out by his mother's laugh. He loved her laugh.

Matt's dad started to sing the last few lines of the song and Matt smiled as he heard his dad's voice crack while he sang. As his mom laughed, Matt could tell that his dad was not singing the words correctly to the song.

"Let's fly way to the clouds
Away from all the crowds
We can sing in the glow of a star...
Where lovers find peace of mind...
Volare....."

Matt watched the sun go down from the rickety chair and eventually fell asleep on the porch. He awoke to his mother tapping him on the shoulder. "Go to bed, honey. We have a big day tomorrow," she said as she kissed him on the forehead and wandered back into the apartment.

The next day, Matt and his family left the small apartment in the hills and arrived in a small, seaside village after a six-hour train ride to the Cinque Terre. They checked into a small hotel in the first of the five small towns. Matt's dad and brother had barely been in the room for five minutes when they rushed out the door in their swimming trunks on the hunt for the pool. Matt's mother dropped her bags on the bed and grabbed Matt's hand.

"Get your hiking shoes on. I want to show you something," she said as she kissed her oldest son on the cheek and winked at him, her cheeks flushed from excitement. Matt's mom didn't give him a chance to respond and was tying her shoelaces before he knew it.

His mom had always been athletic and didn't really fit in with the other moms in Idaho. He tried to imagine some of his friend's moms lacing up their hiking shoes in Italy and laughed at the thought. The majority of his friend's moms stayed home taking care of younger siblings and making sure the house was clean. He was sure most of them had never been on an airplane, let alone been to Europe. There was nothing wrong with his friends' moms' lives, but in this moment, he realized his mom was different. She had a job in marketing in Boise and wore heels and went to the gym after work. She was a *Renaissance Woman*, which was her self-proclaimed title he overheard her use many times while complaining to his dad that she didn't have any friends in Idaho. Although, she had made friends with Zoey's mom. The two matriarchs had formed a close bond watching their children fall in love over the years. They often drank wine together while Zoey and Matt went on their bike rides near their houses. He always wondered what they talked about. Sure, they had lives, but mostly, their lives seemed to be consumed with their kids' lives.

Just then, Matt's mother looked up and saw him watching her tie her shoes. He was happy she had planned this trip and happy to see his mom doing more than working and taking care of him and his brother.

"C'mon, kid, I am not going to live forever. Let's see the sea."

Within an hour, they had climbed to the top of a rocky path that overlooked the village. Even with all his pre-trip research, Matt wasn't quite sure which village they were staying in and which village they were looking at. It had become a blur of beautiful pastel homes and deep green ocean waves. There was not a cloud in the sky and Matt was often overcome with amazement that this place really existed. They were far from Idaho, and he had never felt more like this was where he was meant to be.

Matt's mom sat with her legs crossed just off the trail in the grass. He saw her take a long breath and lower her head. Her eyes were closed, and he thought for a minute she was going to pass out.

"Mom. Are you ok?" Matt rushed to her and sat next to her on the grass.

Her smile appeared before her eyes opened and she took another long, exaggerated breath. She raised her head and slowly opened her eyes. Tears were streaming down her face.

"What's wrong, Mom? You are scaring me."

"Matt, I need to talk to you. Your dad is having this same talk with your brother."

She reached over and wrapped both her hands around his and pulled his hand into her lap. The touch of his mother's hands had always calmed Matt down, but it wasn't working today. He was scared. Her tears had slowed, and she took another breath, this time short and blunt.

With one sentence, four lives changed forever. She had cancer, and they needed to prepare for her to not be here for very long. Her voice was soft and comforting but her words were harsh and horrifying. Nothing was going to be ok, and he was glad that his mother didn't lie to him and tell him it was. His mother was going to die. The woman who brought him into this world was telling him to prepare, at the age of 16, almost 17, to live in it without her.

They sat only for a moment in silence. He struggled to catch his breath after the shock wore off and he realized what her words really meant. He laid his head on her lap and she rubbed his hair like she did when he was a little boy and had a bad dream. He sobbed. First loudly, then he quieted but still could not control the tears. The view was magical from this spot his mother had chosen to tell him she was dying. The colors on the houses and shops below were like a rainbow of pastels with orange, pink, and blue. The ocean was turquoise mixed with deep pockets of dark green. There were little boats sprinkled around the coastline. His mind drifted while his mother's hand continued to stroke his hair and his tears finally slowed. He was brought back to reality when he saw a woman in the distance grab her young son's arm and help him off their small boat. The young mother and son were alone on the boat. He wondered if the boy had a dad and what the boy would do if, suddenly, his mother died. Would he drown in the ocean alone? Would he starve to death or be forced to beg for money and food on the streets of Riomaggiore? Boys weren't supposed to lose their mothers when they hadn't yet become men.

"This is where your father proposed to me, Matt. I wanted to bring you here to tell you this news because I want you to realize that when I am gone, you will still have memories of me. Memories of me and your father and you two boys. This is kind of where it all started. This is where our family began. I want you to think of the good times we had and that I will always be here. Not in body, but in spirit," Matt's mother said as she stroked her son's dark hair.

He needed her here in everything—mind, body, and spirit! He looked up at his mother and she was smiling. She was letting the memory of the day her husband proposed give her strength to share this shattering news.

"I also wanted to bring you here to tell you this to remind you that you will have your own family one day. You will realize what it's like to love someone more than you ever even love yourself. That is how much I love you and your brother, Matt. And your father. And I will always love you."

Matt looked back down to the boat with the young boy and his mother. There was a man now walking toward the pair with his arms outstretched. The little boy let go of his mother's hand and ran toward the man. This was what his mom was trying to tell him. One day, he would have his own family and he would love a little boy as much as his mother and father loved him.

Matt and his mother sat looking down on the Italian village for hours. They watched as the sun set and turned the sky into a blaze of orange and red. He wondered if every sunset was this spectacular from this picturesque spot. He couldn't help but think that Mother Nature had planned this one beautiful sight for them to remember always.

They had three more places scheduled in Italy to go during the remaining week of their trip. Matt's mother had canceled two of the three destinations so that they could spend more time in the Cinque Terre. Matt and his brother had grown to love the beautiful coast and wanted to explore the small villages one by one. Each morning, Matt woke up early and hiked to the spot where he and his mom had seen their magical sunset. He would watch the colors of the sun rising behind him, filling the sky, and brought his notebook up to the patch in the grass to write as he felt the warmth of the sun. He would never actually see the sun rise from his spot on the hill, but he didn't need to see it. Eventually, Matt learned what his mother meant when she said she would be there for him in spirit. Just like the light of the sun rising behind him each morning, he didn't need to see his mother to feel her presence. He would need to learn how to feel her presence when he could no longer look into his mother's eyes and feel her hands holding his.

The months following his trip to Italy were a blur. Matt's mother's health deteriorated quickly, and his father and brother had silently but unanimously determined that Matt would be the glue that kept them all going. Each morning of her illness, she would step into the kitchen of their home in Idaho looking frailer and more delicate than the day before. Most days, she barely ate and was too tired to leave her room. Each night before bed, Matt would climb the stairs to his parent's master suite and kiss his mother goodnight while she laid in bed.

Matt's mother died on a crisp November night. He knew her days were almost gone, and he kissed her on the forehead not once, but twice before he said his last goodbye.

"I love you, Mom. I will never forget our sunset… or anything. I will never forget."

"I love you too, son. Promise to keep making memories and never forget the ones that we have made. I love you more than you will ever know."

Her funeral was on a Tuesday and a week after her 42nd birthday. Matt's father had turned into an emotional wreck, barely able to leave the house. His brother had been in and out of detention since they started school and didn't seem to care what his consequences were for breaking any and every rule laid out for him. They were mourning. Matt was mourning too but didn't feel like he could show it. He had to be the strong one and that meant addressing her friends and family at her funeral.

Together

Together they sat looking down on the waves, smiling in spite of themselves…

Matt's voice cracked as he finished the first sentence of his poem. He scanned the room filled with people in black suits and dresses. His mother's coworkers and college friends and even the kids she used to play with in elementary school were there. Suddenly, he couldn't remember the names of most of the people at his mother's funeral. The woman in the second row with a red scarf was their neighbor from across the street. He had rarely seen his mother speak with her, yet here she was, sitting in a room full of people who had actual memories to remember her by. Matt recalled a time when his mother called the woman a bitch for leaving a note on his bike that he had accidentally parked too close to her precious flower garden. He was suddenly angry that she was there. The woman in the red scarf caught eyes with him and nodded her head toward him as if to say it was safe for him to continue. He shook his head and wondered if everyone could see his annoyance. Behind her sat a strikingly beautiful girl with long, blonde hair and a dress too short for a funeral. The girl was probably in her early 20s. As he took a closer look, he realized she was Matt's old babysitter. She winked at him and smiled. These people were here to say goodbye and listen to her son give them something to remember her by, yet some of them didn't even know her that well.

Matt stood silently thinking of the sunset in Italy. He could feel the breeze off the ocean and his mother's hands stroking his hair while his head rested in her lap. He had a vision of her as she was telling him about his father proposing so many years before. Matt looked at his father in the front row of the church. His heart broke for his father who lost the love of his life. He wanted to imagine his father boldly asking his girlfriend to be his wife on a hilltop overlooking a seaside village in Italy. That was the man his mother had married. His father was tall, dark, and handsome. These were the words you could use to describe Matt. He shook his head again, this time, catching himself quickly with guilt and remorse that he was judging his father on the day he laid his wife to rest. Matt thought his father should be stronger, but he had to realize that his dad hadn't been prepared to be a widow at 43.

Matt scanned the room again and found his girlfriend, Zoey. Her eyes were full of tears and her hand rested in her sister's lap. She smiled at him, and he thought of his mother's smile that day on the hike. He wondered if his mother was thinking of Zoey when she said he would have a family of his own one day.

Matt finished the poem he wrote for his mother in front of the silent crowd at her funeral and knew that nothing would ever be the same. He had changed, and it would be years before he would be able to love someone like his mother had hoped he would. He also realized that day that he and Zoey didn't have what his father and mother had. They were two kids feeling the first pangs of young love, not soulmates destined for a romantic engagement on the Italian coast. He could never imagine he would recover from this heartbreak as he finished his poem.

And in his dream were the trees and the sea and she held him again as they smiled in spite of themselves...

The silence of the room was taken over by his mother's favorite song. Celine Dion's voice was singing "The Power of Love".

Matt had grown tired of his mother's favorite song until that day. She would have been happy with how her final goodbye turned out—apart from the lady in the red scarf sitting in the second row.

As music filled the room, standing alone in front of the crowd at his mother's funeral, Matt smiled as he thought of his mother blasting her favorite song as she drove him home from soccer practice so many months before. Her soft, brown hair blowing in the wind as she tapped her fingers on the steering wheel. She had insisted on watching his soccer practices that summer even though he could drive. She would pack a small blanket and sit on the grass alone, watching her oldest son. He had asked her if her boss was ok with her leaving work early three nights a week to just sit and watch him practice. He had been playing since he was a little boy but watching practice had to be boring for her, and he couldn't imagine her work wasn't suffering with her leaving so early.

"It's fine. I work to live, Matthew, not the other way around."

She would spend the next few months trying as hard as she could to live every moment of every day. Practice wasn't boring for her to watch that summer. Each time he caught a glimpse of her, arms wrapped around her legs with large sunglasses covering her eyes, he saw a smile. What he couldn't see from his distance in the grassy field was her tears under her oversized sunglasses. She was going to have to leave this boy to become a man without her. But during those summer nights, sitting on her blanket, she was exactly where she wanted to be. If only she could have been there forever.

At the time, Matt didn't know his mother was soaking up her last summer with her son. She knew that, soon, the summer would end. She would tell her sons in a few weeks that this would be their last summer with their mom. The days would get shorter, and the time would pass. She would soon be too sick to go outside and watch her son. Her long, brown hair that swirled in the passing breeze would eventually all be gone. She would soon be too sick to even speak, let alone sing her favorite Celine Dion song. Time would eventually run out.

Looking back on those nights, watching his mother sing her favorite song in the car with (what he thought was) not a care in the world, he wondered how she could do it. He wondered how she had winked at him when her voice cracked through the melody, and he shook his head at her and laughed. Matt suddenly grew angry with himself for thinking she was embarrassing singing that song off-beat and too slowly that day when he shook his head to laugh. He wondered now how she could sing the words to a song that she knew she would only get to listen to a few more times—the song she would have played at her funeral. He would finally learn that she wasn't scared of time running out, she was scared of not enjoying the time she had left.

For a moment, he heard soft sobs and the quiet rumble of voices in the crowd as the music in the church stopped. He closed his eyes and saw his mother's brown hair still blowing in the wind. All he wanted to do was to sit in the passenger seat and listen to her sing her favorite song one last time.

CHAPTER 3

WINTER — 1997

Zoey

It was Christmas Eve and over a year had gone by since Matt's mother passed away. I finally could admit, after almost a full year of denial, that I had lost control.

What started out as stress relief and a way to lose a few pounds for volleyball had turned into a full-blown addiction to running and the beginning of my battle with anorexia. It was like I blinked, and a year went by, and I had lost almost a third of my body weight. I had always loved to run, but by Thanksgiving, my runs had gotten up to 10 miles every morning before school. I joined the track team in the spring and the more weight I lost, the more medals I won. It was like I was being rewarded for wasting away. In the fall, I decided to run cross country and even won the state title. I was turning into an athletic phenom, and I was also turning into a freak.

Saying I lost all control actually seemed like an understatement. My soft stomach from the year before had turned into a valley of taught skin stretching from bony hip to bony hip. At first, it felt good to lose a few pounds and to hear friends and classmates ask me if I had lost weight. But before I knew it, it was completely out of control, and I couldn't walk the halls of Kuna High School without stares and whispers.

I was happy to have a few weeks off from school for the holidays to just simply not be stared and gawked at every day. I knew I was wasting away, and this was a mental disease and not even about what I put into my mouth. It was about control and identity. I had gone to enough counseling in the past year to know and understand this, yet I still ran every day and counted my calories. I couldn't stop slowly killing myself. It was funny to me that this disease was about controlling something in my life, yet I felt completely out of control. I barely understood what I was doing to my body and the people around me definitely didn't understand.

Christmas Eve was the first day in as long as I could remember that I didn't lace up my running shoes. I hated the way not running made me feel. I also hated the way my disease made everyone else feel about the girl they once loved. I couldn't blame them though—I hated this disease as much as they did.

Earlier that day, I needed to make a decision that should have been an easy one. I had to decide between enjoying my family on a snowy Christmas Eve day, or pile on layers and burn as many calories as I could before dinner, running swiftly on icy country roads. I chose to sit in a pile with my sister and watch *A Charlie Brown Christmas* like we did every year. I felt more like Charlie Brown that year than I ever had before. He always seemed so down and out to me when I watched him over the years. I wondered if everyone noticed this when they watched. This Christmas Eve, I understood his frown.

When I ran, I was numb. And that was the feeling I was becoming addicted to. It had been over a year, but it felt like it was just yesterday that I was sitting in the car with Matt in the parking lot on the day he told me about his mom's breast cancer. That was the last day I could remember really feeling like myself. That day also felt like the last day of my childhood.

I used to love Christmas when I was growing up. The season meant the warmth of a fire, the lights twinkling on our tree, and watching *A Christmas Story* repeatedly with my sisters. Our house on 40 acres would always be surrounded by snow on Christmas Eve. Outside, colorful lights were strung from the roof and wrapped around the poles that held the awning up over our deck. My mom would walk out to the small conifer tree that stood almost 400 yards from our house and she would trim that tree with white lights and a star. From the road, you could barely see the wreath that decorated our barn that housed our many racehorses. On cold December nights, they stood close to each other to keep warm. From the barn, you could barely see the dim porch lights of our neighbors that lived pastures away from us. This little town was just big enough, and just small enough at the same time. I never felt sheltered, but I didn't quite feel free.

That Christmas Eve, I longed for Christmases of the past. I wanted everything to be like it was when I was little. I wanted to smile and be happy again and I was trying so hard to understand how to break free of the grip this disease had on me and my life. I wanted to relate more to happy Snoopy instead of grumpy Charlie Brown. I wanted it to at least be like it was before Matt's mom died. I didn't like Christmas the year I turned 18. I couldn't feel the warmth of the fire. The twinkling of the lights failed to comfort me. I didn't even feel like laughing while I watched Ralphie's friend Flick get his tongue stuck on the flagpole earlier that night in the living room with my family. Nothing was funny anymore, and nothing was the same. It wasn't about the food or being skinny. I knew this was true, but I knew this disease was causing, or was caused by, a deep depression that I couldn't believe I had in me. As quickly as I felt my childhood slip away was as quickly as this disease took hold of my thoughts every day and every night.

The snow that fell sent shivers through my body as I watched it fall to the ground. And the small conifer tree that my mom decorated each year grew into one blurry, lonely light when I gazed at it through the large frosty window in my room as I laid in bed after a full day of Christmas movies. If I squinted hard, I could see our new baby foal in the pasture. She was trying hard, over and over again, to escape the pack of massive horses huddled around her. She was a rebel at only one week old. She couldn't break free as she wobbled toward the barn away from the pack. She wasn't ready to be so independent and I was sure she knew it, but she kept arrogantly trying. Finally, she gave up and I watched her in the moonlight wander back to the pack with her mother close behind. She stopped to turn back to see if her mom was still on her tail. She felt suffocated, just like I did. She also longed for independence but was scared to truly be on her own.

Christmas was not whimsical, romantic, or magical that year. It had been the hardest year of my young life so far. Although, I had to bet that if I lived 50 or even 100 years, this year would still top the list of the worst. Nobody knew if I would live one more year, and I didn't know if I wanted to.

I laid in my bed with three down comforters piled on top of me with my door cracked open slightly. The top blanket was pink with purple stripes. That was Jasmine's blanket and she had slept with it for more years than I could remember. She took that blanket everywhere and I couldn't remember how I even got a hold of it on this Christmas Eve night.

My sister was enjoying the night as most teenagers were and was still laying on the couch from our day-long movie binge. I could hear her on the phone in the living room down the hall. She was not exhausted and laying in her bed motionless as I had been. Randy Travis and Celine Dion's Christmas albums took turns playing in the kitchen as my mom cleaned the dishes in the sink. My older sister was delayed at the airport in Arizona on her way home from college for the holidays. She was allegedly supposed to make it home in a few hours with a new boyfriend in tow. I hadn't seen her in months. She would be shocked at the sight of me and a part of me hoped she would never end up making it home for Christmas that year just so that she wouldn't have to face the reality of her little sister at home.

My door creaked open, and a light flooded into my room. I closed my eyes. I didn't want to face whoever was casting a shadow on the pink blanket with purple stripes. I didn't want to face anything I was suddenly challenged with that year. I closed my eyes but didn't see sugar plums dancing in my head.

I thought for sure it was Jasmine who had grown silent after hanging up the phone. Her favorite day of the year was just a short night's sleep away. She was so good at putting on a happy face. She needed to be the strong one when her other half had given up, and for that, I owed her the world. I waited for her to pull the blanket off the top of me and say something funny even though she thought I was asleep. She would laugh at herself and then probably start to feel bad the moment she closed the door, pink and purple blanket in tow. She didn't know how to act around me anymore. None of us knew how to navigate this disease. My twin sister had started to feel distant ever since the night of Homecoming a few months ago. I hoped it was her casting a shadow on me that Christmas Eve, but it wasn't Jasmine.

His shadow moved toward me slowly. I felt a gentle hand on my back and heard Randy singing, "Meet Me Under the Mistletoe". I closed my eyes tighter and heard him exhale. He didn't know I was awake. It was the first time I heard my father cry, and his shaky voice began.

"Why are you doing this, Zoey? Why are you killing yourself? You have to pull out of this, sweetheart, or this will be the last Christmas you are here."

He sat beside me for what felt like hours, but when he left, Randy was still just coming to a festive end to the same song as when he walked into my room. Was that all it took to get someone to kiss you?

Hang a mistletoe in the doorway. I had been longing for months to be kissed again by Matt. At that moment, I felt my stomach turn, thinking of our last kiss so long ago. I had read recently that mistletoe was actually a parasite. I felt like a parasite lately. Everything attached to me was suffering, especially Jasmine. And Matt.

My dad stood and closed the door softly behind him to join my mother in the kitchen, where they would finish a bottle of Chardonnay and ignore the purple elephant in the room for just one night. It was Christmas Eve and they needed something to celebrate. For the first time since this disease had taken over my life, I listened to my father. I pulled the blankets up under my chin and cried. He was right. I had to pull out of this disease, or I would die.

My battle with anorexia started a year prior to that cold Christmas Eve. There had been days that year that were vivid in my memory and days that I struggled to remember even getting out of bed. Like a tornado, this disease had taken over my life—and my family's lives—giving us no time to seek shelter. I couldn't recall exactly when it started or how, but laying in my bed, shivering and weak, I knew I couldn't keep living like this. I also felt like I couldn't stop it. I couldn't pull myself out of it like my dad had just urged me to do. Most days, it felt easier to just wish I wouldn't open my eyes in the morning. My dad reminded me that I couldn't wish for the easy way out. But I was exhausted.

One of the days that was vivid in my memory was the day Matt finally broke my heart. It was a dark Sunday night in October when his Jeep pulled into my driveway for the last time, or for what I thought would be the last time. I could see him from the window with his head down walking toward me and I knew the minute I answered the door what he was there to do. He had a piece of paper in his hand like over a year before on the day he told me his mom was dying. It was a letter that he read to me while we sat on my bed in my room. As he read the letter, his voice cracked, and I could tell he didn't want to look me in the eyes. He spoke and I scanned the room, looking at the pictures of us on the wall. In our junior prom picture, I wore a red strapless dress and looked healthy and happy. He was smiling beside me in that photo as if he was the luckiest guy in the school. Just a few inches away hung the most recent picture of us on my wall. It was the Homecoming Dance, just a few weeks before. I was wearing a pink silky dress that clung to my bony body. His face in the picture was not the face of a high school boy excited to be out with his date. He looked serious and worried. I stood next to him in my pink silky dress with a smile I knew took all the energy in the world to produce for the shot. It wasn't until that day that I realized I was frail and weak. It was that day that I realized I was in this fight alone. My parents had a pained look in their eyes as they told me I looked beautiful and to have fun at the dance. Matt's father gasped at me when I got out of his truck for pictures. I had surely reminded him of his wife who had wasted away before his eyes. That was the day I knew Matt had to save himself from this ride I was on. That was the day he started to walk away and the letter he read while sitting on my bed was the day that he needed to make sure he saved himself.

So much had changed that year. Time flew by and, suddenly, I was a different person. I felt so selfish during the first few months of this relentless disease knowing what Matt had just gone through losing his mom. But I was helpless. Even though everyone from my parents to my twin sister to my therapist was telling me I could fight this disease, I didn't have the energy, and neither did he. I didn't feel like I was in control, but really, control was what this disease was all about. I had no control over anything in my life. I was losing my first love and there was nothing I could do about it. I was going to have to decide about college soon and leave the only home I had ever known. I was going to have to leave my twin sister, the one who made it possible for me to never have to face anything alone in the past. At the same time, I longed for independence. I was losing control, but I could control what I ate. I could control how much I worked out. There was so much to this disease that I wouldn't understand until I had conquered it... if I could conquer it.

As Matt and I sat on my bed that Sunday night, I listened to the words he read from his letter. He was coming over that night to finish what he couldn't do at Homecoming. He wanted to end it the night of the dance. As I sat, listening to his words as he read from the paper, I thought of the Homecoming Dance and how he looked at me right before he walked away. He left so much unsaid that night but was here now to say it all.

Matt said he felt like he lost his mother and then he lost his best friend. I had changed and so had he. But he didn't know how to react to my change. Months into my gripping disease, I lost so much weight, he didn't know what to do. He didn't want to walk away but he was in no position to stand by and watch me slowly kill myself. He had gone through this with his mother, watching her disease take over, but I could prevent this disease. Couldn't I?

Matt didn't understand that I didn't think I could prevent it, just like my dad didn't when he warned me months later on Christmas Eve that I needed to pull out of it. Anorexia was a disease, just like cancer was a disease. Matt pleaded with me to stop and told me he didn't understand why I compared purposefully starving myself to his mother's breast cancer.

"I can't watch you do this to yourself, Zoey. I love you and I can't lose you like this, so I have to choose to walk away and hope this is the wake-up call that you need."

Matt was folding up the letter and shaking his head. Tears streamed down his face like they had at his mother's funeral. He was saying goodbye to me like he said to her. Before I had a chance to say anything, he was gone. He left my room that day for the last time. Through the open door, I watched him pass Jasmine in our narrow hallway without even looking at her. She peered down the hall and into my room where I sat, heartbroken and alone on my bed. Somehow, she knew what had just happened and I longed for her to comfort me. Jasmine grabbed the door handle and whispered, "You probably want to be alone." And pulled the door toward her closed. I didn't want to be alone, but there I was, alone.

I laid in my bed that Christmas Eve, thinking about the Sunday that Matt had been sitting there just an arm's length away. The two men in my life had told me I had to do this myself. They were not going to be able to protect me from this. I guessed my dad had wiped his tears away in the hallway before heading into the kitchen to my mom. She was so worried about me and he had to at least protect her from his pain.

I wondered what Matt was doing on Christmas Eve. It would be the first one home since his mother died. The month after her death last year, they went to the Cayman Islands for the holidays. The less it felt like Christmas to them, the less they would have to face that it was Christmas without their mom. I desperately wanted to feel what Christmas really felt like again. I wondered that night if I would live long enough to see the foal run her first horse race. I closed my eyes and listened to the sound of silence in my childhood home. A part of me wanted to stay there forever, and a part of me couldn't wait to leave. I had to figure out what I was running from and why I was trying so hard to disappear.

My door opened again, and this time, it was Jasmine. She struggled to pull the curtains closed and then crossed the room to pull back my covers. I didn't know if she thought I was awake or not as she climbed into my bed and reached for the covers and folded them back over both of us. Mia jumped into my bed and I felt her warm body lay down on my feet.

That night, I didn't know if Jasmine wished I was asleep or awake. I was sure she hoped it had all been a dream.

"Zoey. There is something I need to tell you about the night of Homecoming."

CHAPTER 4

FALL – 1997

Matt

It was a Saturday night in October when Matt decided he needed to break up with Zoey and leave her to fight her disease on her own. The letter was almost four pages long so far and he was going to read it to her the next day. He knew that if he didn't write everything down, he wouldn't get his message across to his first love. He worried if she didn't get the message, she would only get worse.

Matt was sitting at the black desk in his small bedroom. He was reading the letter for the third time. He knew it didn't sound right, but it was too hard to put into words that he was deciding to be a teenager. He needed to live what was left of his exhausting childhood and not worry about someone else he loved dying. That meant he had to tell Zoey he didn't want to be her boyfriend anymore. She had to have known by now, but he needed to tell her. He wanted her to get better, but he was making a choice that meant she was going to have to do it without him by her side. This wasn't a job for the boy who knew her the most and loved her for the majority of his young life. What Zoey faced was a job for professionals. What Zoey faced was also ruining what was supposed to be the best years of his life. His mom's death the year before had already proven to be the worst time in his life. He was ready to start living again, and Zoey was not.

"Matt! Phone is for you!" Matt's little brother, Brandon, yelled from the kitchen holding the phone in the air over his head. Just as Matt reached out, the receiver dropped to the floor and the long cord began to stretch. Little brothers are so annoying. Brandon ran into his nearby room and slammed the door shut, laughing hysterically. Ever since their mother died, Brandon had been a mess. He was always in trouble in school and seemed as though every move he made was in order to draw attention—negative attention—to their family. Matt wondered what was even left of his family as he shook his head and pulled the receiver to his ear.

"Hello." On the other line was a familiar voice. She didn't sound exactly like Zoey, but if he didn't know them both so well, he could easily have thought Jasmine was her twin sister on the other line.

"Hi, Matt. It's me, Jasmine. We need to talk."

He had been waiting for this call since the night of Homecoming. The night he wished he could take back. There were so many reasons he couldn't stop thinking of that night.

"Jasmine, I have been meaning to call you. I just didn't really know what to say. I didn't mean anything that night. What I am trying to say is, I would take it back if I could. I didn't mean to hurt anyone. I don't know what happened."

Matt closed his eyes as he spoke quietly into the phone. He didn't want to hurt her feelings, but he had to protect himself. He also wouldn't really take back what happened that night. He wasn't acting out of anger; he was acting out of confusion—and passion if he was honest with himself. The sound of the TV turned on in Brandon's room and he knew his brother wouldn't hear their conversation.

Matt's dad was working late that night. He had been working late for what felt like every night since his mother's funeral in November last year. His dad decided that the best way to mourn was to do it alone and let everyone fend for themselves. Matt had never felt more alone. He lost his mom and pretty much lost his dad too. He vowed to be a better father than his father had been this past year. Jasmine exhaled on the other line.

"Well, if you were thinking of calling me, why didn't you? I know this is a lot to process. I know it's getting close to the holidays, and I know you still have to figure out what this means." Matt waited for her to say "But…" And it never came. If Jasmine was one thing, it was patient. She was also beautiful.

It had been almost two weeks since the Homecoming Dance. That night, Matt got out of his Jeep to pick up Zoey, feeling excited. He hadn't seen Zoey dressed up in a long time and was anxious to see her in something other than sweatpants and a ponytail. Sure, they were going through some hard times, but he loved her. He knew she had started going to see a therapist and he hoped giving her some space would help get her healthy again. When Zoey answered the door, she looked like a ghost. Her dress straps hung across her frail shoulders, and he could see she was shivering.

"Um. You look beautiful. Your dress is beautiful," Matt lied as he searched her eyes for the girl he once loved.

Fall break was that week and he hadn't seen her in 10 days. That was it. Ten days and she had transformed even further into a stranger before his eyes.

"Thanks. You look so handsome, Matt. I really missed you. Sorry, I need to grab a coat and I think my parents want pictures." Zoey bowed her head as if she wanted to block out the shocked look in his eyes and turned to grab her coat from the coat rack near the door. Behind her, he saw Jasmine standing on the stairs. She had her long hair wrapped up in a towel and oversized gray sweatpants on. It was as if the twin sisters were trading places for the night. It would be Zoey's night to feel glamorous, although he knew that was the last thing she felt.

"I did her hair and makeup. Don't give me too many props, Matt, and don't screw it up when you make out!" Jasmine frowned softly. She knew what he was thinking. Why would he even try to touch Zoey? She looked like a 10-year-old boy. He saw pity in her eyes that matched his and they both smiled weakly. Jasmine scurried up the stairs and disappeared into her room. She wasn't going to the dance that night. School dances weren't really her thing, she had said to the number of boys that asked to be her date. She literally was washing her hair that night.

Matt and Zoey pulled into the parking lot of Kuna High School and parked in the same spot Zoey had parked in when Matt told her his mom was dying the year before. Matt remembered the passionate kiss they shared in her Audi that day. He longed to feel that passion again.

"Do you want to leave your coat in the car?" he asked, knowing the answer as he opened his door.

"No, I should bring it. I think I will get cold." He was relieved that her coat would hopefully hide her emaciated frame from the gym full of teenage assholes they were approaching. Through the windshield, they could see groups of girls with bare shoulders and legs walking awkwardly in their high heels and sparkling short dresses. They wanted to show off their dresses that night and would sacrifice being exposed to the cold late September breeze to impress their dates. Zoey watched them with a look of sadness and regret in her eyes. Matt grabbed her hand for what would be one of the last times.

"Are you ready?" he asked as he smiled weakly at her and nodded as if to say, "Let's get this over with." He let go of her hand and hurried out of the driver's side door. He closed the door hard and caught himself walking away from the car without helping her out like the gentleman everyone thought he was. He turned quickly and jogged over to the passenger side to open Zoey's door and help her out. He thought he saw her roll her eyes at him. He had changed. But not as much as she had.

The dancefloor was a blur of side eyes and covered whispers. He knew what everyone was gossiping about. It was Zoey. She was starving to death and their classmates couldn't look away. She still had her coat on, but her hollow cheeks and thinning hair had drawn stares and gasps. He had just spent the last year passing whispers in the hallway. He was the boy whose mom died and now he was the boy whose girlfriend was dying. Poor Matt. Was that what everyone was thinking? He didn't want to care what they thought, but he was a 17-year-old boy, and caring about what your peers think goes with the territory. He could hear Janet Jackson singing "Together Again" over the speaker as they moved through the crowd.

Matt wondered what was going on in Zoey's head at that moment listening to Janet talk about not belonging. Zoey didn't look like she belonged in the gym full of giddy teenagers. She looked like she belonged in a hospital. She looked like Matt's mother did right before she took her last breath and said goodbye. Matt shook his head to try to ignore his thoughts as he pulled Zoey through the crowd.

"Let's get a picture," Zoey said as she grasped his hand tighter to stop him. The photo booth was just a few feet away and Matt wondered if she realized she would have to take her coat off and show the gaping crowd of their peers her skeletal body. She smiled softly as if this was going to be her way of forcing the situation to be normal as she pulled her coat off and dropped it in front of the enormous camera lights. Matt and Zoey stood in front of the camera holding onto each other. The lights shone on them for the entire gym to see. Zoey had goosebumps on her arms and a fake smile plastered across her lips. The photographer moved Matt's open palm to rest on the small of Zoey's back. He felt an empty space under his palm where her warm skin used to fill it. He had loved her body before this. He knew she had always thought she needed to lose a few pounds, but he always told Zoey she was perfect just the way she was. He meant it and he wished she had listened to him. But she wasn't the way she was any longer—she was starving to death.

Matt was relieved when the pictures were done, and he reached quickly for Zoey's coat. The gym was hot, but her arm hair stood, and her hands were clammy and cold. They stood as the music blasted around them.

"Do you want to dance?" he asked as he grabbed her elbow to stop her from her b-line to the bleachers.

"No. I am ok." Zoey smiled softly and pulled her coat closed tight. She was aware everyone had seen what she was trying to hide all of those months. Her dramatic weight loss was easy to hide when she could throw on baggy pants and hoodies. Tonight, she couldn't hide it. He could tell she was shocked at the stares from her classmates. Maybe she hadn't noticed how sick she looked because she was living with this disease every day.

Matt suddenly felt his heart racing and his face flush with anger. This wasn't what young love was supposed to be. Matt had felt like this was Zoey's rock bottom. He almost laughed at the thought that just a few weeks earlier, he believed that this night was going to be the night they finally had sex for the first time. Instead of what he hoped would have been a night they would remember for the rest of their lives, they were standing in the middle of the dancefloor barely touching as he saw her eyes fill with tears. You only get one Senior Homecoming Dance and Matt was suddenly pissed he was spending it with a girl who didn't even seem to care about herself, let alone him. She wouldn't be doing this if she cared about him or this relationship.

"You know, Zoey. You have got to try to have fun. You have got to try to live a little if we are going to be boyfriend and girlfriend. We should be kissing and laughing, and at the very least, we should be dancing. Hell, I thought we would even maybe be having sex at the end of this night! I don't know if I can do this. This isn't what I want for my last year of high school."

Matt was almost yelling in Zoey's ear as the music blared behind him. He had barely raised his voice at anyone in his entire life and, suddenly, he was moved enough to let his emotions turn him into an aggressive jerk. They stood, staring at each other in the middle of the gym, for what felt like forever. He was a few inches taller than her with her heels on but felt as though he was seven feet tall, yelling at a child looking up at him with tearful, hollow eyes.

"Answer me!"

Matt knew he didn't even ask a question for her to answer but he needed her to say something. He needed her to do something, and she just stood there, closing her eyes tightly at his words. Her tears finally fell as she squeezed her eyes tighter as if she was making a wish to disappear. She had to open her eyes and face him. She had to face this disease and it shouldn't be his job to speak up. He was already acting as the only parent left in his family, he didn't have the energy to act as the only one in his relationship that seemed to care whether Zoey lived or died.

Matt already felt like he lost control of his emotions that night, but just then, he lost control of his body as he turned around and began to walk away. He left his girlfriend of so many years standing alone on the dancefloor. His mind was telling him to stop, turn back around, and get her out of there, but his feet were walking away. He wasn't an asshole like most 17-year-old boys in this town. He was a gentleman who had bought flowers for Zoey's mom that night and wrote poetry on Friday nights instead of getting drunk and being obnoxious like the rest of his classmates. Tonight, however, he was out of patience with being the nice guy. He was tired of worrying about everyone else. Janet Jackson was no longer singing. Matt heard Zoey's favorite song come over the speakers, Blackstreet's "Let's Stay in Love" as he moved further through the crowd. His heart ached for the girl he once loved as he listened to the words of her favorite song. He pushed through the crowd and knew all the eyes that had fixated on Zoey when they walked in were now on him. Did everyone understand what it was like to be the boyfriend of the girl who was starving herself to death? No one understood him. No one except Jasmine.

Couples were merging into one and swaying together melodically as Matt was pushing through the crowd to the door. He made the mistake of looking back at Zoey. She almost looked like an angel standing there with the light creating a halo behind her upswept hair. She stood motionless and he was immediately overcome by guilt and regret when he realized she was shaking. He was abandoning her right there in the gym of Kuna High School, but it was too late to turn back around. It was too late for them. He just wanted his old girlfriend back, but she was gone. He obviously couldn't save her, so he had to save himself. Tears were rolling down her cheeks and her eyes were wide as though she couldn't believe he was doing this to her. She was now looking around as if trying to find someone to help her disappear. If Jasmine had been there, she would have rushed to her side and whisked her out of the nightmare that had become her Senior Homecoming Dance. After all she had done to support him through the last year—he was simply walking away.

If he could only get out of that gym, he would be free. He wanted to be free of what had become of his beautiful, funny girlfriend. He wanted to be free of the stares of sorrow, but he knew that when he reached the doors leading out of the gym, he would never be free of the guilt he would assume that night—all of it.

"Matt! Are you there?" Jasmine's voice on the line brought him back to the present. Matt blinked quickly to pull himself out of his daydream as he sat in his kitchen on the phone with his soon-to-be ex-girlfriend's twin sister. He shook his head, trying to forget about leaving Zoey that night. But Jasmine had called to talk about exactly that—the night of Homecoming.

"Are you going to tell her, Matt? I need to know what your plan is so I can make sure that my sister doesn't hate me for the rest of our lives."

"Then what, Jasmine? You think if we get our stories lined up that she won't hate us forever? She is never going to forgive either one of us for what we did. I don't want to keep lying to her, but I can't keep watching her do this to herself. This might be something she won't ever get over."

Matt looked down at the letter he had written to Zoey. He was going to tell her everything. He had to be honest. She knew what was coming. He had barely spoken to her since that dance, but they hadn't officially broken up either. He was sure she held onto the hope that he just needed space. He crumpled up the letter. He should be honest and tell her everything, but he was tired of always doing the right thing. Sometimes he just wanted to do what was going to be easiest for him. Sometimes he just wanted to do what felt good.

"I am breaking up with her, Jasmine. Tomorrow. I am going to tell her I am breaking up with her because of the real reason, which is that she is not the girl I fell in love with. This has nothing to do with you. Zoey is a wreck. She is fucked up. She is choosing to do this to herself, and I am not going to just watch it. That is my plan, ok? I can't do this anymore."

Jasmine was silent on the other line.

"Hello?" Matt said with frustration in his voice.

"Nothing to do with me? Ok, Matt. Do what you are going to do. Forget that night. Forget everything. Just be gentle on her then and don't worry about me. I am going to be fine."

He heard a click. Jasmine was gone. He knew he would never forget about that night, and he also knew that Jasmine was not going to be fine. If he was honest with himself, he would know that he wouldn't be fine either.

Matt went back to his room and pulled out a fresh piece of paper. It took him hours to write the last words he planned to say to his first true love. Finally, he had the words he thought would be sufficient in ending the first chapter in his book of many love stories to come.

The next day was a Sunday in October. Matt did what he said he was going to do. He drove over to her house, sat on Zoey's bed, and broke her heart. She barely said a word, but he said everything he needed to say to the girl he spent years caring so much about—well, almost everything.

All Matt could think about as he got back into his Jeep and tossed the letter on the floor was how good Jasmine smelled when he passed her in the hallway of their home on his way out of the house.

CHAPTER 5

WINTER – 1998

Jasmine

It was the first few hours of the new year and the snow had been falling hard since Christmas Eve. Jasmine sat on the dark brown leather chair in the hospital room with her favorite pink and purple blanket pulled up just under her chin. It was 2 a.m., but the streetlights outside of the fifth-floor window made it look like the middle of the day.

Through the window, Jasmine could see the bar across the street slowly empty. Every few seconds, she heard the festive sound of whistles blown by drunk people ringing in a new year. The small and ancient-looking TV on the wall was playing "Auld Lang Syne" over and over. Jasmine loved that song even when it wasn't New Year's Eve. It made her wish for a future full of traveling to other countries where everyone spoke another language, and nobody knew her name. She was beginning to hate this small town and couldn't wait for the summer when she would graduate from high school and be able to get out on her own. After this year, she needed a fresh start—she just didn't know if that fresh start would include her twin sister or not.

The twinkle of the red and green Christmas lights that Jasmine had hung on the first night she stayed in room 532 made the room look a little less sterile than it really was. Zoey, who had been asleep for hours, would be woken up soon by the night nurse to check her pulse. The last nurse that checked Zoey's pulse looked at Jasmine with wide eyes and joked about her pulse being so slow, she didn't know if she was dead or alive. She was not funny.

Jasmine hadn't imagined she would spend the last New Year's Eve of high school watching her sister sleep in the pediatric unit of St. Luke's. But here she was, peeking over her favorite blanket down on the crowds that were actually celebrating a new year while her sister laid in a hospital bed for the seventh night in a row. Jasmine hadn't left the room for more than a couple of hours each night since Christmas Day when Zoey checked in. She was physically close to her sister but felt so far away. She couldn't help but feel like her actions were a part of the reason they were there that night. Jasmine longed for something to celebrate.

Just a week earlier, on Christmas Eve, Jasmine sat in the living room gazing at the ornaments decorating their tree. Her dad had just closed the door softly from Zoey's room and joined her mother in the kitchen. She couldn't keep the secrets any longer. Jasmine didn't know if Zoey was asleep when she first walked into her room that Christmas Eve, Mia following closely behind her.

"Zoey. There is something I need to tell you about the night of Homecoming."

At that moment, in the moonlight on Christmas Eve, she saw her twin sister open her eyes. She wasn't asleep. Jasmine lifted the covers and laid down beside her twin sister in bed and watched while Mia laid on Zoey's legs and quickly fell asleep.

Jasmine began to tell Zoey the story she had been trying to tell her for weeks as she laid under the mountain of covers her sister needed to keep her frail body warm. She decided to start from the beginning. She decided she also couldn't tell Zoey everything because it just might be too much.

"All I want is for you to be ok, Zoey. I have never wanted anything else since the day we were born. Do you hear me?"

Jasmine could see Zoey's lips curl into a soft smile in the moonlit room as they laid together. Her mind filled with memories of them as little girls giggling late into the night on Christmas Eve when they shared a bed so many years before. Their mother would barge into the room and tell them that Santa was not going to come until they were asleep. She would slam the door and the two sisters would burst into laughter. Amazingly, and against what their mother had proclaimed, Santa arrived every year even though they stayed up all night.

"I did something. It wasn't to hurt you, Zoey. It was… I don't know why it actually happened."

Zoey's eyes shut for a moment as if to prepare for what her sister was about to say. Her soft smile was gone. Jasmine paused to wonder why exactly it had happened. Not knowing was not an acceptable answer. Why had she chosen to betray her sister, especially in the state she was in? The more she thought about the reasons why, the less they seemed to have to do with Zoey at all.

Jasmine began to tell her sister what happened. It was the night of Homecoming. She had no idea that her sister would be left standing alone in the middle of the dance as her boyfriend of years simply decided to walk away. She would never imagine that Zoey's favorite song played as the only love she had ever known exited through the doors of the gym, leaving his date alone in a sea of hormonal teenage couples. Jasmine wondered if the night would have turned out differently if she had been there for what had to have been Zoey's worst nightmare. She wasn't there. And she wouldn't always be there for her sister, she was learning as she took a deep breath.

Jasmine watched her sister closely in the Christmas Eve moonlight as she continued to tell her the truth—mostly the truth. She told her sister how Matt had pulled up to their house without Zoey in the passenger seat of his Jeep. It was early still, and the dance couldn't have been over already, Jasmine thought. Her parents had just left for dinner and a movie, so she was enjoying having the house to herself. Jasmine was sitting on the front porch in the chair that was normally occupied by their mom. She had been listening to the water fountain and the frogs in the distance in the dark on the porch when he pulled up. Jasmine's towel that was wrapped around her hair earlier in the night was now laying on the concrete and the book she was reading for AP English, *The Scarlet Letter*, laid open on her lap. Matt joined Jasmine on the porch and sat on the edge of the fountain her mom had built the summer before. He removed his long tie and jacket and unbuttoned the top two buttons of his dress shirt. He seemed disheveled and like he was there to vent.

"What is going on, Matt? Where is Zoey?" Jasmine sat up and pulled her damp hair into a bun.

Jasmine looked again at her sister in bed as she continued her story. She left out the part where Matt told her that he left Zoey at the dance because he just couldn't do it anymore. He couldn't watch his girlfriend slowly starve to death and the only other person he thought would understand what he was going through was Jasmine. The real story was that Zoey's boyfriend and her twin sister had bonded that night over the misery of being her support system. And one thing led to another and Jasmine had comforted him more than Zoey ever could. That was not true—they comforted each other. The truth was that both Jasmine and Matt were tired of thinking and worrying about Zoey, and that night, they worried about themselves without thinking of Zoey at all. It felt good and Jasmine felt bad when she longed to relive that Saturday night in September with her twin sister's first love.

She told her sister how bad Matt felt at the dance and how he pleaded with Jasmine, asking her how she thought he could help her sister to get better. She told Zoey that she thought the only reason he had kissed her was because he was lost. This was the story she told Zoey that night. They kissed. She didn't tell Zoey that it was more than a kiss. She didn't tell Zoey that she knew Matt hadn't showed up that night on their porch to talk about Zoey. He was there for Jasmine.

"It was just a kiss." That was all Jasmine told her sister that night on Christmas Eve.

"Then he left." As she laid in bed next to her sister listening to her story, Zoey's eyes were glossy, but she wasn't crying. She had just dried her tears after her dad left the room almost an hour before her sister came in. Zoey looked numb. Jasmine strained to look closer, but it was almost as if Zoey didn't really care. Maybe she should have told her the whole story. They laid together on Zoey's bed in silence on Christmas Eve. Jasmine couldn't think of anything to do but hug her sister.

"I love you, Zoey. I am sorry about Matt. I am sorry about what Matt and I did. It was selfish and we didn't mean to hurt you. I am sorry I didn't tell you sooner."

Within minutes, Zoey fell asleep. Jasmine was shocked at her sister's response—or lack of response—to the news that her best friend/sister and boyfriend had kissed. What she did not know was that Zoey did care. She cared more than she would ever tell either one of them. Her heart was broken laying in that bed on Christmas Eve listening to her twin sister tell her that she had kissed the only boy she ever loved. But she was exhausted. Zoey didn't have the strength or energy to fight anymore, so she closed her eyes and fell asleep. At this point, her broken heart was working hard to just keep her alive. There was no more capacity for dealing with pain or heartache.

On Christmas morning, Jasmine woke up in Zoey's bed and looked over at her sister. Zoey was barely breathing. Their dad was hovering over them with a worried look in his eyes. He had the phone close to his ear.

"Wake her up. Her heart rate is too slow so we are going to the hospital." Suddenly, the news Jasmine gave Zoey the night before seemed so simple and small. Her dad never worried. Jasmine shook Zoey hard and she opened her eyes. She had the same blank stare from the night before.

"Let's go. I am here for you, Zoey." They left for St. Luke's on Christmas Day.

That was a week ago and Zoey and Jasmine had barely spoken a word to each other since. All Jasmine knew to do was sit in the brown chair in room 532 and wait for her sister to get better. Matt had left many messages with their parents, but she didn't know if they were for her or Zoey. She was angry with herself for even wondering.

Jasmine heard another sound of a whistle from outside the bar across the street and looked down to see a couple kissing passionately as the snow fell around them. She wondered if Matt had kissed someone at midnight to celebrate the arrival of a new year and couldn't help but think of the true story she had kept from her sister about what happened when Matt joined Jasmine on the porch that night of the Homecoming Dance in September.

Jasmine didn't tell Zoey that Matt stood up from sitting on the edge of the fountain and bent down to move Jasmine's book from her lap. He was tired of talking about Zoey. He was tired of holding back from acting on what he had been thinking about for months. He was tired of not acting on what every boy in their town had probably thought about for years, in fact. Matt reached for Jasmine's hand and pulled her up to stand before him. She looked shocked and, at first, pulled her hand away. He put his other hand behind her neck and pulled her lips towards his. Suddenly, they were kissing. Jasmine and Matt were kissing and neither one of them wanted to stop. Matt's hand moved around her waist to pull her hips close to his and she could feel the front of his pants swell against her stomach. In moments, he was laying on top of her on the large couch on the porch near the fountain. His hands were under her shirt and hers were in his hair. He stopped kissing her for a moment to take her hair out of the bun and watched it fall down around her neck. They paused and looked into each other's eyes on that dark Saturday night in September. She could see the eagerness in his gaze, and he began kissing her again. Jasmine reached for Matt's belt as his hands moved down to her sweatpants. Jasmine was experienced and knew what she was doing. She also knew he had never done this much before with a girl. She knew he and Zoey had really only made out. He was a senior in high school and ready to lose his virginity to her that night, and that was what they were going to do.

"Are you sure this is what you want, Matt?" It seemed like a ridiculous question to ask in the heat of the moment. Looking back, Jasmine wished she would have said something else.

"Jasmine. All I have ever done these past few years is worry. I worried about my mom; I worry about Zoey. I need something for myself. Right now, I need you. I want you. I have wanted you for a while now and I am sorry if this is not the right thing to do but we shouldn't have to always worry. The right thing to do right now doesn't matter. Nothing seems like it matters to anyone else, so why can't we just do something that I know we both want to do?"

Jasmine could tell he was trying to avoid using Zoey's name. He didn't want to make this about her.

His eyes were full of passion and what felt almost like desperation as Jasmine reached to pull his body into hers. For the first time in over a year, Matt and Jasmine were not worrying about Zoey. And months later, Jasmine longed for that forbidden feeling again.

In the small hospital room on New Year's Eve, Jasmine focused on the couple across the street kissing and tried to pull her mind away from that night in September with Matt. Her heart raced as she thought of the look in his eyes that night. Jasmine hadn't felt that feeling with any other boy, but she was going to convince herself that it wasn't because it was Matt, but that it only felt like that because it was forbidden. It took her years to realize that she was wrong… it was because it was Matt.

Jasmine looked across the room at her sleeping sister. Zoey had a feeding tube in her nose and looked peaceful sleeping in the hospital bed. It felt as though she had been asleep for the entire week while Jasmine had barely slept at all. Zoey didn't fight the doctors that piled into her room on Christmas Day and told her "The plan", which included no exercise, a feeding tube, and a team of medical and mental health professionals. She looked relieved to hand over the fight to this team of professionals and had promised her family she would do whatever they asked so she could get through this disease. This was officially her rock bottom. Although the sisters were barely speaking, Zoey made it clear throughout her stay that she needed Jasmine to stay. She needed Jasmine to stay by her side just as much as she understood why Jasmine and Matt had done what they did. Maybe in some way, they would be even now.

Jasmine listened hard to the lyrics of the song playing again on the TV as she climbed back into the brown chair with her blanket. She didn't understand the words of "Auld Lang Syne" but she loved the melody and knew what the song was trying to say. She figured it was something about friendship and new beginnings. Maybe not everything needed to be clear to have a meaning. Zoey and Jasmine weren't speaking much during that week in room 532 but they had an understanding that would get them through anything.

"Happy New Year. Thank you for hanging the lights. And thank you for being here for me, Jas." Zoey had woken up and startled Jasmine with her first words to her in seven long days.

"I will always be here for you—you know that, right? I am sorry," Jasmine said as she moved from the brown chair to sit on the edge of her sister's bed.

"I do. And I am sorry for what I am putting our family through. And Matt through. Or, what I put him through. I get it."

Zoey pulled her hand out from under the blankets and held on to her sister's hand tight.

"Jasmine, I love this song, but it's been playing all night. Time for something new," Zoey said as she waved the remote in front of Jasmine with a smile.

"I couldn't agree more."

Jasmine turned the TV off and walked over to the window to close the blinds. The couple was gone and the lights outside the bar had been turned off. The door creaked open and the nurse crept into the dark room.

Zoey smiled at her sister as the nurse took her pulse.

"Much stronger, Zoey." The nurse smiled as she tucked Zoey's arm back under the covers.

"She ain't dead yet!" Jasmine and Zoey burst into laughter like they had so many years earlier waiting for Santa on Christmas Eve as Jasmine raised both her fists in the air.

It felt good to finally laugh again.

CHAPTER 6

FALL – 1998

Zoey

It was the last Sunday in August and today was the day. I was finally leaving this small town. I was also leaving my parents and Jasmine. I had graduated in May, and now, I was leaving the small, sleepy town in Idaho and moving to Oregon where I would start my first semester at Portland State University in one week. Jasmine was off to The University of Denver, and for the first time in our lives, we would have to have a few "firsts" without each other. I couldn't wait and I was terrified all at the same time.

"Honey, is the car full of gas?" My mom was a wreck. She had asked me this same question three times in the last hour.

"Yes. And I promise to call you every few hours. Portland is really not that far." I had insisted on driving a rental car one way because all I needed was a bike to get around the new city I would call home. It had been a rough couple of years for my family and it was an act of God to convince my mom and dad to let me even go to college. But I was getting better. I was in therapy and had gained enough weight for my family to be comfortable with letting me go. And, in room 532 in St. Luke's on Christmas Day, I had finally hit rock bottom and decided there was nowhere to go but up. I made a promise to myself and my family that day that I would figure out how to survive the horrible disease. I wasn't completely better, but for the first time in two years, I felt like I wanted to live again. For the first time in two years, I was relieved when I opened my eyes each morning.

I can't explain exactly how I pulled myself out of wishing I wouldn't wake up each morning, but I can try. Some days, I would still wake up full of dread. The thought of making it through each day was easier, but I had to admit, I knew I wasn't completely better. This was a feeling I tried hard to keep to myself. The fact that my parents were letting me move to another state proved I was a great actress, not necessarily that I was completely over my disease. Don't get me wrong, it was getting easier each day to just open my eyes and decide to live, but there were so many days I had to try so hard to forget. The day I was getting ready to move to Portland alone was the first day in years that I felt actual excitement for the future.

"We love you, Zoey. Drive safe and call us right when you get there." My dad was kicking the tires of the Nissan Altima I rented for the drive. I couldn't wait to just turn on the radio and get on the road. My parents had decided to fly to Denver with Jasmine later that day to drop her off at her dorms. I didn't quite know how they decided between going with Jasmine or myself, but I was glad that they trusted me to go alone. I was also glad that they understood that their other daughter needed some help too. I had taken up the emotional resources that every family member had to offer for the past few years, and now it was Jasmine's turn.

"Love you too!" I opened the door to get into the rental car and took a deep breath, realizing I was about to leave my childhood home. We laughed as Mia jumped into the car and sat in the passenger seat, looking at me with her tail wagging. I was going to miss her and thought of how she would wait for me at the end of the lane to come home from my bike rides with Matt the summer of my junior year. Finally, she slowly stepped out of the passenger door and I bent down to hug her.

At the end of the half-mile-long dirt drive, I looked in the rear-view mirror at the only home I had ever known. Vivid memories flooded my mind as I focused on my mom waving aggressively in the distance. I knew she couldn't see me as I blew her a kiss in the mirror and turned out into the street. I didn't know when I would be driving back up the dirt road to my house in Idaho again and I knew she was thinking the same thing as I saw my dad embrace her as I drove away. I wondered what memories ran through their minds, if any, as I drove away. I hoped they were memories from before my disease. We were all anxious to close that chapter, and driving away that morning felt like a good first step to a fresh start.

I took the long way to get to the freeway so I could drive past Matt's house one last time. In the yard was a For Sale sign. I had run into him in the hallways at school a few times. He would pass with a guilty smile and, in his eyes, I could see he wanted to say something. We hadn't spoken again after he broke my heart that Sunday in October. Little did we know how intertwined our lives would end up eventually being. I had no idea if he knew that Jasmine told me about the two of them. At first, she just told me they kissed. I knew better than that. Matt was a horny 17-year-old boy who was dating a girl whose breasts had disappeared and whose butt bone ached when she sat too long. Jasmine was the most beautiful girl in school with long flowing hair and a body that looked anything like a little boy. I was not that naïve. It took a few months for her to finally come clean, but she eventually told me everything.

I can try to explain why I forgave her so quickly. I had put her through so much the last few years that I almost felt like this made us even. It was a strange feeling, but I was almost thankful that she did that so I could rationalize with myself that I didn't completely ruin her last few years of high school. We had an understanding now too that we could get through anything. Heading off to separate colleges was going to be hard, but we both knew it was what we needed to do. In a way, it felt like Jasmine had challenged me to wake up and see what I was missing when she told me she was the one that took my boyfriend's virginity that night when I sat crying behind the school gym on Homecoming night. Life wasn't going to just wait for me to be ready to live it. I had to get ready, or it would pass by. It sounded crazy, but I felt like I had to thank them both for helping me see I needed to pull out of the disease that consumed my life during those years.

I parked and walked up to the front yard of Matt's house. If he saw me, oh well. This would be my final goodbye to my first love. But the house was empty.

"Can I help you?" A woman in high heels teetered over toward me holding a huge sign under her armpit. She was a realtor.

"No. Sorry, I used to know the family that lives here. Just was stopping by to say goodbye."

"Oh. Yeah. They moved—Italy, I think. Open house today if you want to wander through." Her sign dropped to the ground and she bowed awkwardly to pick it up, trying hard to kneel without slitting her tight, red pencil skirt.

Italy. I smiled and shook my head. For the first time in years, my feelings were so clear. I felt joy for Matt starting a new life in Europe. He deserved a new start just as I did. He was always way too sophisticated for this sleepy Idaho town.

I gazed into the window on the side of the house that was just over the kitchen sink and had a vision of his mom. She would always stand in that window and watch us as we sat, swinging in the hammock between the two large trees in the front yard. I had often wondered if she knew we saw her watching us with her head bent slightly and a soft smile in her eyes. Her hair was always piled on top of her head, and she had a kitchen towel tossed over her shoulder. She was a mother watching her son enjoy his first love and it filled her with happiness. I blinked and my vision of her through the window was gone.

"Arrivederci, Matt!" I said dramatically as I squinted in hopes to remember the memories made at this house forever. The realtor smiled and waved her long red fingernails as I turned and walked back to my car between the two trees where the hammock used to be. I couldn't help but wonder if I would ever see him again as I drove back to the highway and left my hometown.

It took just over nine hours to get to Portland. The moon reflected on the Willamette River as I drove over the Hawthorne Bridge into the city. Immediately, I found where I belonged. Idaho felt worlds away as I turned up the music and listened to Destiny's Child singing their own song, "Bridges". I rolled down the window and took a deep breath, taking in the size of the buildings lighting up the dark sky. I was home.

My new home was a studio apartment on Northwest 21st Street. Walking up to the entrance felt almost like a dream. I had to pinch myself as I unlocked the door of the first-floor apartment that would be mine. The door squeaked loudly as I opened it and stepped in. I stood in silence for a moment, in awe that I was standing in my very own apartment. A siren broke the silence and red and blue lights flooded through the large window. I wasn't in my sleepy hometown anymore, that was for sure.

I suddenly thought of Jasmine and my parents, possibly already in Denver. She was going to live in the dorms like most college freshmen. She was going to meet an awkward roommate from Philadelphia that she was praying didn't snore. I was happy to have a non-traditional year ahead of me without frat boys and having to share a shower with my entire floor. I was thrilled to avoid an awkward roommate that I would have to make small talk with when I wanted to be alone. I could hear the giggling now and see Jasmine rolling her eyes and turning her headphones up as she tried to pretend to study to avoid socializing with her new roommate's equally awkward "squad". I was shocked that Jasmine hadn't also chosen to live alone after so many years with me as her constant companion, but I was happy it was her and not me preparing to divvy up the 400-square-foot dorm room on this August night. This was my new life, and I would be following the road less traveled. I had spent my life thus far as a half of a whole—one of the twins. Today was going to be the day I started a fresh life. I spent the summer trying to prepare to be lonely as I knew I would miss my family. But this was a chapter I was ready to open. A new city and a new future had arrived.

The next morning, I woke up early to the sound of rain on my window. I was living in a studio apartment by myself, and it finally hit me when I opened my eyes that I had spent my first night alone. I wondered if Mia slept in my empty bed. She had spent almost every night of her life sleeping on my feet in my small bedroom in Idaho. I waited for fear or anxiety to take over and it never did. The rain fell harder as the sun rose and filled my small apartment with light. The room was about the same size as my bedroom in Idaho but came furnished with a twin bed, a papasan chair, and a small kitchen table with two chairs. My new life fit into 300 square feet. Suddenly, I wondered who, if anyone, would sit at my kitchen table with me.

I dug through my suitcases to find my running shoes and threw on a long-sleeve shirt and shorts. I couldn't wait to explore my new city on foot. I was still getting used to my body growing back to a normal teenage size, which meant most of my clothes were a little tight. Some days it bothered me when the elastic on my shorts cut hard above my belly button, and some days it didn't. Today was a lucky day that I didn't care that I was gaining weight. That was what I was supposed to be doing and what I needed to keep telling myself if I wanted to stay here and live my new independent life. I pulled my hair into a ponytail in front of the small mirror above my bathroom sink and smiled at my reflection.

The door creaked loudly as I stepped out and into the small hallway. As I turned to lock my door, I heard his voice.

"Hi, neighbor! Did you sneak in here last night? I thought I heard you moving stuff, but you sure did that quickly. Must not have much, huh? Going for a run? It's raining. But the sooner you get used to running in the rain, the better off you will be in this city."

I tried to take inventory of the questions he rattled off as I caught eyes with the first person I would meet in my new city.

"Um. Hi. I did move in last night. My name is Zoey. I live in apartment 101."

I blushed with regret as I realized that of course he knew I lived in apartment 101—I had the keys and had walked out of 101 just 30 seconds earlier. I felt my face flush as he smiled in an effort to help me feel not so dumb.

"I see that. You know the old lady that lived there before you died in there and they didn't find her for a month! How's the smell?"

"What?" I said as I dropped my keys on the old hardwood floors. I bent down to grab them and felt the elastic in my shorts tighten. I stood quickly and locked eyes with him.

"Just wanted to get a reaction out of you. She didn't die. Well, she didn't die in that apartment, but she might have died since last week when she moved out. She was probably 100 years old. Her daughter finally picked her up and moved her into her house. Took her long enough. She was a sweet old lady, but I think she was racist. Age is no excuse for that shit. Anyway, my name is Kofi."

He extended his long arm, exposing a sleeve of intricate tattoos telling a story on his skin. He flashed a bright smile as he stepped toward me. He was gorgeous. My new neighbor was tall, dark, and handsome in the flesh. He had big brown eyes and the beginning of a perfectly cut beard. The hair on his head was cut so short that I didn't know if you would even say he had hair. He was very handsome. As he shook my hand, I found myself wanting to know everything about him.

"Nice to meet you, Kofi."

I smiled and noticed our hands were still locked together. I caught a glimpse of my hair in the small window behind him near the front door. I looked as though an eight-year-old had tried to put my hair in a bun, and not the cute messy buns that models wore on beaches in magazines. I never imagined I would have a gorgeous neighbor to impress on my first day in the hallway of my new apartment. I remembered my older sister telling Jasmine and I earlier that summer that she always tried to look her best at the grocery store. She would rather meet a man in the grocery store than the bar or at the gym. She was meeting men while she was still in Arizona in her last year at ASU. Up until today, I had only ever worried about meeting boys. My new neighbor, Kofi, was a man.

"You too, Zoey. I look forward to running into you again… or maybe having coffee with you tomorrow…"

"Oh, um… I have class tomorrow, it's my first day at PSU." I was realizing how bad I was at this and should have offered some alternative instead of just saying I couldn't and seeming like I didn't want to.

"Ok, well then, dinner tonight? Unless you are busy, of course," Kofi said, seeming to have read my mind.

He pulled his hand free and put both hands deep into the pockets of his black sweatpants. He raised his eyebrows, waiting for my reply. I almost laughed out loud thinking of how not busy I was that night. He was the first person I met in this city. Maybe he would be the first person to sit in my kitchen with me in one of my two black plastic chairs.

"Oh. Ok. Yeah, that sounds good." My cheeks were almost burning, I was blushing so hard.

"I will pick you up… um… knock on apartment 101 at 7 p.m. See you then!"

I nodded and turned quickly as he smiled and retreated into his apartment.

And just like that, I had a date with a gorgeous man at 7 p.m.

With two hands, I pushed open the doors to the building and stepped on the sidewalk. The rain was coming down hard and my bun was now a wet ball of hair weighing heavy on my drenched head. The sirens whirled on Burnside Street in front of me as I passed the old light posts that flanked the cracked sidewalk leading up to 201 NW 20th Place Apartments. With the light layer of fog, the light posts made me feel like I was in a romantic black-and-white movie from the 1920s. I looked up into the sky and let the rain wash over my face. The raindrops were cold and refreshing.

I took a deep breath and exhaled and put one soggy foot in front of the other for my first run in my new city. I had a date, and I couldn't wait to tell Jasmine.

CHAPTER 7

FALL – 1998

Kofi

Kofi watched through the rain-soaked window as his new neighbor struggled to parallel park on the street in front of the apartment complex. He knew she was his new neighbor only because Monica, the complex manager, had gone out of her way to tell him there was a cute young girl moving into Mrs. Rochelle's old apartment that morning when he ran into her in the laundry room. Monica and Mrs. Rochelle were constantly trying to set him up. He had lived in the building for two years and was yet to be even slightly attracted to any of the long list of women either of them had tried to push on him over the years. He figured a single 40-something apartment manager and a 90-something old cat lady could never guess what type of a woman Kofi was in the market for.

As he peered through the window, Kofi remembered when he arrived at his empty apartment for the first time years earlier. He had walked over a mile from the bus stop in the pouring rain that night.

Nobody warned him about the depressing Portland weather, and he had never taken enough time to figure out how to take the bus. Had he taken the time to understand the city bus route, he would have been dropped off right in front of the building as opposed to a mile away. Instead, Kofi got off the bus at the Waterfront Park with a backpack full of clothes, which was everything he had to his name. When he stepped off the bus, he had never seen such a beautiful sight as the city lights twinkling off the water in his entire life. He didn't mind the walk but was amazed at all the homeless people along the waterfront and under the bridge. What had all the people done to not have a bed to sleep in? Kofi looked up and thanked God he had arrived in what would now be his new home. Portland was as far away as he could travel with what he had to spend on a one-way bus ticket. Two years later, as Kofi looked back on the day he arrived, he felt what was his first glimmer of hope that he wasn't completely alone.

He would end up being pleasantly surprised when his new neighbor finally emerged from her car after what must have been 10 attempts to park. She took a few steps backwards and sized up her parking job with both hands on her hips and her head cocked to the side. He noticed her looking around to see if anyone was watching her 10 attempts to park. *She must not be a city girl,* Kofi thought as he squinted and lifted the slats of the blinds to get a better look. She had long, brown hair pulled tight into a high ponytail. She wore running shoes and short spandex shorts that were almost fully covered by a baggy University of Oregon Track hoodie. She was skinny but looked like an athlete. He watched her as she struggled again to open the trunk and loaded what must have been 20 full grocery bags onto her arms. She was determined to make one trip!

"This girl is efficient," Kofi said out loud to himself as he laughed, watching her shuffle quickly with the bags to the front door.

She got lucky and caught the door as Kofi's upstairs neighbor, Jon, swung it open aggressively. Jon jumped onto the steps below, lit a cigarette that was almost falling out of his mouth, as he gasped at almost knocking her over. He was drunk already. It was Saturday night and Jon was off to a bar or a club or any number of places he could smoke and get just drunk enough to come home and keep Kofi up most of the night. This was par for the course for Saturday night at 201 NW 20th Place Apartments. Jon would arrive back to the front step hours later, half-empty bottle of something in his hand, and loudly stomp up the stairs to his one-bedroom apartment directly above Kofi's studio. He would turn some form of Seattle grunge music up and have a rotating parade of strange girls with him that Kofi would hear moaning loudly minutes later. Kofi scoffed, thinking that Jon was some sort of lover boy while he had spent most Saturday nights alone. The girls that Jon brought home to NW 20th Place Apartments weren't the types of girls Kofi was interested in regardless. Kofi would rather be alone than drunkenly entertain strangers every Saturday night like his upstairs neighbor did. If he had a dollar for every poor, hungover club-rat that he saw sneak back down the stairs before Jon woke for a Sunday morning walk-of-shame, Kofi would be rich!

The new neighbor gasped at Jon and quickly stopped the door with her foot and smiled, not dropping a bag or missing a beat. Kofi could see her eyes widen at the sight of his obvious intoxication. Jon looked back at her and raised his eyebrows.

"New neighbor? Much hotter than Mrs. What's-Her-Face. Not really my type though. Sorry, sweetie." Kofi heard Jon stutter through the crack in his window.

"Asshole!" Kofi's voice was loud in his head as he wondered if anyone had ever just punched Jon in the face before. This guy was truly a jerk.

Jon stumbled onto the sidewalk and the new, brown-haired neighbor adjusted her foothold on the door and regained focus on the task at hand. Kofi immediately felt protective of her even though he hadn't even met her yet and made a mental note to keep an eye on Creepy

Jon around the new girl. Monica was not wrong though… she was cute.

Kofi pulled the curtains closed and smiled as he plotted "running" into her the next day. He wondered how old she was. He was going to be 21 in just a few hours. She didn't look old enough to share a drink with him on his big day. If she had been his age, he imagined ordering a bottle of red wine to go with his birthday dinner they would share at the fancy Italian place on Northwest 23rd. He would make sure her glass was full and she would smile at him through the candlelight. Kofi shook his head, annoyed at himself for jumping ahead to their first date when he hadn't even met the girl. He was just tired of being alone. He had been alone for what felt like his entire life. Meeting friends was hard in Portland. Meeting a girl to have a drink with seemed almost impossible. Well, he had met one, but she was gone now and living a new life.

Kofi looked around his studio apartment, suddenly feeling a wave of loneliness. The rain started to come down hard again after what ended up being just enough time for his new neighbor to empty her car without getting drenched. He wondered if it had felt like a sign to her that the weather let up just long enough for her to get settled. Would that help her feel at home in a brand-new strange place? Kofi hadn't really felt at home since he moved to Portland two years ago from Kentucky. He knew, though, that this was probably the best he could ask for after leaving Kentucky.

He wandered into his small kitchen and turned on the radio that sat on the windowsill above the sink. His favorite song by The Fugees filled the silence, reminding him that everything's gonna be alright.

Kofi wondered if his new neighbor could hear the music as he turned the volume knob to full blast. The walls were thick in the old brick building. Mrs. Rochelle couldn't hear anything. Kofi made a mental note to ask his new neighbor tomorrow if his music bothered her.

Music had been a constant companion to Kofi over the years. He would fall asleep most nights listening to Miles Davis or Sade. He wondered if his new neighbor knew who either of them were. He smiled, imagining playing her his list of favorite songs.

It had not been an easy 21 years so far for Kofi. He had secrets about his past you would not expect anyone to be able to carry around with them. One glance at him and you might mistakenly assume he breezed through life. The music had a way of drowning out the thoughts in his head and the anxiety he felt when he was alone for too long. Kofi sat on the edge of his bed and fell back, his head gently hitting the pillows propped up behind him. The music was loud but not loud enough for him to forget. He needed someone to talk to.

The next day would mark two years since the accident. The day his life changed forever was the anniversary of the day he was supposed to celebrate his life with those that he loved. After that day two years ago, he would never be able to do that again. He dreaded his birthday after the accident changed that day for him forever. This year though, he hoped to start a new tradition and reclaim that day as his birthday and not the anniversary of the worst day of his life. He was going to ask out the new neighbor tomorrow. If Kofi knew anything, he knew that life was short, he was lucky to be alive, and everything was going to be alright.

As he laid in his studio apartment, listening to the rain fall on the window, Kofi remembered his birthday just the year before. He hoped time would help him forget that awful day, but it didn't seem to make a difference. He had barely been able to enjoy waking up each day without a feeling of guilt overwhelming him. Kofi woke up that morning one year ago and didn't feel thankful to be alive and to be celebrating another year of life. All he could think about was that day, two years before. Kofi tried numbing the pain of his past in many ways. Alcohol, sex, and even drugs had only been able to keep his mind idle for so long. Once the numbness wore off, Kofi could not think of anything but that day.

Kofi closed his eyes and felt as though he was back on that bridge the year before. He woke up on his 20th birthday alone and depressed as he had every day since the accident. He stepped outside of his studio apartment and into the rain that fell the hardest he had seen it come down since he moved to Portland one year earlier. Kofi unlocked his blue 10-speed bike and rode down to the waterfront before heading toward the Hawthorne Bridge. He felt as though he hadn't woken up yet physically and mentally and he just needed to end a terrible nightmare. The rain fell harder. Kofi abandoned his bike when he finally arrived at the bike lane to cross the bridge. It hadn't been more than two minutes before a homeless man ran up behind him, claiming the blue bike as his own and pedaling away into the rain. The man abandoned his clear plastic bag full of soda cans where Kofi had left his bike. He turned and watched as the man's long stringy blonde hair flopped in the wind as he sped off on Kofi's blue 10-speed bike. Kofi jogged quickly to what he felt was the tallest point of the bridge overlooking the city. He stood near the guard rail and pressed his stomach to the cold concrete. He gazed through the rain at the city he was supposed to now call home. The city was full of people and yet he had not one person to call his friend. He realized at that point he was crying as he tasted salt in the rain running down his face.

Kofi closed his eyes and saw her face, clear as the day she died. Clear as the day he killed her. She was the one that always visited him in his dreams. She was the one that he could never forget about. Her eyes were light green and striking. Her skin was dark and clear, and she wore her hair tight in two cornrows. He closed his eyes tighter and saw her smiling, laughing maybe at a joke he told her before bedtime. It was the image Kofi saw every night that kept him up, wishing he could have taken her place that day two years before.

Kofi opened his eyes as the rain poured down and the little girl disappeared. In her place was a woman. She was all grown up. Her hair was no longer in two braids but pulled into a ponytail that flowed down her back in tight, black curls. Her striking green eyes were staring at him. She had to be 20 now—his age.

"I am so sorry. I can't ever forgive myself for what happened to you, Naya." Kofi's tears fell harder, and the woman stared at him silently as she stood next to him on the Hawthorne Bridge.

"What are you talking about? Are you ok? I was on a run and I saw you dump your bike back there, so I followed you to make sure you were ok. Was that your blue 10-speed? I think that man took it. My name is not Naya. Um, I think you need some help."

Kofi lowered his head as the woman who was not Naya reached for his hand.

She held both his hands tightly as he imagined falling into the water from the bridge. He had come there to end his nightmare and be with Naya again. This woman had stopped him. Naya died two years earlier and was not the woman who stood in front of him. Not many people would have ever known or cared if Kofi died that day except his neighbor, Mrs. Rochelle, Monica, the apartment manager of his building, and his best friend, Reggie, from home.

"Ok. Let's get you home." The girl who was not Naya was looking around as if to find the quickest way off the bridge. She didn't know Kofi's story. In fact, nobody knew his story. She did know he needed to get off that bridge and she was going to be the one to get him home.

"Everything is going to be alright. We will get you home and we need to get you some help." Kofi nodded and followed her off the bridge in silence, tears streaming down his face.

Kofi opened his eyes quickly as he heard Jon, his neighbor, singing loudly outside of his window in the courtyard. He was not on the Hawthorne Bridge anymore on the day he tried to end his life a year ago. It had been 365 days since the homeless man stole his blue bike. Kofi was laying in his bed and it was officially his 21st birthday. Jon was drunk and had gone from singing loudly to trying to open the door. Kofi heard keys fall to the ground over and over again and finally heard the door swing open and Jon's slurred singing fade off as he made it to his apartment upstairs.

Kofi turned up the radio and closed his eyes. He had slowly learned how to sleep without seeing Naya's sad eyes. Maybe two years was the turning point for him and his healing. Maybe the day of his 20th birthday was his official rock bottom.

Just like the woman who saved him from jumping off of the Hawthorne Bridge and the Fugees said, finally he believed that everything was going to be alright.

CHAPTER 8

FALL – 1998

Jasmine

Jasmine loved this city so far. Denver had been the place she felt like she was meant to be. She didn't much care for her roommate, Cali, and her slew of obnoxious sorority sisters. Jasmine actually didn't know for sure if they were in a sorority, but from what she saw in every terrible college party movie, they fit the mold.

They lived on the 12th floor in one of two towers on campus. From her dorm room window, she could see the lacrosse field on one side, and the Rocky Mountains on the other. It was the most beautiful view she had ever seen, and she wondered each morning how she got so lucky to have that room. Jasmine had a full academic scholarship but knew that most of the students were paying the hefty private university tuition in addition to room and board. No wonder she didn't really fit in with her roommate. Cali was a spoiled, east coast rich girl like the majority of the student population.

Jasmine prided herself on being the daughter of two hippies that met in South America in the 70s and raised their family to work hard and be thankful for what they had. Sure, her dad was a doctor, but she didn't grow up like these kids at her school had. Although she and her sisters don't remember, her parents told them stories of their first home in New Mexico where they were born having dirt floors. Her roommate had a Range Rover parked in the student lot outside. They couldn't be more different, but still, Jasmine liked being a student at the University of Denver. She would find her friends sooner or later in her new home.

Surprisingly, Cali didn't even argue with her about which bed she wanted, so Jasmine promptly arranged her belongings in the twin-sized bed that looked west toward the sunset and the mountains.

Jasmine's parents had left that morning after a few nights in a bright white boutique hotel in Cherry Creek North Shopping District. Her mother had fallen in love with the small shops and diverse array of restaurants. Jasmine always felt like her mother was too classy for the small Idaho town they grew up in and she saw her smile fade quickly as she packed her suitcase to leave Denver to go back to the home she knew just hours earlier. Jasmine wondered what her childhood home would feel like to her parents now that all their children were gone. They had no more kids to worry about running around the house, just kids out in the real world to keep them up at night now. At least they had Mia still, and the horses.

"Jas, have you heard from your sister today?" Her mother asked her the night before at dinner in a small Italian place off of University Blvd in Denver. The tables had small, red candles on them similar to what you might see in Lady and the Tramp. Even though she had never been to Italy, Jasmine imagined this was how cafes on the sidewalks of Venice looked. Jasmine couldn't stop staring at the flame.

"Jasmine, your mother asked you a question…" Jasmine's dad had his arm around her mother's back and was gazing into her green eyes.

Something about this trip seemed like her parents were falling back in love. After all these years putting their marriage second to their three daughters' needs, Jasmine had hoped they were doing just that—falling back in love. She shook her head and moved her focus from the candle flame to her father's blue eyes. He was handsome, even at the age of 55. She knew her friends all had crushes on him and wondered what he looked like at their age. He had dark hair with more and more flecks of gray each day. It suited him and he almost gave off a George Clooney vibe with his pretty eyes and charming personality. Jasmine's parents were a knockout couple in their day and still were with three grown children and an empty nest.

"Sorry. Um. Yes, I did hear from Zoey. She seems pretty excited about the hot neighbor… and her place, of course. She said it never stops raining though," Jasmine said as she grabbed a buttery roll from the breadbasket and ripped it in half, imagining her sister running through the rainy streets of Portland.

"Hot neighbor? Oh, jeez. I hope she doesn't get her heart broken again after all she went through with Matt." Jasmine's mom shook her head and took the last swig of her white wine. She kept her eyes focused on Jasmine as she tipped her neck back to get the last drops from the wine glass. Jasmine knew her parents didn't know anything about how she was actually a part of the reason Matt had broken her sister's heart. Still, her palms grew sweaty as her mom watched her through her wine glass as though she might know something about it after all. It really did seem like her mom knew everything or eventually found out, just as she had threatened them multiple times when they were younger.

"Fresh start for our girl in Portland. And a fresh start for you in Denver, Jas. We are proud of you. Even though you aren't going to study medicine, we are happy to see you on your own." Jasmine's dad was smiling and pouring another glass for her mom from the almost empty bottle on the table. He had hoped one of his daughters would pursue medicine like he did but had three strikes on that dream. He was still a very proud dad to three girls that were all in college.

"I am going to be the best journalist you ever meet!" Jasmine said as she shoved the second half of the buttery roll into her mouth.

"Yep! And the only!" her mom muttered and playfully rolled her eyes.

Jasmine was going to miss her parents. She loved spending time with them alone without Zoey. It had been years since it was just the three of them and it felt good to see them laugh. It felt even better to know they were proud of her.

Jasmine smiled to herself thinking of her last night in perhaps the next few months with her parents in Denver. They had already called to tell her they made it home safely and to not forget to call them any time. She missed them already.

"Hey. Do you want to go to brunch with us, Jas?" Cali said as she burst into the room with her blonde crew in tow. *Nobody calls me Jas except my family,* Jasmine thought as she took a deep breath.

"I am good. Thanks though," she said as she wondered if she rolled her eyes in reality or just in her head at her new roommate and her friends.

"Um. Ok. See ya, girl." And just like that, the room was silent with only the leftover scent of too much perfume and hairspray to fill the air.

Jasmine fought the urge to pick up the phone and call Zoey. She was learning to wean herself off the comfort of always having her best friend around. She assumed Zoey was feeling the same. Or, perhaps she was being comforted by that hot neighbor she was so excited to talk about a few nights before.

Jasmine decided to put on her tennis shoes and take a walk around the park that she could see from the window at the end of the hallway. It looked about a mile away and had two ponds from what she could tell. It was amazing how Jasmine could barely breathe in the mile-high city just walking up and down the stairs of her building. She imagined her sister running around it each morning and knew she would be excited to visit her and stay in the dorms just so she could run laps around that beautiful park. Jasmine was excited to start a new tradition of walking around Washington Park. That tradition would last the entire four years she went to the school.

The park was bigger than Jasmine had thought. It took her almost half an hour just to get there from her dorm. When she finally got to the park, it was bustling with runners, walkers, and even girls laying in the grass in bikinis.

"I am so sorry! She is nice, I promise!" A runner stopped to pull her black lab from jumping on Jasmine's legs at the stop light.

"No worries. Your dog is so cute." Jasmine almost felt like she knew the girl with the lab. Her hair in a tight ponytail and an Oregon Ducks t-shirt on—she reminded Jasmine of Zoey.

"Do you know how far it is to walk around this park? I just moved here and don't want to get in over my head." Jasmine was on a mission to make some friends that didn't drive Range Rovers that their father bought for them for Christmas. This girl seemed fairly normal compared to the sea of rich girls from her dorm.

"I run here every day… almost. It's 2.6 miles around. You can do it! Are you a runner? I can always use a friend to run with. No pressure. I sound crazy. Sorry. What is your name? This is Jimmy." The girl pointed to her dog as though it would then present its paw for a formal handshake and introduction. The dog looked up at Jasmine as if trying to get permission to lay down. Both girls laughed as he plopped onto the middle of the running trail, watching as runners and walkers moved around him in the middle of the trail.

"He really isn't much of an athlete, is he?" Jasmine's new friend shook her head as she pulled hard on the leash.

"My name is Jasmine. Sorry… no running for me. I will walk though. I might be more Jimmy's speed than yours." Jimmy looked up at Jasmine and back toward his owner as if he knew they were talking about him.

"I would walk with you too. Damn, I sound desperate for friends. Sorry. I just moved here and really haven't met anyone worth hanging out with and you seem really cool. My name is Cassidy," she said with a smile.

Just like that, Jasmine had her first friend in Denver. She even came with a cute dog and a healthy habit.

"Cool! Want to meet here tomorrow to walk?"

"Let's do it! Does 9:00 a.m. work?" Cassidy asked as she lifted her sunglasses to display a set of striking green eyes. Jasmine hoped her expression didn't show how shocked she was at her new friend's beauty.

"See you tomorrow!"

Cassidy jogged off with Jimmy in tow as Jasmine slowly crossed the street into Washington Park. She walked around the entire park in pretty much exactly an hour as her new friend had predicted.

Jasmine arrived back to her room and was relieved to come home to an empty place. She kicked off her shoes and placed her CD player on the small desk as she picked up the phone. Zoey answered on the first ring.

"I made a friend. You should be jealous. She has a cute dog and green eyes!" Jasmine laughed into the phone, feeling at home hearing her sister's voice on the other line. She was also feeling slightly awkward at mentioning Cassidy's beautiful green eyes.

"Well, I just might be in love, so I think I beat you in today's game of one-up, sis!" Zoey sounded happy and relaxed as they talked for hours.

Jasmine hung up the phone and climbed into her twin bed. Cali hadn't gotten home yet from her all-day brunch and Jasmine was thankful to have the place to herself. The normal chatter outside her door had been taken over by silence and she knew it must have been past midnight. Through the window, the moon filled the night sky and illuminated the mountains below. Jasmine could see herself living there forever.

The next morning, Jasmine started a tradition that lasted through college. It was a tradition she had hoped to keep for longer, but life had a way of surprising her. She met her new friend, Cassidy, at the corner of Franklin and Louisiana Streets at the tree near the creek in Washington Park. For the next many years, through rain and snow, they would meet to walk and talk and eventually became the best of friends.

That morning, they walked for almost two hours, telling each other the stories of their lives. Jasmine told Cassidy about her sister's anorexia and how she fought to stay alive.

"It was the hardest thing I have ever had to do that I wasn't actually doing. Ya know? Like I had to be there and support her, but I really couldn't do anything to save her. I just had to hope that she would figure it out and pull herself out of this horrible disease. I felt really guilty. Still do." Jasmine lifted her sunglasses to the top of her head to look into Cassidy's eyes as they walked.

"Wow. I can't imagine. Your sister sounds strong." Cassidy met Jasmine's gaze with her crisp green eyes.

"So, why did you move here?" Jasmine asked her new friend.

"Well, I fell in love with someone that couldn't love me back. Word to the wise is to never fall in love with someone who can't even love themselves. I moved here for a fresh start." Cassidy stopped walking and squatted down to pet Jimmy. Jasmine noticed that Cassidy was not used to talking about herself.

"You remind me a lot of my sister actually," Jasmine said.

"Let's get coffee after this. Sound good?" Cassidy stood up quickly and smiled. Jasmine could tell Cassidy had a lot on her mind. She would spend the next four years listening to her and telling her everything she had on her mind as well. They would eventually know everything about each other's past—well, almost everything. They had no idea on that beautiful morning at Washington Park how much their pasts were intertwined and how much their futures would be determined by fate.

CHAPTER 9

FALL – 1999

Zoey

September in Portland was bittersweet. The summer was over. It was full of days that the rain stayed away so everyone remembered why they moved there in the first place. I didn't live in Portland over the summer, which meant that September was my favorite month of the year in the city. Driving back to Portland from Idaho felt like I was really coming back home. I felt like I finally belonged somewhere.

It was my birthday. I was starting my sophomore year and I was happy. The summer had been full of family time and therapy appointments. I felt like my old self again and was doing everything in my power to stay that way. It took me a long time to get back to a place where I felt happy in my own skin again. It felt like my struggle with anorexia was over. At least, I didn't struggle enough to really feel it for the most part.

It felt like a century had passed since I felt my first heartbreak over Matt. I was happy in my new life. And I was in love. It had been a year and a half since I was in that hospital room on New Year's Eve with Jasmine at my side, wondering if I would wake up to a new tomorrow. I often thought about that night in the hospital bed. That was one of the last days I struggled to want to wake up the next day.

I missed Jasmine the minute we parted ways after our summer together at home. We went for bike rides, to the movies, and just talked for what felt like every night over the summer. Two weeks earlier, we each headed off, back to our homes for the next nine months with a long hug and too many tears to count. Jasmine was happy in Denver and couldn't stop talking about her new best friend, Cassidy. I was happy she had someone in Denver, and I had someone in Portland. I told her all about Kofi and how he made me feel like the most beautiful girl in the world. I would go and visit her for New Year's in Denver, and she would come to Portland in the Spring. The day that we had to say goodbye at the end of the summer, we reminded each other that we had so much to look forward to!

It had been over a year since I moved into apartment 101 and met the handsome stranger across the hall that I now called my boyfriend. It had been a magical year since our first date, which was also our first kiss.

Kofi and I had spent almost every night together since that day he knocked on my door and we headed out on our first date. That night was the first of many nights we would wander up NW 23rd Street, hand in hand, sometimes under an umbrella in the pouring rain. We ended up eating at a Thai place with dark tables and only candlelight to light the room. A year flew by, and it felt like yesterday since that day we met. On this September morning, I couldn't help but smile as I reminisced.

"So, I have a confession to make. It's my birthday today," Kofi said to me with a shy smile halfway through dinner on our first date.

"What? Holy shit… I am so sorry, I didn't know." I blushed and slapped my hand on my forehead, realizing at that very moment how incredibly awkward I am in front of the opposite sex.

"How would you know, we just met!" Kofi said as we both laughed.

"How old are you?" I was relieved to get to ask the question I had wondered since I met him for the first time earlier that day.

"Actually, I am 21 today." Kofi picked up the plastic menu under the candle that had the list of drinks available and raised his eyebrows as he gazed at me past the candlelight.

He was gorgeous. I looked into his dark eyes and smiled. I hoped at that moment that I would look into those dreamy eyes forever. I felt my cheeks flush and tried hard not to stare at him.

"Are you getting an alcoholic beverage? Don't let me hold you back! FYI, I am not 21." I smiled across the table at my date as he set down the plastic menu in front of us.

Kofi lifted his cup of tea with both hands and held it in front of me with his elbows on the dark table. I did the same with my cold cup of water. My curiosity about this sexy man was mounting as my glass touched his lukewarm cup of tea.

"Cheers. Happy Birthday, neighbor, and to many more."

That night, Kofi and I finished our dinner and wandered back to our apartment complex. The entire walk, I was longing for him to grab my hand. I hadn't felt these butterflies since Matt. These feelings felt much different though. They felt mature. We arrived in front of the building and stood facing each other on the steps. I could hear cars honking on Burnside and could see the lights of the city out of the corner of my eyes. I was still in shock that I lived in this city and had actually left my small Idaho town. If this night was any indication, I was going to be perfectly happy here for the next four years, at least!

"Well, thank you for spending my birthday with me, neighbor. Although, it must have seemed like I tricked you into being my date on my birthday since you didn't know when you said yes. You are a lot more fun than Mrs. Rochelle," Kofi said as he moved closer and finally took my hand in his.

He was tall and looked down at me as we stood on the porch. Although I had only known this man for hours, I was shocked at how comfortable I felt in his presence.

"You are quite fun yourself, Mr. Birthday Boy." I realized I didn't even know the last name of this man I was falling for quickly.

"Dean. Kofi Dean is my name." He bowed to me as though I were royalty.

We stood on the steps in silence, and he reached for my hand again.

"Zoey, to be honest, I don't want this night to end. I haven't enjoyed my birthday in a while, and I am having a great time with you." Kofi tilted his head and suddenly appeared shy to me for the first time since I met him.

"Me too. There is a coffee shop that stays open all night on Glisan Street. Do you want to go there?" I said, very unsure of myself and surprised at the bold words coming out of my mouth.

I had asked the barista that morning what their hours were as I ordered a black coffee on my way home after my run. I expected I would need a quick response to Kofi's idea of us extending our date but thought for sure I would chicken out if it came time for me to speak up. I wanted to spend all the time I could get with him.

I wanted him to come in and lay in my bed in my studio apartment. I wanted him to kiss me and play with my hair. I wanted to trace every one of his tattoos on his arm with my fingers and hear the story of what they all meant. But I didn't want Kofi to get the wrong idea. I was still a virgin at almost 19. I'd had one boyfriend in my entire life, and if Kofi kissed me right now, he would be only the second boy—man—I had ever kissed in my life.

"That sounds like a great plan," Kofi said with a smile so innocent that I almost felt like he could hear my thoughts.

It would be hours until we made it to that coffee shop on Glisan street. I ran into my apartment to grab a sweatshirt and came back to

Kofi sitting on the steps. I joined him and we sat on the front porch, his dark kitchen window behind us to the left and mine to the right for hours talking. It was 2 a.m. when we were finally interrupted by Jon, the neighbor from upstairs, as he stumbled up to the entrance with a beautiful woman on his arm. She reminded me of a 21st-century Marilyn Monroe with bleached blonde hair and a clingy white silk dress. Her nipples were hard as though it was the middle of winter, and her strap was falling off her thick shoulder as she smiled at us. You could tell what this woman looked like as a little girl when she smiled through her red-stained lips. It was a shame that she tried so hard to look older than she really appeared. She was beautiful but fit the description of a racehorse my dad often used so many years ago. Jon's date looked as though she was "rode hard and put away wet." I hated that expression but was amused at how well it described my current situation and the beautiful woman in front of me. I wanted to know more about her as we caught eyes as they passed.

"Ah. The two lonely lovebirds found each other; I see. This guy hasn't had a date in a year! Even though he is so hot, I would fuck him." Jon gazed into his date's eyes, hoping to have shocked her with his confession. He was drunk. I secretly hoped that she wasn't drunk in case she needed to fight this jerk off at some point later in the night. I caught eyes with Kofi and he seemed to be thinking the same thing. She was still smiling at us and winked as she reached for her strap with fingers decorated with long red nails. At any moment, it seemed her breast would be fully exposed, and I wondered if she had said a word all night or just listened to her obnoxious date and smiled.

"He is hot," Jon's voluptuous siren whispered in his ear on cue, fully realizing her comment would ignite the appropriate amount of jealousy to make the night exciting. As they walked away, I wondered what she could ever see in this guy. He had to have been at least mid-30s living in the same apartment complex as a fresh out of high school girl was. My parents had taught me at a young age to never judge a book by its cover, but some days, that was a harder notion to follow than others.

Jon slapped her round butt and managed to push her through the door and up the stairs without a second glance. Suddenly, it was silent again.

"Wow. So, that is our upstairs neighbor, huh? I feel like they just gave me chlamydia. I think I saw him yesterday." I glanced at Kofi as he shook his head and smirked.

"You did." He laughed and then stopped quickly as though he had accidentally told me a secret.

"Ah. So, do you watch every neighbor move into this building from your window?" I said, looking at his dark kitchen window behind him.

Kofi looked up as though he was trying to think of something clever to say.

"You did… I mean, you got chlamydia from them just now." His expression seemed as though it was funnier in his head than it was when it came out of his mouth. I could tell he wanted to take back his comment insinuating I had an STD as he shook his head just once. Finally, his big brown eyes met mine and he leaned in and did what I was waiting for all night. He kissed me.

My stomach dropped as I felt his hands in my hair. Kofi's hands were big and strong, not like my high school boyfriend's hands. These were the hands of a man, a beautiful man, who seemed like he couldn't get enough of kissing me. I never wanted it to end.

When he finally pulled his lips away from mine, I felt a raindrop on my shoulder. He looked up almost exactly as the sky opened up and decided it was time for us to get off the front porch. It was pouring on us now.

"Ok. Time to make moves, beautiful." My heart dropped hearing him call me beautiful.

Kofi grabbed my hand and pulled me off the porch and we jogged down the middle of the street to the coffee shop. It felt like the city was abandoned except for me, my handsome neighbor, and a few homeless people shuffling through trash bins to collect pop cans. The lights from the restaurants, closed hours before, reflected off the dark rain on the streets and it felt as though we were running on glass.

Kofi and I sat in that coffee shop on Glisan until the sun rose. He told me the story of every tattoo that sprinkled his arm. He told me he dreamed of being an architect and was saving up to go to school by working at another coffee shop in the art district. He told me about his love of music and how hard it had been for him to make friends in Portland. Kofi listened to me tell him about Jasmine, and the horse farm I grew up on in Idaho. I told him about my classes at PSU and how I didn't know what I wanted to study yet. I told Kofi that I ran every morning, rain or shine with no music, just my thoughts. I also told Kofi about my last New Year's Eve, and how I had to will myself to want to wake up each morning until just a few months ago. He told me he understood more than I would ever know. Finally, I told him about my first love, Matt.

That was the first of countless nights we spent in the coffee shop on Glisan Street. One year and two weeks later, I was in love with the gorgeous man across the hall. I had gone from spending every minute with my sister to every minute with my boyfriend, except for my runs, of course.

The sound of the phone ringing loudly brought me back from the night of our first kiss and to the morning of my birthday.

"Happy Birthday!" Jasmine sang when I picked up the yellow phone near my bed.

"Happy Birthday, sis! What are you doing today?" I asked her, knowing the answer already.

"I am going for my walk soon with Cassidy and then I am doing what I always do on my birthday." I could almost see the smile on her face through the phone.

Jasmine was referring to her tradition that I had embarked on with her for so many years. She would buy a ticket to a movie and then spend the entire day watching every movie that was playing in the theater. I was sad to see her carrying on our tradition without me for the second year in a row.

"I think I can talk Cassidy into movie day with me. It's my birthday, so everyone… well, my only friend, should do what I want!" Jasmine said with a laugh and a fake deep voice.

"Well, that sounds fun. I miss you and I wish I was with you today." I suddenly felt so thankful for my sister.

"Alright, bitch. Go get some birthday booty from that hot neighbor slash boyfriend of yours. I still can't wait to meet him." I could hear a hint of envy in her voice wrapped with happiness for me.

"Love you, sis. Happy Birthday!" I said as I hung up the phone and made a kissing sound into the receiver.

I looked out my kitchen window into the courtyard. It was a beautiful sunny morning. It was a rare occasion that I woke up alone, but Kofi had to go back to Kentucky the week before and would be arriving back to Portland tonight. I had to admit, although I loved spending time with him, I needed a week to remember who I was—without a boyfriend and without a twin sister.

As I tied my shoelaces, I heard a knock on my door.

"Good morning! I have a delivery from Mr. Dean." Monica, the building manager, was smiling as I answered the door. She had a full face of makeup and a long black ponytail so tight I was willing to bet her head was pounding.

"Hi, Monica. Thanks! I wonder what it is?" She handed over a paper bag and almost looked as though she was rolling her eyes at me. I expected she was jealous of us since the first day she realized we were together. After all, Kofi was the most handsome man I was sure either of us had ever met. But it wasn't just his looks that attracted people to him, there was something else that I was still trying to put my finger on. He was mysterious.

"Well, I dunno. Have a good day and thanks for always paying rent on time!" Monica twirled and her long black ponytail followed her violently. She was an interesting woman. Kofi had always told me she was sweet, but I was yet to see this alleged sweetness directed toward me. She seemed like the kind of woman that was only sweet to very handsome men. I made a mental note to ask Kofi more about her.

I unrolled the brown paper bag and reached my arm in to pull out a CD player with a set of headphones attached. Under the player were two CDs and a note.

"Happy Birthday to the most beautiful girl in the world. I adore you. Kofi."

The CDs were both Prince. I turned over the first album to look at the list of songs. There was a piece of tape with an arrow pointing to the last song called "Adore". On the second album, there was the same piece of tape pointing to the first song called "The Most Beautiful Girl in the World". Sure, I had heard Prince before, but I never really listened to the words in the songs. *Purple Rain* was the first movie we watched together on his couch the night I finally lost my virginity to him. It was a magical night and just thinking about it gave me chills.

I smiled, thinking of Kofi picking out these songs for me to listen to. He loved music and couldn't believe I ran every day with just the thoughts in my head to entertain me. I never needed to listen to music while I ran but was excited to hear the songs he picked out for me on my birthday.

Running alone with no music had been my therapy all these years. Today would be the day I was going to introduce music into my therapeutic runs.

I stepped into the sun with my CD player in my hand and the headphones singing in my ear. The sound of horns and Prince's unique voice filled me with energy. I suddenly felt I had been missing out on my entire running career. It was a gorgeous September morning, and I was another year older. Prince was the perfect music for my run.

Together, we ran along the waterfront and to the highest point on the Hawthorne Bridge. I stopped and looked down to the water below. I was another year older, and I was in love. I suddenly felt an overwhelming thankfulness for Kofi. It was as though he was there, pushing me along on my run, making it easier to put one foot in front of the other, making it easier to breathe. I leaned over the cold concrete on the bridge and turned up the CD player as loud as it would go. I was alive. For the first time in years, I felt like I didn't know that girl in the hospital on New Year's Eve. I felt like I was right where I needed to be. I was with a man who thought that I was the most beautiful girl in the world, and I adored him.

I watched the water rush swiftly below the bridge and removed my headphones to hear the water. I imagined the view from where I stood at night with the city lights glistening on the water. It was beautiful yet eerie.

"Don't do it. Don't jump. I tell everyone that. If you do, then give me that CD player before you do. It would be a shame to kill a brand-new CD player while trying to kill yourself."

I turned around to see a homeless man leaning against a blue 10-speed bike. He was thin and had long, stringy hair parted down the middle. A clear plastic bag full of soda cans was attached to his bike. For some reason, I felt like I knew this man.

"I am not going to…" and before I could finish my sentence, he hopped on his bike and rode away, mumbling under his breath.

I looked over the bridge back down into the water. I couldn't imagine jumping to my death from the top of a bridge with cars and pedestrians zooming past behind me. I thought back to the mornings during the worst part of my disease, feeling more thankful than ever to not have to fight overwhelming sadness each and every day.

I put my headphones back on and began my run back home. No matter how loud I listened to my music, I couldn't stop thinking about the man with the blue 10-speed bike. I wondered how many people he had approached trying to jump off that bridge. I wondered how many people he had collected their belongings from after they had jumped.

I arrived back at my apartment and tossed my CD player and headphones on the bed. I picked up the yellow phone and dialed the number Kofi gave to me in case I needed to get a hold of him in Kentucky. The number was disconnected. I tried again to make sure I got it correct.

There was a loud knock on my door as I hung up the phone after my third attempt dialing the number.

"Happy Birthday, beautiful!" It was Kofi, standing in front of me with a bouquet of yellow roses hours before he was supposed to arrive.

"I am so glad you're home. I missed you! You are early," I said as I wrapped my arms around him and felt his lips kiss my sweaty cheek.

"Me too," he said as he pulled me away and looked me up and down with a smile on his face. He looked different to me, almost older, more mature. I pulled him back into my arms and he exhaled deeply.

CHAPTER 10

FALL – 1999

Kofi

Kofi sat on the second step on the porch of his friend Reggie's house just outside of Lexington, Kentucky. It was Kofi's second home and the place where the two childhood best friends made countless memories. Kofi looked into the distance as he waited for his friend to come back from the kitchen. Even though it was around 10 a.m., Reggie brought Kofi a glass full of bourbon and water. Everybody drank bourbon in Kentucky. Everyone chewed tobacco, watched basketball, and drank bourbon. Reggie handed Kofi the glass and sat down on the same step next to his childhood best friend.

It had been three years since they had seen each other, although it felt like an eternity. Reggie smiled at Kofi and shook his head as if he was still in shock that he was finally visiting the place they both called home.

Reggie and Kofi were born in Lexington just a few houses apart from each other. They had gone through a lot in their lives and Reggie, for one, was happy they actually both made it this far. Every memory that Kofi had, Reggie was there. They used to ride their bikes together each morning to their first job at the stables, cleaning and feeding the thoroughbreds and hauling hay. They won the state title two years in a row for basketball in high school. Reggie was 6'4" and the leading scorer in the state. Kofi was the point guard and had a way of pretty much being able to read Reggie's mind. They were mesmerizing to watch. Reggie and Kofi even double-dated to prom and ended up both getting grounded for missing curfew that night. Kofi couldn't remember the name of his date, but he remembered laughing so hard that he cried with Reggie as they rushed home, knowing they were about to be in trouble. And when Naya was born, Kofi's mom made him go over to Reggie's house while she was in the hospital. Kofi remembered that day like it was yesterday. Every 10 minutes, he would ask Reggie's mom if she had heard from his mom yet.

"Is it a boy or a girl?" he would ask as he sat across from her at the small kitchen table that Reggie still had. Reggie's mom would shake her head, ignoring his question, and remind both boys to "eat up or you will stop growing". Those memories flooded Kofi's mind as he stared off into the woods.

"I am glad you came home for the week, man. I missed you. No time to say goodbye or nothing, huh?" Reggie smirked as if to let Kofi say he understood why he had left in such a hurry three years ago, but he wanted him to know it still hurt to have lost his best friend. Kofi still had never talked to his best friend about the day he left and the tragedy that drove him away from his hometown and everyone he thought loved him. He knew it had nothing to do with him, but Reggie was still hurt that his best friend left with no goodbye. Reggie wanted to be there for his best friend, but Kofi gave him no choice when he ran away and never looked back—until today.

"I can't say it's good to be back, but it's great to see you, Reg. I am sorry for how I left. You understand, right? I had to leave and start over. I should have kept in touch with you. It was just too hard." Kofi swallowed almost half of his cold drink he hoped would help numb him for at least that day.

Kofi lowered his head and waited for forgiveness, thinking about how Reggie was the only one in their entire town that seemed to care about him. He was all Kofi had left of his childhood. Kofi really was so thankful for Reggie, and it was hitting him as he sat on Reggie's porch that day how he had failed him as a friend. He was thankful that he had such a forgiving and understanding friend in Reggie and vowed at that moment not to take this friendship for granted again. He would eventually see how much Reggie was willing to sacrifice for his best friend.

The year before, both their moms left Kentucky and moved to Los Angeles for a fresh start, leaving everything behind and seemingly forgetting about their sons. Neither one of them had ever been close with their fathers. Reggie was all Kofi had after Naya died. It was hitting Kofi that he was also all Reggie had. Kofi needed to be a better friend. He had spent the last three years trying to understand why he couldn't open up to the people he loved.

It was going to be Zoey's birthday in a few days and Kofi still hadn't told her about his past. The time would come. Today, the time had come to finally talk to Reggie about that day he would never forget. He had been there a week already and kept everything so superficial with his best friend. They played pool, went to the local YMCA and shot hoops like old times, and ate the best food Kofi had eaten in years. It was the last day of his trip and they needed to finally talk about the painful stuff.

"Of course, man. I get it. I need to know what happened though. I haven't talked to my best friend in three years, and I don't know how to feel. There are all sorts of rumors you probably need to settle while you are here. You probably need to talk about it too, for your own good. Honestly, Kof, you probably need therapy, man." Reggie sipped slowly on his drink and rested his hand on Kofi's shoulder.

Reggie was a good man. Kofi was sure Reggie had spent the last three years defending him against any rumors that he wasn't there to defend himself against.

Reggie and Kofi had been friends since the day Kofi was born. Their moms were best friends and Kofi was almost exactly one year younger than Reggie. They were like brothers. And Naya, Kofi's little sister, was also like a sister to Reggie. Reggie was an only child, so when Naya died and Kofi left, he lost more than Kofi would really understand until that day on the porch.

"I am hurt too about her. She was like a sister to me, and you know you are like my brother. You know, time is supposed to heal, but it's not really working for any of us now, is it?" Reggie nodded to his friend. He knew Kofi more than anyone on Earth. He knew his friend had been alone and trying to deal with the accident on his own. That was what it was—an accident. Reggie sent Kofi a plane ticket every year on his birthday since he moved to Portland to come home. This was the day that he finally showed up, three years later.

Kofi finished the rest of his drink and told his best friend what happened on the worst day of his life as if he wasn't also there. Reggie nodded his head, understanding that Kofi had to walk through it like that to help him heal. He needed his best friend to listen, and Reggie kept his hand grasped tightly on his best friend's shoulder as the words fell numbly out of Kofi's mouth, recounting that horrible day. It felt good to talk about it and Kofi felt like he had cried for the first time in three years, replaying the story to his best friend. He didn't leave any detail out and Reggie cried just as hard as Kofi did sitting on the porch in Kentucky.

The two men sat on that porch until the sun came up the next morning, listening to the sounds of the woods and catching each other up on the last three years of life. Although three years had passed, Kofi felt like he only really started living the year before once he met Zoey. They finished every drop of alcohol in the house and reminisced about their childhood after Kofi finally told Reggie about that horrible day. Kofi also told Reggie about the girl on the top of the Hawthorne Bridge with the green eyes and dark, curly hair on the first anniversary of Naya's death. Kofi told Reggie about Zoey and how he felt like he might actually be in love and that she might be the one. His eyes lit up every time he said her name.

"I'm so happy for you, man. You really deserve to live the rest of your life as a happy man. It was an accident. You can't beat yourself up for this any longer after today. You hear me? I know it's hard to talk about but I'm glad that you finally told me. I needed to hear your story and I can tell that you needed to tell me yourself. I still think you need to see a professional, but I'm here for you, man, and I don't want you to ever forget it. And don't forget to call me when you need a best man." Reggie smirked and finally stood up and stretched his arms above his head. He missed his friend and he also felt more alone than Kofi realized. Reggie had so much love to give but no one to give it to but his best friend.

"Oh, shit. I gotta go, my plane leaves in an hour." Kofi stood as he looked at his watch and gave his friend a long overdue hug. He couldn't help but wonder… if he would have talked to Reggie sooner, would he have ever had that day looking into the water below on the Hawthorne Bridge? They might have lost a little sister, but in each other, they still had a brother.

An hour later, Kofi left his best friend for the second time in his life. As he sat in the back of a yellow taxi driving through the hollers of Kentucky to the Lexington Airport that day, he realized how lucky he was to have a friend like Reggie. Kofi admired Zoey and Jasmine's relationship and always loved how close she was to her parents and older sister in Arizona. He wanted that. He had that with Reggie and would have had that with Naya if that terrible accident never happened. Kofi didn't know when or if he would ever see Reggie again in person or sit on the porch in Lexington looking out into the woods with his best friend. He made a mental note to send Reggie a plane ticket to Portland for his birthday just as Reggie had done for him. Reggie had never left the state and he knew he would get a kick out of the Pacific Northwest, and he would love meeting Zoey.

Hours later, Kofi arrived back in Portland and couldn't wait to knock on the door of apartment 101. As he stood on the other side of the door, holding a bouquet of yellow roses, he finally felt what would be the first glimpse of peace. He couldn't wait to see Zoey and spend her birthday eating, drinking, and making love. He felt excited to open up to her more and wanted her to meet Reggie and learn more about him than just his favorite music or favorite food. She had opened up to him so much over the past year and it was time he did the same. He couldn't wait for her to meet Reggie.

Kofi smiled to himself as he heard the high angelic voice of Prince through the door. Zoey looked beautiful as she opened the door and flung herself into his arms.

She squealed and put her hand behind his neck and reached her lips up to his. It felt good to kiss her finally.

"I love you, Zoey." Kofi looked deeply into her green eyes. She was beautiful. Zoey was the type of beauty who didn't realize how pretty she was, which made her even more beautiful. He had yet to see her really wear much makeup and she almost always had her hair in a ponytail. He loved when she pulled her hair out of the ponytail and let it fall over her shoulders. She was completely clueless at how sexy she was. She was the first woman he had ever said those words to and meant it.

Sure, Kofi ended up loving the woman who saved his life that day on the Hawthorne Bridge, but that was different. He wasn't in love with her, and she came into his life for a specific reason. It almost felt as though she left just in time for him to meet Zoey and find out what being in love really felt like. Kofi felt a pang of guilt just at that moment thinking of all of the secrets he was still keeping from

Zoey. He knew he had to open up to her soon. She pretty much knew nothing about his childhood in Kentucky, the accident, and the girl he met on the Hawthorne Bridge. He had a lot to share with the woman standing in front of him. It just wasn't time yet. He was close, but he wasn't ready to tell her how broken he had been.

"I love you too, Kofi," she said as she kissed him softly on the cheek.

Kofi grabbed Zoey's hand and pulled her to the bed just feet away from the kitchen. He pulled her gently on top of him as he laid back. He was exhausted from his trip and the day of traveling but felt a sudden rush as he felt her body on his. She pulled herself close to him and kissed his neck.

"Oh, wait. I need to shower. I just ran. I am really sweaty." Zoey rolled over with a sigh and stood at the foot of the bed with her arms on her hips.

"I will hurry," she said as she wandered toward the bathroom, stripping a piece of clothing with each step.

Almost an hour later, Zoey finally emerged from the bathroom with a towel on her head. She was naked and smiling at Kofi, noticing he had dozed off to sleep. She pulled the towel off her head as she laid back down on top of him on the bed and kissed him softly to wake him up. Kofi opened his eyes and moved his hand behind her lower back to pull her close and pulled her damp hair into a ponytail. She closed her eyes and smiled. Zoey loved nothing more than when he played with her hair.

The next morning, Zoey and Kofi laid in bed all day and made love before they walked to dinner that night to celebrate her birthday. They ate at the same Thai place they went to on their first date—Kofi's birthday. After dinner, Kofi bought a bottle of Malbec from the small liquor store across from their building. They sat on her bed and drank the bottle while listening to the CDs he bought her for her birthday.

"Oh, my machine. I missed a call… I bet it's from Jasmine," Zoey said as she poured the last few drops into her glass.

"I think we need more. And since I am the only one old enough to buy it, I will be right back," Kofi said as he kissed Zoey on the forehead. He hadn't ever seen her drunk, let alone seen her drink more than one glass of alcohol. It seemed tonight she was on a mission.

"Thanks! It's my birthday!" Zoey said with a smile and pulled his face down to kiss him playfully on the lips. She rolled over to press play on her answering machine as he closed the door behind him.

In the hallway, he could hear the muffled voice of Zoey's sister along with her friend on the answering machine singing Happy Birthday. Kofi laughed as he heard Zoey begin to sing along to the two happy voices on the answering machine. He was definitely in love.

CHAPTER 11

NEW YEAR'S EVE — 2001

Jasmine

Jasmine and Zoey arrived at Jasmine's new apartment just in time to get ready to go out for New Year's Eve. They had been planning this trip for almost a year and it had been months since they saw each other. Jasmine was so excited to show Zoey her place and finally introduce her to Cassidy. She had been in Denver for almost three years now and Zoey only managed to visit her twice so far. Zoey was busy working at an internship at a local news station. She was still going to school in Portland and dating Kofi, whom Jasmine also hadn't met yet. Jasmine just started a new job at her school and spent most of her time with Cassidy, who was now not just her best friend but her roommate.

"I am so happy you are finally here. We are going to have so much fun. I promise, next year I will meet you in Portland for New Year's Eve." Jasmine was almost running down the hall to her door with Zoey trailing with her luggage. She had waited months to show her sister her new apartment. They turned 21 that year and hadn't even shared a legal drink together yet! This New Year's Eve would be amazing.

"This is so cute, Jas. I can't wait to meet Cassidy. I am sorry Kofi couldn't come. He really didn't want his friend, Reggie, to be alone for the holidays but he said he was sorry," Zoey said breathlessly as she hurried behind her sister.

Zoey seemed impressed by the building so far. Jasmine told her sister on the ride from the airport that the building had a rooftop pool, elevators, and marble floors in the entrance. Jasmine had been working almost full-time and Cassidy had a good job. Together, they were able to get one of the nicest apartments near campus. Jasmine knew that Zoey still lived in her studio but was planning to move into a bigger apartment with Kofi in the spring. They were both full-blown adults now and it always felt shocking to realize.

"I love it here. I feel like I deserve it. Ya know?" Jasmine finally found the key in her pocket and flung the door open, turning to see her sister's expression at the light, airy place she called home.

"This is so you, sis. I love it. Really. I am so proud of you. This place must cost a fortune." Zoey left her bag in the entry and plopped onto the large white couch. She ran her fingers over the soft blanket and fell back.

"Alright, bitch. It's not that long of a flight. Don't get too comfortable… time for a drink!" Jasmine said as she pulled two martini glasses down from the floating shelves over the kitchen sink. She couldn't believe they were about to have their first drink together. Jasmine couldn't help but feel a sadness wash over her, realizing they had grown apart over the past three years. They had spent so many years spending every minute together that it felt like they were missing out on each other's lives when they only saw each other a few times a year. Sure, they talked on the phone pretty much every night, but she still felt the distance. It was as if them finding Kofi and Cassidy challenged their own friendship. Jasmine hoped that being together in the same city for a week would bring them as close again as they were when they were little.

Jasmine did, however, appreciate that the two sisters seemed to be growing into who they were meant to grow into. The closer they lived to each other, it seemed like the more they looked alike. When she spotted Zoey at the airport, she almost didn't recognize her. She imagined she would find her sister wearing an old hoodie and track pants. Her hair would be in a ponytail as always. Jasmine was pleasantly surprised when she saw Zoey standing with her luggage, wearing a long flowy dress, a brown wrap coat, and her hair in a loose braid down her back. Jasmine admired Zoey's new look as she watched her twin sister sit up on the couch. She looked like a woman, and she looked healthy and happy. Jasmine couldn't believe this was the same person that she watched sleep with a feeding tube in her nose in St. Luke's on New Year's Eve their senior year of high school.

"You look really good, sis," Jasmine said as she pulled four different types of vodka from a cabinet.

"Thanks. I am actually trying to look good. Turns out you were right… boys don't like hoodies and ponytails. Well, sometimes they do," Zoey said with a smile and wink.

"Ok, but please don't be the type of girl that changes just for a man," Jasmine said, finally deciding to just pour all four flavors into the cup with a small splash of cranberry juice. She shook the cup over her head and poured the drink into the two martini glasses as though she had done it hundreds of times. She smiled at Zoey and winked.

"No way. I just feel better like this than I do in my sweats. Kofi likes me however I feel best about myself." Zoey couldn't help but smile as she talked about him. Jasmine was happy to see her sister like this.

Jasmine turned on the radio and Aaliyah's raspy voice filled the room. Through the large window, the snow began to fall outside. Jasmine made sure that wherever she lived, she would be able to see the mountains. The pink outline of the Rocky Mountains was almost lit up from the sky and she watched as her sister gazed at the view in awe.

"Ok. Let's get ready. We are going to dinner first and then a party. I can't wait. Drink up!" Jasmine turned the volume up as loud as it would go and pulled her sister from the living room into her bedroom. She was thrilled that any distance she felt seemed to be long gone after just a few hours together in the same city. Jasmine also had a surprise for her sister that she knew she would love. She couldn't wait to get the night started.

Zoey and Jasmine looked beautiful. Zoey wore a black dress and a long, red coat. Her hair was pulled high into a tight ponytail. This was not a high school tomboy ponytail. Zoey wore her brown hair in a sophisticated, sexy ponytail and red lipstick. Jasmine almost couldn't believe this was the same girl that barely knew how to put mascara on and wore the Oregon hoodie their entire junior year. Jasmine had a white pantsuit on and large green earrings that brought out her eyes. Her blonde hair was straight and flowed down her back.

"Oh! There she is." Jasmine grabbed Zoey's hand and pulled her toward Cassidy, who was sitting at the bar with a beer in front of her. Cassidy was two years older than Jasmine and spent a lot of time out at bars and clubs. As they got closer, Jasmine noticed a man raising his drink toward Cassidy from across the bar. She nodded and smiled. Jasmine was sure she had told at least 10 guys already that she had a boyfriend. Cassidy did not have a boyfriend.

"Hi! I finally get to meet the famous Zoey!" Cassidy said as she stood and pulled Zoey in for a tight hug. She was wearing heels and tight jeans with a red sparkly sequined top. She towered over Zoey and had the same tight ponytail, but her hair was full of dark brown curls. Cassidy almost had the exact same color of striking green eyes as Jasmine had, but against her caramel complexion, they looked even more gorgeous.

"Wow. Jas never told me her best friend was a supermodel." Zoey blushed as she pulled back from Cassidy's hug and glanced at her sister. Jasmine smiled at Zoey and raised her eyebrows.

"Well, that wasn't awkward." Jasmine laughed and plopped down where Cassidy had been sitting. She took a long swig of her beer and turned slowly to catch eyes with Cassidy with the empty beer still to her lips. She could always make both Zoey and Cassidy laugh.

The three women ordered two more drinks each before closing their tab and heading across the street for dinner.

The snow started to fall lightly as they crossed Broadway and piled into the small sushi bar lobby.

"I thought this place was supposed to be good, Jas?" Zoey said to her sister, looking around the empty restaurant.

"It's amazing. No one knows about it yet. I wanted to actually be able to talk." Jasmine was waving to the hostess and smiling. She was excited to show her sister her favorite restaurant. She just wanted them to be able to sit down and catch up before they went to the party where she was sure they wouldn't be able to hear each other over the music.

The three women sat at a small table and ordered almost every sushi roll on the menu. They split two large sakes, and each had a beer. It was the best restaurant in Denver and Jasmine was happy to see her sister and her best friend having such a fun night and finally getting to know each other. On this night, they had no idea what their futures held. It was the last day of the year and each of them had more surprises ahead of them than they would ever imagine.

"So. What is the story with you, Cassidy? Why did you move to Denver? I don't think Jasmine ever really told me. And how in the hell are you single? There were so many guys looking at you in the bar. You could have anyone you want," Zoey asked as she elbowed Jasmine and raised her eyebrows.

"I know, right?" Jasmine said, shaking her head and agreeing with her sister.

"Well, I moved here for a fresh start and honestly to get over someone I loved that I don't think had the capacity to love me back. He took a piece of me I will never get back. I honestly don't think I would ever be able to forgive him." Cassidy sipped from the warm cup of sake in front of her.

"You know, you haven't really told me much about him either. I remember the first day I met you and you told me about him, but otherwise, you never talk about him much." Jasmine had been meaning to ask Cassidy more about her past every time they went for their walk, but Cassidy was a listener and never really talked much about herself.

"It's not a great story, that's why. He never really loved me. I think he was actually sort of using me to get over his past. I fell in love with him, and he would start to make me feel like he was falling in love with me too and then, poof, he would disappear. It's hard to be the one who always has to be supportive. It was toxic. He disappeared when I needed him most. You know what I mean, Jas." Cassidy was referring to Jasmine and Zoey. Jasmine wasn't shy about telling Cassidy that she had always been the one listening and supporting her sister. She told Cassidy that the first day they met. Jasmine looked at Cassidy across the table quickly.

"That's not what I meant." Cassidy grabbed Jasmine's hand and lowered her eyes. Jasmine knew she didn't mean to cause an argument. Cassidy was just being honest but almost seemed like she forgot Zoey was with them.

"Cassidy, you don't need to pretend that Jasmine hasn't told you everything about my fucked-up past. It's ok. There will be a time in my life when I need to support Jas. She was there for me when I couldn't even be there for myself. It's nothing to be ashamed of to talk about reality." Zoey put her arm around her sister and kissed her on the cheek. Jasmine was relieved that Zoey understood.

It had been hard to always be the one to support her sister all through high school. Jasmine couldn't help but think that contributed to them growing apart in college. She was exhausted, always being the one who had to be strong. It was a part of the reason she was so thankful for Cassidy's friendship. Cassidy listened and was always there for Jasmine. It actually made Jasmine feel guilty sometimes for talking too much. It was nice to see her friend finally open up, especially to her and Zoey.

"So… what happened? With the guy?" Zoey asked with her arm still around her sister as they both watched Cassidy take another long sip of her drink.

"I don't know. Honestly, I feel like he might be dead. I wouldn't be surprised. He had a lot of secrets I don't know if he ever worked out. He told me everything, but he really needed to go to therapy or something." Cassidy raised her hand to the server and pointed at the empty beers, suggesting another round.

"Holy shit. You think someone killed him?" Zoey's eyes were fixated on Cassidy.

"No, I think he might have killed himself."

"What? That is terrible." Zoey glanced at Jasmine as if asking her if she knew this about her best friend. Jasmine shrugged her shoulders as Cassidy told them the story of the man that she used to love. Jasmine realized then more than ever that Cassidy hadn't opened up to her. She vowed to be a better listener to her best friend going forward.

"How do you even fall in love with someone like that? I can't imagine," Zoey said as she ate the last piece of sushi on her plate.

"I did fall in love with him, but love shouldn't be that hard. And he didn't love me back. He said it, but I knew he didn't mean it. He was broken. I can't imagine him ever loving anyone the way they deserve. It is best to keep him in my past." Cassidy was staring at the flickering candle in the middle of the table. Suddenly, Jasmine's strong, confident, beautiful best friend looked like a heartbroken, sad, and desperate woman sitting across from them.

"Well, honestly, it sounds like you dodged a bullet. He sounds like he wouldn't deserve you," Jasmine said as she picked up the bill that the server had just placed in the middle of the table. They split the bill three ways and grabbed their coats.

"Let's go and ring in the new year. The party is a few blocks away. I will get a cab," Jasmine said as she left her sister and best friend in the warm restaurant and headed out into the cold night to hail a cab.

Within minutes, they were inside a beautiful loft overlooking the city, each with another drink in their hand. The music was so loud, they could barely hear each other. Jasmine was so happy her sister and best friend were hitting it off. She was having the best New Year's Eve she'd had in her life. In less than a minute, she would make sure it was her sister's best New Year's Eve as well.

"I am going to get more drinks. Stay here," Jasmine said loudly to Zoey with a mischievous smile. She heard, *Auld Lang Syne* start to play over the speakers and realized she needed to hurry for her last-minute surprise to be a success. She thought back to the last New Year's Eve she had spent with Zoey in the hospital room when her twin sister was fighting for her life. She was so happy they were together again.

"I am really glad I finally got to meet you, Cassidy. Maybe soon you and Jas can come to Portland and stay with me and Kofi. We are getting a place together soon. I would love for you to visit and meet him," Zoey yelled into Cassidy's ear as the countdown to midnight began.

"Five, four, three, two…" the crowd sang in unison as Zoey searched the room for her sister. She wanted to make sure to ring in the new year with her sister by her side.

"Sorry it's so loud. What did you say his name is?" Cassidy leaned down and looked at Zoey with her striking green eyes.

"One. Happy New Year!" The crowd sang again as the new friends lifted their glasses to cheers.

"Kofi?" Cassidy said as she realized her past was standing right behind her new friend.

"Yes. His name is Kofi." Zoey leaned in close to Cassidy with a smile.

Jasmine stood next to the man that Cassidy had met on the top of the Hawthorne Bridge so many years ago with a wide smile on her face. Her smile slowly started to fade as she realized her best friend knew her sister's boyfriend. Jasmine held her breath as she waited for her sister to turn around.

"Cassidy?" Zoey turned quickly as she recognized her boyfriend's voice.

The crowd drunkenly sang what they thought were the words to *Auld Lang Syne* and Jasmine felt as though time was standing still. Cassidy rushed past Zoey and pushed her way through the crowd of couples kissing to ring in a new year.

Jasmine and Zoey caught eyes, realizing that they each had so much more to learn about Kofi and Cassidy. Jasmine didn't know if she should follow her best friend or stay to comfort her sister.

"You should go and get her, Jas. She needs you." Zoey nodded at her sister before looking back at the man she had been in love with for over three years. Jasmine felt a wave of gratefulness wash over her as she looked at her sister. She had forgiven Jasmine for sleeping with Matt so many years ago, and now, here she was, facing another heartbreaking surprise. Zoey had grown up and Jasmine vowed to be as mature as her sister was. She couldn't believe what was happening.

Jasmine kissed Zoey on the cheek and glanced at Kofi. This wasn't his fault. His eyes were wide, still, and full of surprise. He called Jasmine two months earlier to set up this surprise and spend the week with Zoey and Jasmine in Denver. He was the man her sister wanted to be with, and Jasmine hoped that Zoey would give him a chance to explain. She couldn't imagine him being the man Cassidy described at dinner. She couldn't imagine him wanting to jump off a bridge to his death. Jasmine turned to go and find her best friend in the sea of drunk partiers.

"I have a lot to tell you, Zoey. I am sorry," Jasmine heard Kofi say to her sister as she turned to leave, chasing after Cassidy.

"I know. But first, Happy New Year. Thank you for coming here to surprise me." Zoey pulled him in close and kissed him. Jasmine reached the doorway and turned to see her sister in the crowd of her drunk friends. She was surprised to see her sister with her arms wrapped around Kofi. Jasmine's surprise wasn't entirely ruined. Zoey smiled at her sister and mouthed the words, "Thank you." She knew her sister would be alright after she talked to Kofi, but Jasmine needed to find Cassidy.

Jasmine saw her best friend quickly shuffling a few blocks in front of her on Broadway. Cassidy had her coat pulled tight around her thin frame, curly hair bouncing down her back.

"Cassidy, wait. Please talk to me. I am so sorry, I had no idea Kofi is the man from the bridge… er, your ex," Jasmine yelled ahead of her. Cassidy finally stopped and turned around, her striking green eyes were smeared with mascara. Jasmine had never seen Cassidy cry and she was sobbing. She felt strange calling him the man from the bridge but that was all Cassidy had ever really told her about him.

"I am sorry, Jas. I can't believe he is really here. He said he couldn't love someone. It wasn't me; it was him, and look at him now. She has been gushing about him all night. He was a wreck from losing his sister, but I lost someone too because of him. I was pregnant, Jasmine. The last time I saw that man, I was carrying his child. Can you imagine carrying the baby of a man that was suicidal? And then he left. He just left."

Jasmine's heart dropped when she looked into Cassidy's green eyes. Her heart broke for her best friend. Jasmine took her hand, and she finally understood all the pain in Cassidy's eyes.

"Oh my god, Cassidy. Let's get you home." Jasmine's mind was racing as she put her arms around her friend's waist and guided her home.

CHAPTER 12

FALL — 2001

Zoey

The rain fell so hard, I couldn't sleep on the first night Kofi and I slept in our new apartment together. I couldn't think of a time the rain had ever kept me up. Usually, it was the sound that helped me close my eyes and fall asleep.

I was sad to leave 201 NW 20th Place Apartments but couldn't wait to move in with Kofi. We had spent every night together in either his or my place for the past three years. But tonight, we slept in the middle of the living room in our new apartment on a makeshift bed surrounded by Chinese takeout boxes and a large, empty wine bottle. The king-sized bed we ordered wouldn't arrive until the next week, so we decided to camp in the living room for now. I looked around at all of the boxes still to unpack as the rain fell harder outside the window. I couldn't wait to make this place feel like home.

I looked over at Kofi, sleeping so hard that his opened mouth was pressed awkwardly against his tattooed arm. He was even more handsome than the day we met. I was more in love with him now than I ever thought possible. It had been a rough few months for us but we made it.

I thought back to the night of New Year's Eve in Denver when I realized I didn't know the man I wanted to spend the rest of my life with. I saw my future flash before my eyes when Cassidy looked at him with more pain than I had ever seen in anyone's eyes before. It was almost as though I could feel her heart break when she saw him stand in front of her that night as the new year began. The expression on her face took me back to the night of Homecoming when Matt left me on the dancefloor to fend for myself. That was the moment I knew that everything in life was a choice. Sure, there was a part of me that believed in fate. But ultimately, everything that happens to us is because of the choices we make. That night, in the gym on Homecoming, I watched Matt walk away because I hadn't fought for us. I needed him to walk away so I would realize that I had to fight for myself. Now, looking at Kofi on New Year's Eve in Denver, standing in front of his past, I knew that I was going to have to fight if I wanted him to be my future.

Once Jasmine left Kofi and I standing there in a party full of strangers, I knew we had to start from the beginning, and that was exactly what we did that night into the early morning of the first day of 2001.

After Jasmine chased Cassidy through the crowded party, Kofi and I left with no destination in mind. We couldn't get out of that party fast enough and we couldn't go back to Jasmine's, so we began to walk. We walked for miles through the streets of Denver that night and, finally, on a park bench near where my sister met her best friend three years before, Kofi told me everything.

"This is the park that Jasmine walks around every single day. She always said she couldn't wait for me to run here," I said to Kofi as we stood in front of a sign that read "Washington Park". I had no idea how long we had been walking but I could see a slight glimpse of the sun trying to peek into the sky behind the mountains. It was as if the entire city had fallen asleep and the only sounds were the birds landing on the water. The lights from the boathouse and the falling snow on the water made it look as though we were in a painting. It was a beautiful view from that park bench.

"Listen, Zoey. I am really sorry I didn't tell you everything. I just thought you wouldn't want to have a boyfriend with a past like mine. When I met you, I never intentionally kept this all from you. I just didn't want to ever chance losing you," Kofi said as he wrapped his jacket tightly around my shoulders.

"You didn't not tell me 'everything' Kofi… you didn't tell me 'anything!' Why would you think you would lose me if you told me the truth about you? You don't think I can understand you have a past? I told you everything about my past. I told you about my anorexia and my twin sister sleeping with my boyfriend. You can ask my sister; I can handle the truth."

"The accident. It was my fault. I was really all my sister had and I let her down. Naya and I didn't grow up like you did. Our mom… she ended up leaving, you know. Well, she left me. Naya was already gone. My mom. She left a year or so after the accident. I honestly don't even know if she is still alive. It was like she just decided she didn't want to be a mom to me anymore after Naya died."

"This wasn't your fault, Kofi. You can't blame yourself." I tried to imagine watching my sister die as I watched the tears stream down his cheeks.

"Naya was sitting on my lap. She was eight and we were pretending that she was driving. We always did this. I had two beers. That was it. I wasn't drunk. I was just being her big brother and having fun with her in the empty field in front of our house. But I shouldn't have driven that truck with her on my lap. It was my birthday, and we were just having fun. Reggie turned up the music and let the dog out of the house and I was driving the truck and laughing and singing to the music he was playing from the porch. I wasn't paying attention. I didn't think anything would happen. She was having so much fun." Kofi was shaking his head as he relived the worst day of his life to me that night in Washington Park with the snow falling lightly on the water in front of us. I realized that Reggie was the only familiar name in his story. My boyfriend of three years failed to mention he had a little sister and that he didn't even know if his mom was still alive. A mix of emotions filled me as I reached for his hand.

"The dog ran in front of the truck and Naya screamed and I lost control and hit a tree. All I could hear was the song Reggie was playing and the dog barking. I didn't hit the dog, but my sister died that night in the hospital from internal injuries. I was completely fine, Zoey. Not a scratch on my entire fucking body. The dog was fine. I can still hear her scream for me to watch out for the dog. She didn't want me to hurt the dog. I remember Reggie running over to me and he was talking but I couldn't hear a word he was saying." Kofi had a blank look in his eyes as he rubbed my legs to warm me up. If his hands weren't rubbing my legs, I knew for sure they would have been shaking. He exhaled for what felt like 10 minutes and closed his eyes.

"I am sorry I never told you this," he said finally and opened his eyes to look at me.

My boyfriend was a stranger sitting next to me. I understood it was hard to talk about, but I couldn't understand why he never felt he had to tell me. We sat in silence as I looked up at the sky, trying to comprehend what the man I thought I knew was telling me.

"I am sorry this happened to you, Kofi, but you can't keep stuff like this in. I am your girlfriend. I deserve to know who you are. Cassidy said something about how she thought you might have killed yourself. What was she talking about?" I tried to seem calm as I asked him the first of so many questions I had. The sky seemed to be endless as I kept my gaze on the stars above to keep from crying. It felt selfish to be hurt that he didn't feel like he could tell me these things, but I couldn't help how I felt.

Kofi stared at the water on the lake and took a long, deep breath.

"I met Cassidy at the top of the Hawthorne Bridge. I was going to jump. It was my birthday and a year after the accident. I couldn't sleep without seeing Naya's face screaming for me to watch out for the dog. Every single night, I felt like I relived that day. I wanted it to stop. I never paid any consequences for her death and that felt like what I deserved… to die." He was crying now, and his hand gripped my knee.

"Honestly, Cassidy and I spent pretty much every night together after that. Not because I loved her, but because I couldn't be alone with my thoughts and memories." Kofi seemed ashamed as his eyes lowered.

I remembered the sad look in her eyes earlier that night when Cassidy told us she thought the man who broke her heart was using her. I hoped she was ok, but a pang of jealousy took over as I imagined him in bed with anyone but me, especially the most beautiful woman I had ever met.

"Do you still feel like that?" I was afraid of his answer. Suddenly, all of the nights he stayed up into the early morning listening to music endlessly made sense. He was trying to numb the pain with music, red wine, and possibly me.

"I don't. I want to live a long, happy life with you, Zoey. I want to marry you one day and have a family. I am fine. I promise you. When I met you, it was almost the two-year anniversary of her death. I think if I hadn't met you, I would have gone back to the place I met Cassidy and I would have jumped. I love you, Zoey. In a way, you saved me. I am so sorry."

Kofi moved his hand from my knee to my cheek and pulled me close. It felt like it was the first time we had ever kissed.

"Is that everything? I want you to tell me everything, Kofi."

"There is one more thing. There is a reason Cassidy is so mad at me and acted like she did tonight. It wasn't just how one-sided our relationship was. She was pregnant, Zoey. I asked her to have an abortion. I gave her money, she agreed to have an abortion, and I left. I couldn't bring a child into the world in the state I was in. I also couldn't face her after asking her to do that. It was obvious I wasn't in love with her and bringing a child into the world would have not changed that fact. I knew she didn't want to go through with it, but she told me she would. I knew she would never forgive me, so I just disappeared. I was too young; I was too messed up." Kofi looked away, ashamed to admit what he had asked Jasmine's best friend to do.

"I tried to find her months later when I realized how she must have felt after I disappeared. When I finally got enough nerve to face her, she had moved away. I had no idea where she moved to, and I definitely had no idea she was your twin sister's best friend. We weren't together long but we went through what felt like a lifetime of ups and downs together. I was never good to her. It wasn't fair for her. Especially what I asked her to do the last time I saw her."

There wasn't much left to say. Kofi and I sat quietly on that bench in Washington Park until the sun came up on the first morning of 2001. I felt betrayed yet closer to him than ever at the same time.

As I watched Kofi sleep eight months later, on the first night of us officially living together, I tried to imagine all the times Kofi had wanted to tell me about his past. I wondered if he wanted to tell me that first night we went to dinner at the Thai place on Northwest 23rd, or the many times we sat on the front step drinking wine straight from the bottle and making fun of Jon and his dates. Our first date was the two-year anniversary of his little sister's death. As I looked at my beautiful boyfriend sleeping in a makeshift bed in the middle of our new apartment, I wondered what Kofi and Cassidy's baby would have looked like. I wondered what our baby would look like. I wondered if he was truly healed or if he would ever be ready to really let me in. I loved him more than I felt I could handle sometimes.

The rain fell harder and a loud crack of lightning woke Kofi from his sleep.

"Hey. What are you doing up?" he said as he rolled over and pulled my body close to his. He looked tired as he smiled at me through the moonlight.

"I was just thinking about New Year's Eve. I was thinking about me and you. I was thinking about how I never want you to want to jump off a bridge again." I searched his eyes for a sign of confidence.

"I will never want to jump off a bridge again. I can promise you that. Just don't leave me and I will be alright," Kofi said as he kissed me with his soft lips. He brushed my hair off my face and moved his eyes sharply to the door.

"I thought I heard Jon and his date for the night. But I just realized we are in our new place and Jon isn't our neighbor anymore! I love you, Zoey."

I laughed and rolled my body on top of his. Kofi moved his hands from my lower back to my butt and pulled me close.

"I love you too."

I flipped my hair behind my shoulder and kissed his chest. I could see my reflection in his eyes.

"Do you ever deal with depression or anything anymore? I just can't imagine you ever not feeling comfortable in your body. You are so confident and happy. Sometimes I forget you had a past, and I think we need to check in with each other sometimes," Kofi asked, looking at me eagerly.

"Not really. I feel like being so close to death made me who I am. It made me more confident today. It made me thankful to wake up each morning relieved instead of disappointed. You get that, right? Don't be fooled... I still have my days and I wouldn't wish those few years on my worst enemy. For the first time in a very long time, I feel in control. And happy to open my eyes each day and see who I see in the mirror. And to see you, of course."

I kissed him on his forehead and was overwhelmed by how much I was in love with this man. I hoped more than anything that he felt in control too.

"What made you think of that? Are you ok?" I asked as I rolled off his body, back into the makeshift bed on the floor of our new apartment. I loved the sound of that… 'our apartment'.

"I was just thinking about how I am truly happy right now. This is a fresh start for us. You make me so happy."

Kofi smiled the first genuine smile I might have ever seen. We had a rough year, but he had a rough life, and I had a rough adolescence, but we found each other. Nothing had ever felt so right.

Kofi and I made love that night until the sun came up.

It was still raining hard the next morning. When I opened my eyes, I saw Kofi standing over our small TV. He was adjusting the rabbit ears we had bought at Fred Myer the night before and was staring down at the morning news.

"Augh, turn that off. The news is so depressing," I said as I threw a pillow in his direction.

"Zoey. Wake up. You have to see this."

CHAPTER 13

FALL — 2001

Matt

Matt was getting used to San Diego as his new home. He drove along the coastal freeway on his way to the Los Angeles airport. The sun was barely rising, and he could see the dark ocean slowly fill with yellow, pink, and purple from the light over the hills behind him. The whole state must have still been dreaming and the road was empty.

Matt loved California, but not as much as he had loved living in Florence, Italy for the past three years. He moved to San Diego three months earlier after his junior year in college in Italy was complete. Matt hadn't been back to Idaho since his senior year of high school and would probably never go back again. He often thought of his friends from his hometown… and of Zoey and Jasmine, of course. He wondered where they were and if they were together or not. He imagined they went off to college together and came back to Idaho to see their parents every chance they got. Sometimes he felt like he and

Zoey never got a proper goodbye, but he hoped she was happy, and he wished her the best. He hoped most of all that she was healthy. He vowed on the day he left his childhood home that he would find her one day and apologize for their relationship and everything he did to hurt her. Matt also thought about Jasmine more than he realized. On this September day in 2001, Matt would have no idea if he would ever see Zoey or Jasmine again. Eventually, he would be shocked to realize that their stories were far from over.

For now, though, Matt was happy, and he was also in love. He was in love with an Italian girl, and he was picking her up from the airport in just a few hours to start their new life in California.

His dad was not too happy when Matt told him over dinner five months earlier that he was dropping out of school and moving back to the States. He was following a girl and his father told him over and over that it was a mistake. Matt knew he would enroll again in school in San Diego eventually, but that summer had been spent finding an apartment and working as much as he could to save up for this day. His girlfriend would be doing a paid internship at the local newspaper in La Jolla, and he would wait tables until he figured out which school he could transfer his credits to. Maybe, he thought, he would finally start writing a book.

On the day that Matt boarded a plane to California in June, he promised his brother and dad he would be back to visit. He actually thought he would be back soon for a big Italian wedding with his small family and Francesca's enormous Italian family. She had the biggest family he'd ever seen, which was a nice contrast to his small family of three. It was a wonderful three years in Florence, but he was willing to sacrifice living in Italy and leaving his dad and brother if it meant he could be with what he hoped would be the love of his life.

Matt met the beautiful Italian girl he had hoped to soon call his fiancé when she walked into the small restaurant he was waiting tables at two years before and ordered a lemonade.

"That is all you want?" he said to her in Italian. The place was so small he actually was not just the waiter but the host, the cook, and bus boy too. When Francesca walked in that day, he was glad it was just the two of them so he could be the one to serve her. She was beautiful with long, dark hair and big green eyes. He was surprised he hadn't seen her before and was hoping his Italian was not too broken for her to understand.

"Yes. Just a glass of lemonade please," Francesca replied to him in English with a shy smile.

"Coming right up." Matt moved quickly to the kitchen and returned with a large glass full of lemonade.

The beautiful Italian girl sat down at a small table on the patio in front of the restaurant and took a few sips of the drink. She reached into her bag and pulled out enough lira to cover her lemonade with a small tip for Matt. He watched her stand and pull her long, black hair into a low ponytail. She looked up and smiled at him watching her as she tied her sweater around her thin waist.

"Thank you. I hope you come again," Matt said to her through the window as she pushed the chair in, only half of her lemonade gone.

"In Italian. You should speak Italian to practice and I will speak English. I will see you again," she said to Matt with another shy smile. He watched her get on her bike and ride away down the narrow cobblestone street. Matt couldn't wait to see her again.

Matt and Francesca spent every afternoon together the summer they first met. She would come into the restaurant at the same time every afternoon. Matt told her the second time she came to visit that she should come at 2 p.m. because the owner would have made his daily visit by then and he would be free to join her on the patio if there were no guests in the restaurant. He would help her with her English, and she would teach him Italian. When he arrived home after work, he would teach his dad and brother what the beautiful Italian girl taught him that day.

The only day that Francesca came and Matt was not there was the anniversary of his mother's death. He didn't show up to work that day and instead took the train to do the same hike he had done with his mom so many years ago when she told him she had cancer. He sat, overlooking the ocean for hours thinking of the last few months he had spent with his mom so many years before. He could almost remember their entire conversation from that day of the hike—a conversation that he could finally say he fully understood. The next day, Francesca asked him where he was and he told her all about his mom and dad getting engaged on that same hike, about him losing her when he was in high school, and how after he graduated high school, he left everyone he knew and moved to Italy to start a new life with his dad and his brother. He even told her about Zoey—his first and only girlfriend. He told Francesca that, somehow, after that hike with his mom in Italy on the day she told him she was going to die, he knew there was someone else out there for him. His mom made him realize that he hadn't found her yet.

"Oh, really? How did you realize that she wasn't the one? Just from what your mom said to you that day?"

Matt looked at his beautiful new friend in a way he hadn't looked at her before that day.

"I don't think it was what she said. It was how she said it. She was talking to me, and I could tell all she was thinking about was my dad and all the great memories they had together. Twenty years later. Can you imagine feeling that for 20 years? That's what I want. I knew that day that every time my mom thought about my dad, it made her smile. She didn't settle. Even on the day she had to tell her son she was dying; the thought of her husband made her smile." Matt looked at Francesca and hoped she understood everything he said. She was getting better at English than he was at Italian, and he was proud of how much he had taught her.

"Settle?" Francesca thumbed through her book to look up the translation before Matt grabbed her hand.

"Settle means... um... don't give up on what you want. Don't settle with being together if you aren't in love. Don't settle with just my definition. You should look it up." They laughed as he rolled his eyes at himself. She touched his hand and smiled.

Years later, as Matt listened to the music and felt the air on his cheeks as he drove to go and pick up his potential future wife in LA, he realized that it wasn't going to be too soon to ask Francesca to marry him tonight. He had worked all summer to make enough money to pay for all of his bills and to save up for a ring. If he learned anything from his mom, it was that life is short and that he would know when he found the one. Francesca was the one, he hoped. He wanted to propose to her in Italy, but he couldn't wait until they got a chance to go back to see their families. And when they still lived in Italy, he didn't have enough money for a ring. He knew his dad would give him his mother's ring if he had asked but he wanted this to be his own love story, as much as he had admired theirs. They were starting a new life together in California and that was exactly what his mother had told him to cherish. She wanted him to start a family of his own. He was anxious to start the second chapter of his love story with Francesca today, in their new home together.

Francesca had spent the summer interning at the Boston Globe and would be arriving in Los Angeles in a couple of hours. They spoke on the phone about every other day, and he couldn't wait to finally hold her again after three long months without her. Matt pulled into a gas station about halfway between San Diego and LA to get a cup of coffee. He checked his glove compartment to make sure the ring was still where he left it and got out and leaned on the hood of the car, admiring the ocean in front of him. He was going to propose at their apartment that night but didn't want to chance leaving the ring anywhere that wasn't right by his side. In his pocket, he felt his phone ring. He still wasn't used to carrying a phone and had probably only used it once or twice. He flipped it open and struggled to remember how to answer it. Finally, he heard his dad's familiar voice.

"Hey, Dad. So good to hear from you. How are you? What time is it there anyway?" Matt heard his dad's muffled voice on the other line. It was rare they spoke on the phone because of the price of long-distance but he was happy to hear his dad's soothing voice. It had been a lonely summer in California with Francesca in Boston and his only family in another country. If he was honest, Matt really had no friends yet either. He couldn't wait to show Francesca around San Diego and to have some company on the lonely nights. He hoped they would soon have their own new group of friends to spend Friday nights making pizzas or playing volleyball on the beach with.

"Hey, Matt. I am glad I caught you. Are you at the airport yet? Have you heard from Francesca? I have some bad news for you, son. Are you sitting down?" His dad's voice suddenly sounded an ocean away.

Matt's heart began to race. The last time he heard bad news, his mother died.

"I haven't heard from her but have her itinerary right here. She lands in a few hours unless something has changed. I am pretty close but was going to get something to eat and kill some time waiting for her. I definitely don't want to be late." Matt pulled the email he had printed with her itinerary on it from his pocket. He unfolded it and pushed his sunglasses to the top of his head. He looked closely to make sure he had the times right.

"She isn't coming, Matt. Her mother stopped by a few minutes ago. Apparently, she got a job offer at the Boston Globe too good to pass up. Her mother begged her to tell you, but she insisted she didn't want to hear the disappointment in your voice. She said she didn't want to hurt you. I am so sorry, son. I can't believe she doesn't have the heart to tell you. Her mother said she told her to get on the plane and figure it out with you when she arrived, but she said she couldn't face you. Matt. She must not be the one." Matt's father's voice trembled as he delivered the news the he knew would break his son's heart.

Matt couldn't believe the words coming through his phone. He looked at the ocean and it seemed as though the waves had stopped moving and everything was still. The colors reflecting off the water turned to gray instead of pink, purple, and blue. The seagulls that normally sang so loud he couldn't hear himself think were silent.

"Are you sure, Dad? That is not something she would do. What exactly did her mother say to you? We have a plan, there is no way she is just not going to show up. There is no way Francesca just wouldn't get on the plane." Matt heard nothing from the other end of the phone and pulled it away from his ear to make sure he hadn't lost his connection.

"Dad?" Matt could feel his stomach turn as he waited for his dad to reply with a different answer. He would get back on the phone and say he was kidding. He would say it was April Fool's. Except, it wasn't the first day of April. It was September 11th.

"She isn't coming, Matt. I am sorry. I will send you a ticket home if you want. I love you." Matt felt tears well in his eyes as he flipped his phone closed and looked around the empty parking lot to make sure no one would see him cry once his hot tears escaped his eyes. He was alone. He looked inside the gas station and realized it was actually closed. He looked down at the email Francesca had sent him weeks earlier with her flight information. The email said she missed him so much and couldn't wait to see their new home.

As the ocean lit up with the early morning sun and he gazed at the last glimpse of the moon from the night before, Matt realized he didn't know where his home was anymore. He had never felt so alone. Finally, almost an hour later, he got in his car and pulled out of the empty gas station parking lot. He shook his head as he read the sign for Los Angeles Airport just 20 miles ahead. He was supposed to pick up the love of his life 20 miles away to bring her to their new home and ask her to spend the rest of her life with him. Matt drove back to San Diego in silence.

The red light of the answering machine was flashing when Matt opened the front door of what was supposed to be his and Francesca's first apartment together in San Diego. He tossed his keys on the small kitchen table and hit the button, imagining it would be his dad or brother calling to check on him.

"Matt, I am so sorry. I was scared. I wasn't going to come, and you probably heard. I made the biggest mistake. But I changed my mind, and I am on the plane. But I don't think I will make it. I love you. Goodbye and promise me you will try to find a love like this again—" Francesca's voice was suddenly cut off as it seemed she was about to say something else when the phone hung up sharply.

Matt played the message again. The muffled voice on the line didn't sound like Francesca. His dad had just told him she wasn't getting on the plane. As he went to push play again, the phone rang. Matt picked up on the first ring, hoping to hear his girlfriend's soft voice.

"Matt," his dad said loudly.

"Dad. Do you know what's going on?"

"Matt, thank God she didn't get on the plane. Turn the news on." Matt's father's voice was dull as Matt realized something horrible must have happened.

Matt turned the news on, and his heart sank. He pulled Francesca's email from his pocket again and unfolded it. The same flight number that scrolled at the bottom of the television and read "Hijacked… No Survivors" was the same flight number from Francesca's email that was signed "Love Always, Francesca."

"Dad. She was on the plane. Please. I need to come home."

CHAPTER 14

SUMMER — 2003

Jasmine

Jasmine read the letter twice. All four pages. She felt guilty holding a letter like this in her hands. Her boyfriend, James, would be furious if he found out that she received a letter like this from someone from her past. He was more than just the jealous type. Just the night before, he accused her of cheating on him with her best friend's boyfriend because he found some emails from him about a surprise birthday party they were planning for Cassidy. Jasmine's boyfriend was jealous and crazy. He made her think she was the crazy one with his mind tricks and outbursts. Her heart raced as she looked down at the letter. She felt a mixture of happiness and fear in the same moment as she folded the letter and put it back in the envelope.

"Why don't you just call him? He obviously wants to reconnect. He sounds like a great guy too. After all the shit you go through with James… call him!" Cassidy stood in the doorway ready for work with half a bagel now hanging out of her mouth. She was tired of hearing of all the times James, Jasmine's boyfriend of just over two years, had disappointed her. Honestly, Cassidy didn't even know half of what Jasmine had been going through.

The letter was from Matt. It was sent from Italy and addressed to her home address in Idaho. Surely, he knew she didn't live there anymore but knew her parents would forward it to her. Jasmine appreciated that her parents hadn't asked her why her twin sister's first love was sending her mail. She hadn't talked to Matt in years and wondered why suddenly he felt the need to reach out. Why had he waited all these years to finally tell her exactly how he felt? She wondered what Zoey would think of the letter and if her parents were at least curious about it. They didn't question it and forwarded it to her address in Denver. To say she was shocked was an understatement.

"Call him! Oh, and dump James before you do. We don't want to see you on Dr. Phil talking about how your boyfriend killed the man you are actually meant to be with. If you are worried about Zoey, you are crazy. She didn't care at all when she found out about my past with Kofi before her. She will be fine. Do something for yourself for once!" Cassidy winked and smiled as she pulled the door shut behind her, leaving a scent of perfume lingering in the hallway.

Jasmine grabbed her cup of coffee and sat down on the large white couch. The living room was full of boxes. Her friend was right. She rarely put herself first. It was obvious in her current relationship. Jasmine never wanted to be the one to rock the boat or cause any drama. But here she was, miserable in a relationship and lonelier now than she had ever been. She often wondered if this was how Zoey felt when she was anorexic and depressed in high school—hopeless.

Cassidy was moving in with her new boyfriend soon and Jasmine was happy for them. Cassidy hated James and wasn't shy to make it clear to her best friend that she deserved better. Jasmine knew she was right. She couldn't decide if this letter from Matt could be a sign or a curse. Either way, she needed to make a change. She had to get out of this toxic relationship with James whether she left him for Matt or left him to be alone.

Jasmine met James at a University of Denver alumni basketball game the year before. He was attending law school and she was in her last semester of undergrad. Jasmine was standing behind him at the concession stand and noticed him turn slyly to check her out. He was handsome and seemed shy. She was surprised she hadn't seen him before. When she got to the front of the line and opened her purse to pay for her candy and drink, the young man working told her that the man in front of her asked to pay for her. Eventually, she found out that was part of how he would control her—with his money. It was as if he wanted her to always feel like she owed him something, starting on the first night they met. If she was honest, Jasmine had never cared about money to begin with. On that day, she was flattered that he paid for her candy and drink. Now, after two years of his emotional and sometimes physical abuse, she knew better, but she still couldn't find the strength to leave.

"He gave me a 50-dollar bill and said to cover what you get. Are you sure that is all you want?" The young concession stand worker raised his eyebrows at her, holding the 50 with both his hands.

"I am sorry, did you say he paid for me? Why would he do that? He doesn't even know me," Jasmine asked the student holding the 50 as though he would know the answer. He couldn't have been more than 17 years old and was acting as though he had never held a 50-dollar bill before.

"He probably thinks you're cute." Jasmine smiled and the young man looked at her amused as he slipped the 50 into his pocket. He shrugged and she smiled and pointed at a large box of Junior Mints. The student handed them over and winked. Jasmine slid a 10-dollar bill across the table to ensure the kid could keep the 50 he put in his pocket without any questions and winked back at him and smiled.

Jasmine looked around to find the man that paid for her drink and candy and realized he had been watching from a few feet away the entire time. It wasn't long until he wandered over and asked for her phone number. He called her the next day, and they began to date... well, sort of date.

James and Jasmine had been hooking up for months by the time she finally asked him what exactly they were doing. At that point, she hadn't seen any of his red flags that she saw almost daily now that they were far into their relationship. She thought he was just playing hard to get or was maybe just not a one-woman man. She didn't realize he was playing a much more thought-out game to eventually try to control her. Toxic might be the word she was looking for to describe their relationship.

During the first few months, he would see her at school and ignore her or pretend like he didn't know her when they ran into each other at parties or events. Finally, she called him and told him it was over. She didn't like being treated like she was someone he was embarrassed to be dating and wanted him to stop calling her. Jasmine ignored his phone calls for a few weeks until he was finally fed up. He wasn't used to not being in control. He showed up at Cassidy and Jasmine's apartment and said he wanted Jasmine to be his girlfriend. He would change, he promised.

That was the day he made sure Jasmine understood that their relationship would be on his terms. That was long ago, and Jasmine had never felt worse than when she was with James. She hated to blame a man for how she felt about herself, but it was true. He spent most of their time together putting her down or comparing her to his ex-girlfriend. He even often brought up his ex to make Jasmine jealous, calling her "The Great White Buffalo... The one that got away." James made sure that Jasmine knew she was not his first choice. Jasmine had always been self-confident, but this man was tearing her apart. She fully understood that she was being verbally abused by him and he also might be a sociopath... at the very least, he was a narcissist. But she couldn't get the strength to just walk away. Jasmine looked down at Matt's letter and just knew this was a sign, maybe even fate.

As she sat with the letter on her lap, Jasmine was overwhelmed with embarrassment about her current relationship. She was dating a verbally and sometimes physically abusive man and she wasn't strong enough to leave. It wasn't for lack of trying to break up with him, but she just could never stay away long enough to escape him coming back and manipulating her into thinking she was the problem. She would plan to break up with him after one of his rages and then he would show up with flowers, begging her not to leave. It was a ritual she was embarrassed to be a part of but not strong enough to finally put an end to. She also didn't tell her family or friends about how he made her feel. Jasmine told Cassidy as little as possible, but just being around the couple, Cassidy picked up on his behavior quickly. Jasmine's best friend despised her boyfriend. *She would love Matt,* Jasmine thought, looking down at the pages in her hand as she stood.

She pulled her hair into a ponytail and walked past a mirror in the hallway on her way to the kitchen. The night before had been one of the worst nights so far with James. As she caught a glimpse of herself in the mirror, she remembered the last words he said to her when she shut her car door in his driveway.

"Next time, put on some makeup before you come over here," James said to his girlfriend as she got into her car. The man was serious, and Jasmine couldn't believe she let him talk to her like that without saying a word back. Tears rolled down her cheeks as she sat in her car alone in his driveway, angry at herself for not rolling down her window to cuss him out. She had to get out of this relationship. Jasmine's eyes filled with tears, and she looked at herself in the mirror. She didn't know where the strong, independent woman she was on her way to being was hiding, but she needed to find her. Sure, this letter from Matt could be a sign, but it was a complicated one.

The doorbell rang as Jasmine poured her second cup of coffee. She wiped her eyes and opened the door to find two dozen pink roses. She didn't have to open the card to know they were from James. After reading the letter, she wished they were from Matt. James didn't feel bad about telling Jasmine she needed to wear more makeup next time she came over, basically calling the most beautiful girl he had dated ugly to her face. The more he put her down, the less chance she had of leaving him. He just needed her to think he felt bad. It was a vicious cycle, often ending in dozens of roses.

Jasmine returned to the mirror in the hallway on her way back to the living room with her arm full of roses. She didn't have one drop of makeup on, and she knew she didn't need it and she didn't need to live up to James' standards of beauty. She came home after leaving his house and scrubbed her face hard the night before. She knew she didn't need makeup to be beautiful. She knew she didn't need him to validate that she was that or anything else. Looking back at her in the mirror were striking green eyes and plump, pink lips. She pulled out the tie in her hair and her blonde hair fell down her back. She knew she was beautiful but sometimes a girl had to hear it from the person she was dating. James had gone out of his way to put her down. It was as if he was intimidated by her beauty, so he played it down.

Jasmine sat down and read Matt's letter one more time. As she read the last paragraph, it was as if she could hear his voice reading it to her. She had so many emotions running through her that she couldn't tell what she really felt about him reaching out so many years later.

I want to give us a chance. I am tired of not being honest with myself. I am not willing to lose another person I love because I don't fight for them. I need to see you and know if it's real.

Love, Matt

In the pages before, Matt told her he had lost his future fiancé a few years earlier. It felt as though she was reading a manuscript for a movie as she read about his Italian girlfriend dying in an airplane on September 11th. He told her about his heartache just as he had on the night of the Homecoming Dance their junior year on her porch in Idaho. The night they betrayed her twin sister and his girlfriend was also a night that Matt was coming to Jasmine to heal his broken heart. She realized then that she couldn't see Matt in person. He didn't want Jasmine, he wanted a distraction from the most recent loss in his life. In high school, it was Zoey he had lost, now his girlfriend in a crash. Jasmine knew she deserved a better boyfriend than James, but she also knew she deserved more than being Matt's second option, although the gesture was romantic.

She pulled her journal from the shelf in the living room and closed Matt's letter where her bookmark had been. She would call Matt if and when it was really their time. Until then, his letter would stay safe inside her journal with all her thoughts. Maybe she needed a real sign to know it was their time, but he would have to wait.

The door opened slowly, and Jasmine jumped.

"Hey. I am just grabbing a few boxes. Care to help? I will pay you in mimosas when we are done." Cassidy had returned with her boyfriend and his best friend in tow. They looked around the bright apartment as though they had never seen so much sunlight in their lives. Jasmine smiled, imagining Cassidy living with a man that didn't appreciate her fresh flowers and coconut candles. She knew Cassidy was excited to move in with her boyfriend but expected her to miss the comfortable and cute home she and Jasmine had made for themselves over the past few years.

"Flowers, huh? What did he do?" Cassidy's boyfriend had the note from the roses in his hand as he raised his eyebrows.

"Don't read the note. Jeez. That is personal. Please tell me Matt was romantic enough to send flowers after he knew you read his letter and they aren't from James!" Cassidy said as she plucked the note from her boyfriend's hand.

"I haven't actually read it. Go for it," Jasmine said as she pushed a large box out of her way with her foot.

"Oh my God. He wants you to go to Europe!" Cassidy slammed the note on the kitchen island and stared at Jasmine.

"They are from Matt?" Jasmine asked in shock as she grabbed the note from her friend. He was living in Italy still—it had to be from Matt!

"No. James. He got a fancy new job and invited you to some conference in September in Amsterdam," Cassidy said as she pulled the note away from Jasmine and shoved it back into the bouquet.

"You know I hate this guy for you, but I kind of think you need to go on this trip… then you can break up with him. He owes you a trip to Europe after all you have gone through."

Cassidy pointed to the boxes and motioned her eyes to her boyfriend and his friend. She pulled a bottle of champagne out of the fridge, grabbed two glasses from the cupboard, and poured each glass almost to the top.

Jasmine drank the glass of champagne before Cassidy had a chance to add orange juice.

"You are right. I might as well go on a vacation. This will be my final goodbye to my relationship with James. Oh, and Matt isn't ready for me. He thinks he is, but I know he isn't. And I don't want to bring this up to Zoey… it's just too complicated."

Cassidy watched as the two men emptied the room of her boxes as she sipped champagne with her best friend.

"I am going to miss you," she said, kissing Jasmine on the cheek.

"Me too. I don't want to live alone."

Suddenly, Jasmine thought back to the day that Zoey left for college so many years before. She felt an eerie similarity between that day and now, where she was preparing for Cassidy to move out. Her sister, who used to be her best friend in the world, left and found what was appearing to be her soulmate in Kofi. Now her new best friend was moving out and into a home with her boyfriend. Jasmine deserved better than James. She knew she would always have Zoey and Cassidy and that she wouldn't technically ever be alone. But where was the love of her life? She knew it wasn't James. Maybe it was Matt.

Jasmine knew she needed to tell Zoey about the letter from Matt. Maybe she would do that after this trip to Europe with James. After all, she had never been out of the country. It would be her way of finally being in control before she ended the relationship for good. She raised her glass to cheer her best friend. It was, after all, going to probably be her last chance at an all-expenses-paid, first-class trip to Europe.

"To freedom after first-class," Cassidy said as she smiled, not realizing she had just read her best friend's mind.

"Wow. This seems a little opportunistic, don't you think?" Cassidy's boyfriend said as he stopped moving boxes and grabbed a beer from the fridge.

"You have no idea what this woman has gone through with James. It's literally the only way she can say goodbye with a shred of dignity." Cassidy rolled her eyes and smiled at Jasmine.

"Tell me how you really feel?" Jasmine laughed and wondered how close Amsterdam was to where Matt lived in Italy.

CHAPTER 15

FALL – 2003

Zoey

My second marathon was just a month away and waking up early for the long runs was getting old. It was especially hard to unwrap myself from the warm comfort of Kofi's arms as he slept, only to have to get drenched with rain for two and a half hours in the Portland fall. But I had worked hard, and it was my last long run before getting to taper and rest before race day. Kofi would hopefully still be here when I returned, and the hardest part of the long run was always just getting out the door.

As I got out of bed, I saw Kofi slowly open his eyes. He closed them quickly and rolled over, facing away from the light I had just turned on in the kitchen. He knew the routine. I broke a banana in half and quickly ate before gulping down some water and heading out the door.

Kofi had gotten me an iPod for my birthday a few days earlier even though my birthday wasn't until the next week. He said he wanted to give it to me early to get me through my last long run, but I honestly preferred listening to the sounds around me and letting my thoughts run wild. It was funny to me that he still couldn't understand how I ran without any music the majority of the time. Running was my therapy. I usually brought a CD player with me on my long runs just in case I needed some motivation to get me through the last few miles, I had to admit, this iPod was much more convenient. Kofi rolled back over as I turned off the light and went to kiss him on the cheek.

The sky was barely glowing from the sun making its debut just a few minutes before I shut the door behind me. I stepped out onto the sidewalk and passed Kofi's bicycle that was locked against the fence. I couldn't help but smile looking at his multiple locks. It was the third or fourth bike he'd had since I met him. They were getting stolen at least every couple of months and he was getting tired of buying a new one at the thrift store where we got most of our furniture. I noticed one of the chain locks had been cut but the others were all still intact and imagined him cursing as he unlocked it later that day.

I zipped my brand-new iPod and headphones into my running belt as I started to run. I was not your typical marathon runner these days and didn't carry water and barely timed myself. I just knew that if I ran a certain loop, it was five miles, another loop was 10. If I did a combination of my routes, I could easily log 20 miles and stop in a coffee shop for a bathroom break or a sip of water. I never wanted to know my times because they were slower and slower the further away from anorexia I got. That was fine with me, but sometimes still hard to process.

I loved running before the sun rose and while the city was still asleep. The first few miles of a long run in the dark sometimes didn't even feel like they counted. They felt easier than the miles I ran when the sun was up.

I headed up NW 23rd and was able to run right down the middle of the sidewalk without having to dodge anyone. There were usually a few people sitting in coffee shops this early, but other than that, the city was quiet. As I ran by the small bakery, a whiff of fresh bread filled the air and I heard coffee grinding as a young employee closed the door behind her. She locked the door and flipped the outdoor light off that had brightened my path. The loop I planned for this morning meant making my way up NW 23rd and eventually to the trails behind the city. I would wind down to the Willamette River and back on the waterfront and through the city to our apartment. It would take close to three hours, and I always tried to leave early enough to get back in time to jump back in bed with Kofi for at least a few minutes before he would start his Saturday.

Kofi worked the second shift on Saturdays and Sundays at a bike shop in the Hawthorne District. During the week, we both worked pretty much 9 to 5, which meant he worked seven days a week. My internship had turned into a real full-time paying job after I graduated from Portland State, and Kofi was getting closer to his dream of becoming an architect and working full-time at a local firm. Some weekends, I enjoyed having the afternoons to myself when he left for his second job, but mostly, I wanted to be with him as much as I could. Spending time with him on a Saturday morning after a long run was my favorite time of the week. We were still young but working and trying to save for our future sometimes made me feel like our lives were moving way too fast. Sometimes it felt like it was just yesterday that I was in high school in Idaho.

As I approached the trailhead, I was just starting mile three. The sun was now hiding behind a thick layer of fog, but the rain held off thankfully. I would run through the trails behind the city for the next five miles to get to my favorite spot that I had discovered running in the city for the past few years. When I finally reached my favorite spot, I decided to stretch and take in the views. It was always amazing to me that just eight miles of running could bring me to what felt like the top of the city. I could see the river, the city below, and all of the beautiful bridges through the trees. I was close to halfway through my long run and felt great.

This run was the last of six long runs I had on my marathon training schedule. I had many routes in the city, but this was my favorite loop, mostly because of the spot I stood right then. As I stretched and took in a deep breath, I thought about how close I came to death just a few years earlier. My mind flashed back to the New Year's Eve I spent in hospital with feeding tubes and a team of doctors meeting every few hours to evaluate the next steps to keep me alive. I was proud of how far I had come and proud that I was able to control my running and come back to a place of being able to enjoy it but be healthy and, most importantly, happy. It had been a tough few years of healing and I hadn't really taken a lot of time to reflect on how thankful I was to be where I was that day—alive.

As I stood, watching the water run swiftly in the river below and listening to the leaves whisper in the wind, I smiled and exhaled exaggeratedly. It felt so good to breathe, knowing it wasn't my last breath. It felt so good to open my eyes and see a future in this new city I called home. I was a different person now living with Kofi in Portland than I was starving myself in Idaho. All those years ago, I would run endless miles just to numb my pain and calm the anxiety I felt every minute of every day. Today, I ran to relax. I ran to feel and appreciate the body I had dedicated myself to restoring and valuing.

I felt the first rain drop on my cheek as I looked up into the sky and took another deep breath of the crisp fall Oregon air. Suddenly, a salty taste of a tear rolled over my lips, and I realized how much I truly had to be thankful for.

The next few miles were a breeze. They were mostly downhill until I reached the waterfront bike path that would lead me under a few bridges and to the opposite end of downtown. I still hadn't pulled the iPod out of my running belt when I reached the end of the bike path. From there, I would run on the sidewalks through downtown and make my way to Portland State, with only my thoughts and the sound of my breath accompanying me.

I took a few minutes to walk when I reached the school and reminisced about all of the classes I took as I passed the football field. I didn't really have the college experience I thought I would have had when I was younger. I met Kofi before I even started classes, so I didn't really prioritize going to football and basketball games or partying like most college students did. I didn't regret anything though. I started running again after passing the library and the green sign that read Portland State University. I got my degree and I felt content with the life I created with Kofi in our apartment near NW 23rd. I missed my family but talked to Jasmine on the phone often enough and usually visited my parents and older sister, Erin, at least a few times a year. I smiled, thinking of the visit Erin and her best friend, Sophie, had over the summer. I was anxious to show my older sister and her best friend my new city and introduce them to Kofi. Just as I had expected, they loved him. They loved how happy I was in my new home, and they were proud of me for getting healthy.

I looked down at my watch to see I had been running for just over two hours now as I took another walk break. The coffee shop I spent half my time in during school was just two blocks away. It was a regular spot for me to stop for water and a bathroom break during my long runs. The baristas knew me well and never hesitated to hand over the key to the bathroom and pour me a glass of ice water.

"Hey, Zoey. Long run today or just coming in to see me?" Cole, who had a long dark ponytail and glasses, asked as I opened the door to the coffee shop. There was a bell attached to the doorknob that reminded me of Christmas as it chimed as I struggled to close the door behind me. Cole was my favorite barista and I had known him now almost as long as I had known Kofi. Cole had seen me stress out over finishing papers late at night or studying for tests for the past few years but had recently only seen me during my long run pit stops.

"Oh, hey, Cole. Long run today. It's my last one until the marathon. I promise to actually order something next time I come in, but could I grab some water?"

Cole was already pouring me a glass when I asked and had the key to the bathroom in his hand. The small key had a long piece of wood attached to it that was decorated with drawings from the staff over the years. I caught a glimpse of his name spelled out in dark green marker. It looked as though he purposefully handed the key over so that I could see his name. He gave me the biggest smile I had seen in a while.

"Don't lose the key!" Cole said laughing as he handed me the large stick across the bar counter. I wondered how many times a day he said those words.

"I won't lose the key…" I said after chugging the ice-cold water and winking at him dryly.

The coffee shop was full of students with their noses in books. There was a man playing the guitar in the corner with a bowl full of dollar bills and change on the ground in front of him. He was playing Pearl Jam and singing a song almost too soft to be heard. I wondered if it bothered him that nobody seemed to be listening to him. I noticed for the first time how loud the buzz of voices was in the small coffee shop. The sounds of grinding coffee and steaming milk were also distracting. I caught eyes with the musician, and he smiled almost as big as Cole had just smiled while handing over the bathroom key. Everyone was happy to be there, together but not technically together, on a Saturday morning in Portland, Oregon. I was happy too. I made a mental note to come back when I wasn't running so I could enjoy one of Cole's fancy six-dollar drinks and give this guitar player a tip to help fill his bowl.

I handed Cole the key back, said goodbye, and stepped back outside to finish the last portion of my long run. The rain had started a steady stream miles ago and was coming down hard now. I looked up as I crossed the street and was surprised to see Kofi pedaling his bike in the bike lane of the busy street across from me. He didn't notice me and had his head down as the water splashed hard around his bike pedals. He didn't have to be at his job for a few hours, so I just assumed he was running an errand or getting some exercise.

Less than 30 minutes later, I arrived back at our apartment and kicked off my soggy shoes outside the door. I looked at my watch and was happy to have finished the 20 miles in under three hours. I was officially in the resting phase of marathon training and smiled as I thought of all of the hard work I had done in the past few months. Almost every Saturday morning, I woke up and ran, rain or shine. Now it was time for shorter runs, rest, and mental preparation for my second marathon. My first one had been at the peak of my anorexia on a whim, and I won the entire race. That one didn't really count in my mind because I truly was a completely different person back then.

There was a pile of letters on the kitchen table as I slugged a full glass of water quickly. I dumped the last inch of water into a plant on the windowsill and turned back to look through the pile. Kofi had opened one of the letters and left it on the table, almost willing me to look at who it was from. It was handwritten and neat. Must have been Reggie or someone from his past. I made a note to ask him about it as I fought the urge to see who it was from and noticed a letter with my name on the front. The return address was Italy. The only person I knew that had anything to do with Italy was Matt, but I hadn't heard from him since high school, and I really had no clue what he was doing. There was no name on the letter, just an address and probably way more than enough stamps than what was required to send it.

I smiled as I read the letter. I was shocked at the words on the page but thrilled to hear from him. It was Matt. I stepped outside as the rain started to die off and pulled out my CD player to listen to the CD Kofi made for me the first year that we met. Minutes later, I saw Kofi heading toward me, walking his bike up the path as I wound the headphone cord around the player and got up slowly.

Later that night, Kofi told me what the letter said that was addressed to him on the kitchen table. He asked me who had written to me from Italy. I was relieved to feel happy as I read the letter out loud from my first love to what I hoped would be my last love.

"Wow. Zoey. You are such a forgiving woman," he said as he poured me my second glass of red wine and turned down the radio that sat near the plant on the windowsill in the kitchen.

"Sometimes forgiveness is the only thing that will heal you. You should try, Kofi. The only way to start is by forgiving yourself," I said as I dropped both letters in the trash and kissed him on the forehead.

CHAPTER 16

FALL – 2003

Kofi

Kofi pedaled his bike to the top of the Hawthorne Bridge. It was raining but he could see the sun trying to peek through the clouds. He hadn't been to the point where he almost ended it all many years before, but something was telling him to visit that spot today.

Zoey had left on a long run a couple of hours earlier and wouldn't be back for another hour after that. She was training for a marathon that would take place in the next month and was waking up every morning and heading out the door for a run. This had been one of the first mornings in more than he could remember that he woke up before she had already left. He knew if he let her know he was awake it would be harder for her to leave, so he pretended to be asleep as she got up and headed out the door. He wanted to just lay in bed with her that morning, but he knew she was too dedicated to training to miss a long run just to lay in bed with him. After she left, Kofi cleaned the entire apartment and went for a short walk, but he needed to get out of the apartment and clear his head.

On the kitchen table, he left an opened letter he had read just after Zoey left for her run. It was a letter from his mom in California. She was getting married and wanted him to know. She told him he would have a new half-brother named Justin. This kid was not his brother. Kofi knew he would never meet Justin and he would never meet the man his mother was about to marry. He imagined his mother, in her late fifties by now, standing in front of a man in a wedding dress. He imagined Justin would be his dad's best man.

Kofi couldn't think of who would be there to stand next to his mother on her big day. Reggie's mother maybe, but all that they really had in common was their sons, both of whom they had abandoned. Kofi wanted to know if his mother had told this man she was about to marry about Kofi, the son she left behind. He wanted to know the story she told him about Naya and the day she died. Kofi was sure his mother had told this man that it was her son who killed her daughter, therefore, they were both dead to her now. She had started a new life and marrying this unnamed man and becoming stepmom to Justin would replace Kofi and the life she left behind in Kentucky. She could be happy now. He hadn't heard from her since the accident, and after this letter, he decided he never wanted to hear from her again. Kofi's own mother had abandoned him when he needed her the most, and for that, he didn't know if he hoped she had a happy life. He did know that he had to move past being angry with her and he couldn't use this as an excuse for anything he did wrong as an adult. He knew too many adults using their messed-up childhoods as an excuse. He had no blood family now. But at least he had Zoey and Reggie. To Kofi, the two of them were enough—they had to be enough.

When Kofi arrived at the top of the bridge, the rain stopped. The sun glistened off the water below and he felt a sense of calm he had never felt before. He propped his bike against the railing and leaned forward to smell the water below. It wasn't the smell of fresh seawater; it smelled like trash. Kofi closed his eyes and thought of the last time he saw his mother. He was sitting in the back of a police car in Kentucky on his birthday, the day his sister died. Red and blue lights were flashing, and his mother was screaming. She was screaming at him and at the world that he had killed her baby.

"It was an accident. I didn't mean for this to happen, Ma!" were the last words he said to his mother as she shook her head and turned away from him, falling into Reggie's mother's arms. Reggie had tried to grab her arm and comfort her and she ripped her arm away from his grasp and walked out of their lives. From the back seat of the police car, Kofi looked at his best friend, Reggie, through his tear-filled eyes. Reggie looked down and shook his head. Reggie knew that day his best friend had lost his little sister and his mom. Reggie would always be there for Kofi—he would even sacrifice himself for his best friend. Kofi would learn soon what it really meant to have a brother, blood-related or not.

Kofi closed his eyes tighter and felt the breeze on his face. The smell of trash was fading, and he could smell the freshness in the air after the rain as the wind picked up. He thought back to the night he watched Zoey unpack her car and move into apartment 101 so many years before. He had no idea that almost five years later she would be the love of his life. They rarely fought, not even when she realized he had kept more than just a few secrets from her years before.

Kofi thought back to the night in Denver when he worried his secrets would be too much for her and he waited for her to walk away. He remembered the exact look in her eyes on that New Year's Eve in Denver when Zoey realized that Kofi had not been totally honest with her. But Zoey never walked away from him like his mother had. She loved him and he loved her.

As Kofi stood on the top of the bridge, he realized he had all he needed in his life. There was nothing he could do to bring back Naya.

There was nothing he could do to try to have a relationship with his mom or even his dad again. They were gone and he had been fine all these years without them. Kofi didn't believe the saying that everything happened for a reason. If so, his little sister shouldn't have died. There was no reason behind that. There was no lesson for him or everyone that loved her to learn from her death. Things don't always happen for a reason. Sometimes, terrible shit happens, and you have to be strong enough to move past it.

Kofi did believe that he couldn't be a victim of the bad things that had happened to him in his life so far. He couldn't change his mother's mind that he was the reason her youngest child was dead. He couldn't change the fact that his father had left without even meeting his own son. Finally, Kofi took a deep breath and smelled only fresh air. He didn't smell the trash below anymore from the top of the bridge at all. He got back on his bike and rode toward his new home to his present life and his future. *The past is behind me now,* he thought as he turned to look at the bridge behind him.

When Kofi arrived back at the apartment, Zoey was sitting on the front steps with a tall glass of ice water and her shoes off. She looked beautiful with sweat dripping down her cheeks and her hair pulled up in a loose ponytail. She was wrapping the cord of her headphones around her CD player and looked up, surprised. He bought her an iPod for her birthday in a few weeks but wondered if she would ever give up her CD player. He noticed the iPod in a pile near her on top of the pink running belt she seemed to never leave home without. Watching her wrap her headphones around the player reminded him of the first year they were dating and he gave her some CDs to listen to. He knew she still listened to his favorite Prince song almost every morning when she stretched before her run on the soft rug in front of their TV. He had heard her singing the week before and smiled as he laid in bed, watching her from across the room as she thought he was still sleeping.

"Oh, hey. What are you doing?" she asked as she stood and began to stretch. The smile on her face let him know she was happy to be done with her long run and happy to see him. Sometimes it felt as though they had just met. Kofi still got chills when he saw her and, to him, even after almost five years together, she was still the most beautiful girl in the world.

Kofi laid his bike down in the grass and walked over to Zoey. He kissed her salty neck and picked her up in his arms. She kicked playfully and then winced and reached for her calf as though she hadn't quite recovered yet from her three-hour run just moments before.

Kofi lowered Zoey to the ground and handed her the ice water she was drinking as he arrived.

"I love you, Zoey. I want you to be my wife."

"Whoa. What?" she asked, pulling away and looking at him questioningly.

"Not today. Not tomorrow. But someday I want you to be my wife."

Kofi pulled her back in and kissed her. He felt her body get weak as he rubbed his hand over her butt. He wondered if their attraction would ever fade and imagined kissing her and feeling the same way in 20 years. He could only hope.

"I think I can do that. We will see if you ever learn to put your dishes in the dishwasher and not the sink. Then we can talk!" Zoey winked at him and kissed him again quickly before picking up her shoes and walking into the building.

She turned and paused, taking in how handsome he was standing next to his bike. Kofi had grown out his hair and had the beginnings of short dreadlocks. His tattooed arms were strong and sexy. She nodded her head in approval and smiled at him. They were lucky and they both knew it.

Kofi glanced at the letter from his mom as he walked into the kitchen. That would probably be the last he would hear from her. He was sure she felt obligated to reach out just to tell him she was moving on. He was relieved to know the ball was in his court, and he was not going to respond. He also noticed a letter to Zoey on the table that was open that looked as though she had just read it. The return address was in another language—Italian maybe. She never got mail and he made a mental note to himself to ask her if everything was ok. She was the type of girl that didn't usually just tell you if she was upset or something was wrong, you had to get her to open up.

Across the apartment, Zoey had taken all of her sweaty running clothes off by the time Kofi returned from putting the glass in the kitchen sink.

"The best part of a long run is the long, hot shower after it. Care to join?" she said with a smile as she peeked her head out from the bathroom, her finger waving him in to join her.

"Oh. And I love you too," she said to him as he pulled his shirt over his head and closed the bathroom door behind him.

Kofi would never speak to his mother again. Two months later, she married a man in California and became stepmother to Justin, the kid she told Kofi was somehow his new half-brother. As far as Kofi knew, she never stopped believing that he killed his little sister. Zoey and Reggie were officially what he considered his only family. He might not have had a big family, but he'd never felt so loved.

CHAPTER 17

FALL – 2003

Jasmine

Jasmine woke up under a heavy white down comforter in the Waldorf Astoria in Amsterdam on the morning of her 24th birthday. The large suite in this charming city in her new favorite country was majestic and decorated with gold-trimmed mirrors and a floor-to-ceiling window that overlooked the bustle of the street below. Jasmine hadn't confirmed yet but was pretty sure their room took up the entire floor. She felt like Princess Diana in more ways than one. When she was younger, she had a fascination with Lady Di. Although Jasmine had always noticed the sadness in her eyes and wondered how she could be so sad living what seemed like a romantic fairytale. She finally started to understand that everything is not what it seems, and sometimes what appears to be Prince Charming might not make your fairytale dreams come true.

Jasmine could hear the rain hit the cobblestone streets from the king-sized bed that felt larger than her king bed at home. She had been here for four nights and the rain fell softer each morning. She rolled out of bed and opened the window to a sea of bicycles whirling through the rainy slim street. Three women were sitting under an umbrella at a table drinking tiny cups of coffee across from the hotel. Jasmine couldn't make out what language they were speaking but they seemed to talk more with their flailing hands than the puzzle of words that flew out of their mouths. Watching the women made her miss her sisters.

The women in Amsterdam all seemed to be blonde and very tall with perfect skin and red lipstick. She was here for three more nights and then off to Venice for another week. She was being treated to an all-expenses-paid European vacation by a man she needed to break up with immediately.

I will break up with James when we get home, she thought to herself as she pulled her long blonde hair into a high ponytail and wrapped the soft white robe around her body. The curls still in her hair were not the only thing reminding her of the night before. Jasmine had a slight headache from the two large glasses of Italian wine she consumed during dinner, followed by a very stiff martini in the lobby.

James had been made partner at his law firm and was here for a ceremony celebrating his and the other partners' new roles in their large company. In this new role, eventually, he would be rich and what he had worked for so many years to accomplish was being celebrated this week in over-the-top fashion complete with a formal ball that would start in about nine hours. Jasmine was his plus one. So far, it had been a trip full of extravagant meals with expensive wine. There were also a few shopping sprees and one very strange "mandatory workshop" for the new partners' spouses on how to basically be a supportive wife who runs charities while your man raked in the dough and worked late into each night. Jasmine had sat in that "workshop" the day before listening to the CEO's wife tell a room full of bright-eyed submissive women about her charity of choice. All Jasmine could think while she told them about the "Books for Bobby" (her husband was Bob, of course) charity that forced the other housewives to read books to inner city children was that there were so many other great causes to support. Weren't children still starving in third-world countries? Weren't children actually starving in their own countries? Did inner-city kids really need the Housewives of Denver to read them books? As she flashed her possibly 10-carat diamond wedding ring, Jasmine did the math in her head and concluded that she could pay for the starving kids in at least two countries to eat for six months with the price of that rock. *Is this lady for real?* As Jasmine scanned the room, she noticed most women taking notes and glancing up occasionally to size up the competition. This was going to be the most exciting thing these women did in their lives that were full of boring afternoon playdates and dinner parties filled with fake friendships and fake boobs. She was almost expecting this "workshop" to teach them how to look the other way while their men bought their mistresses a Jaguar and an apartment in the city. She sat in that "workshop" and listened to housewife after housewife talk about the charity they would start—none of which would actually make a difference in this world of poverty that they knew nothing about. Jasmine didn't have enough appendages on her body to count how many of these housewives asked her when her and James would get married. If they only knew...

It took her years to realize, but she would eventually learn that his confidence was a cover-up, and he was not the man he appeared to be in his black suit and fresh haircut. He was a man that hadn't yet dealt with his childhood. A man that covered up his insecurities with brooding yet fake self-esteem. Eventually, Jasmine would see the worst of his insecurities.

She never thought she would be the type of woman who let a man hit her. It wasn't even the physical abuse that hurt so bad. James had spent the last two and a half years making sure any shred of self-esteem she had built up in her adult life was buried deep beneath his insults. Then, when he felt she had reached her breaking point and she was ready to leave him, he would revert to the charming, handsome, successful man she fell for almost three years earlier. James would shower her with gifts and romantic surprises and plead with her to never, ever leave him. He couldn't go on without her, he would say, as he held onto her hand a little too tightly the last time she told him she was finally done. Just two months earlier, he sent three dozen roses to her job in hopes she would forget about the deep teeth marks in her back he claimed he didn't mean to cut into her skin while he "kissed" her during a back massage he hoped would turn into sex. It didn't. That was just one of the times she was able to fight him off while forcing her to give in to sex when she didn't want it.

But Jasmine forgave him, as she always had, for the bruises, the scratches, and the deeper emotional wounds to her pride. After each wound, he would apologize and tell her things about his life he claimed to have never told anyone before, as if to explain why he did what he did. The stories were typically of growing up poor and seeing his father hit his mother. He told her stories of his big brother going to prison when he was barely old enough to understand that he might not ever come back. He had been abandoned, he said, by everyone. That was why he ended up always begging her not to leave, even after he would force her to have sex with him or say something so hurtful that she wished she could disappear.

Jasmine didn't understand why James told her these stories after he did the same horrible things he said he was ashamed to watch his father do to his mother. She supposed he was trying to explain why he did these things to her as if his life before her was an excuse for what he had done. He was perhaps the smartest man she ever dated, yet he was not smart at all. Eventually, she would be back in his tight grips again right after the bruises healed. That pattern had repeated itself almost like clockwork every couple of weeks. It wasn't like this in the beginning. It took her almost a year and a half to even realize she was in an abusive relationship. But here she was—alone in a hotel in Amsterdam on her birthday staring in the fancy, gold mirror at the large patch of purple and blue on the left side of her neck. He hadn't hit her in over a month, but this bruise on her neck was the last reminder of a jealous, rage-filled night where he accused her of cheating on him with a coworker she had a group happy hour with earlier that week. That night, he lifted her off the ground by her throat. In James' opinion, if you work with a man and he sits at the table with you and a few other female coworkers, you are obviously sleeping with him. His jealousy and control had Jasmine questioning everything she did and everyone she spent time with.

Luckily, James' days in Amsterdam were full of meetings, so Jasmine was alone for most of the trip during the day. Each night when the sun started to subside over the city and she began to put on her makeup and curl her hair for that night's event, she wondered if he would break his month-long streak and hit her again. It seemed that his abuse of choice during this trip was not physical but mental. She was sure none of his colleagues or their wives knew any part of the side of James that she was so familiar with.

Jasmine leaned in close to the mirror to see what she thought he saw when he looked at her. The night before, during the cocktail hour, he whispered into her ear and she froze.

"You are embarrassing. Wear the right amount of makeup tomorrow so the partners don't think I'm dating a grandma. You look like shit."

Suddenly, feeling like the ugliest woman in the room, she caught eyes with one of the housewives from the "workshop" the day before as James leaned back to the table and picked up his drink. The housewife heard every word that James said to Jasmine and her eyes were full of pity. She looked at Jasmine with her eyelash extensions and salon-manicured hair and nails as if to say, "Get out!" Jasmine had spent all that time feeling sorry for her and the other Stepford Wives, but she was the one living the life of shame.

Jasmine splashed cold water on her face from the marble sink and looked again at the face he seemed so ashamed to be seen with. She didn't look old. She was still pretty beneath the makeup he urged her to paint on. How had she given him the power to take that all away?

Jasmine leaned back from the mirror and heard a knock at the door. What must have been five dozen white roses were covering a short man who blurted, "Delivery for you." He pushed past her and put the roses on the coffee table in the middle of the massive living room. Another man followed with even more vases full of light pink roses. The note read, "Happy Birthday. Check the closet."

Jasmine opened the closet to see a floor-length revealing black dress and a box with large diamond solitaire earrings and a matching diamond necklace. It was his gesture to say this is what she needed to wear tonight.

Hours later, Jasmine arrived at the formal ball to meet James and the other partners. She had taken a car from the hotel to the historic art museum where the ball was held. His classes ran so late that day, so they had to meet there. As she pulled up to the museum, she saw him across the street. James stood with two other men in suits waiting for their wives to arrive. Their wives would stand silently on their arms all night while they boasted about themselves and their professional accomplishments. James didn't see her get out of the car across the street from the museum. Jasmine stood and watched as the two wives eventually found their husbands with no greetings or hugs. She wondered if either of the men told their wives they looked beautiful in their gowns or if they were all just like James. *At least the two wives have each other*, she thought.

Jasmine was sure he was looking for the fitted black dress he planned for her to arrive in as she saw him look around the dimly lit streets outside of the museum. She watched as he looked down at his watch, disappointed in her for being late. Crowds gathered, and she finally got the courage to cross the street. As she got closer, she recognized one of the wives standing near James as the woman who overheard him telling her that she looked old and needed more makeup. The wife caught eyes with Jasmine again and gave a slight smile with the same look of pity on her face from the night before. James stared at Jasmine as she approached in the red dress she had bought months ago to wear to this ball. It sparkled in the streetlight, and she felt the wife's look go from pity to admiration. They loved Jasmine's dress. Jasmine loved this dress. James' eyes were filled with fury as he realized she wasn't wearing the black dress he had waiting for her in their room. Jasmine got closer and the housewife from the night before smiled when she realized Jasmine had not one drop of makeup on her face. Jasmine smiled back at her and nodded as she reached James.

"This is for you," Jasmine said as she handed him the black box with the diamond earrings and necklace, and she turned and walked away.

"You both look beautiful," Jasmine said to the two wives as she passed them on her way back to the car waiting across the street.

Jasmine never saw James again after that night in Amsterdam. She got back into the black town car and returned to the luxury suite to collect her bags. She changed out of her sparkly red dress into yoga pants and a hooded sweatshirt she was pretty sure James never realized she even owned. She stood amongst the roses as she pulled her hair up into a bun and tossed her large makeup bag into the trash under the gold mirror. The doors closed slowly behind her and the same man who filled her room with roses earlier that day hailed a cab for her to get to the airport.

"Sorry, do I have a minute to call my sister before we go?" Jasmine asked the cab driver who shrugged and clearly didn't understand a word she said. He looked at the short man who hailed the cab and they both smiled as Jasmine ran back into the lobby to the front desk, her bun flopping on top of her head.

"Yes. Charge it to the room please," she said as she wrote down the international phone number for the front desk person to call.

"Happy Birthday, twin… lots to catch up on but I am heading to Italy a few days early… without James," Jasmine said as soon as Zoey picked up the phone.

"Happy Birthday! I think. What time is it?" Zoey replied sleepily. "Jasmine, go and find him and live happily ever after. You have my blessing," Zoey said. Jasmine could imagine her smiling and shaking her head as she said it as though reassuring her that she did really have her blessing.

Jasmine's eyes filled with tears as she wondered how Zoey knew about Matt's letter and him asking her to come to Italy so many months before. Twin intuition couldn't be that strong… or maybe it could?

As the cab pulled away from the most beautiful hotel Jasmine would ever stay in, she took a deep breath and realized that James could never hurt her again. She looked into the dark sky just as a shooting star blazed lightly overhead. Maybe the timing was finally right.

CHAPTER 18

FALL — 2005

Matt

Matt woke up and rolled over. His lips grazed Jasmine's neck as he rubbed his hand over her back. Her long hair was tangled and sprawled out on the white pillow. Jasmine slept with her hands clasped together under her cheek. Matt felt like he could tell exactly what she looked like as a little girl when she slept like that. She was just a teenager when he met her all those years ago in Idaho when he was her sister's first love. He could watch her sleep forever. That was his plan. It was her 26th birthday and he couldn't wait to celebrate with her. Finally, he felt he found true love.

It had been two years since she showed up on his doorstep in Florence in the middle of the night with an overnight bag and her hair piled on top of her head. When he opened the door, he could see she had been crying. Matt didn't know about James or the abuse she endured while being his girlfriend until almost five months into her stay. He was furious and couldn't understand how the most beautiful girl he had known could have been treated like that. After spending the last two years together, Matt realized that Jasmine was even more beautiful on the inside than on the outside. It took her a while to finally open up and talk to Matt about the man she left in Amsterdam that had tried his hardest to make her feel less than the beautiful woman she was. There were many late nights that Matt and Jasmine spent just laying in bed, catching each other up on the many years of each other's lives that they had missed. After all the late-night talks, Matt had come to realize that his new girlfriend, the woman he hoped to spend his life with, was just getting out of an abusive relationship. It wasn't long before he made her finally feel safe.

It had been years since Francesca died. September 11th, 2001 was the worst day of his life next to the day his mother died his senior year of high school. He told Jasmine all about his Italian lover that he had planned to propose to after a whirlwind romance that started over a lemonade and some Italian lessons. The day that Francesca died was also the day he decided he couldn't keep waiting for love to come to him. He had to go and get it. He spent years after losing Francesca feeling sorry for himself and barely leaving his house outside of work and to visit his dad and brother. He really couldn't stop thinking of Jasmine during that time and he knew he had to listen to the longing that took over his thoughts most nights. Matt always went back to the day on the hike with his mom overlooking the ocean. That day she told him the story of her finding her own love in his dad was the day he vowed to find that love of his own. He had always sort of known in his heart it was Jasmine. It was always Jasmine. To Matt, love felt like it hadn't been patient and kind. It had been full of obstacles. One thing always remained through those obstacles—he always thought about Jasmine.

In high school, Matt had tried to love Zoey—full eating disorder and all. When he thought back on his time with Zoey, he realized that they were friends more than anything else. They weren't in love or meant to be. She wasn't what his mom talked about all those years ago on the cliff in Italy. Zoey and Matt needed each other for very specific reasons. He needed her to get him through his mother's death and she needed him to help her realize that she would miss out on life and love if she didn't pull herself out of her disease.

In college, Matt tried to love Francesca, which met such a fateful ending. On Francesca's last day on Earth, she had to talk herself into coming home to Matt. She didn't want the life he wanted for them. She didn't want to live in San Diego and wear the ring he had worked so hard for. She didn't want him. That wasn't the kind of love he wanted for the rest of his life. Even if Francesca hadn't died that day, Matt knew that she wasn't the one that her mother tried to tell him about overlooking the sea.

Matt needed someone who never made him doubt that it was meant to be. Matt needed someone that made him feel the same way his mother felt about his dad. He saw it in the way they looked at each other through all the years. Through all the pain and struggle, the way that they looked at each other remained the same. That was what Matt wanted. He wanted to dance in the living room in front of their kids and hear Jasmine's laughter until their very last days. He wanted his own family with Jasmine, the family that his mother told him about on that hike.

As he thought of Zoey and Francesca, he thought that being in love just shouldn't be that hard. It wasn't hard with Jasmine, and he couldn't believe that she was there, lying in bed with him after so many years.

It had to be Jasmine. If he was honest with himself, he knew it was her on the day he picked Zoey up for Homecoming and saw her with her hair wrapped up in a towel on the stairs. The way they looked at each other that day, it was as if they understood. Maybe love was patient after all, as long as he had been patient too.

The night that Jasmine arrived in Florence on Matt's front porch in the middle of the night two years earlier felt just like yesterday. She had taken the train from Amsterdam to Florence and arrived close to 5 a.m. Matt couldn't believe his eyes when he opened the door and saw her standing on the porch in the moonlight. Her hair had been piled on top of her head and she wore a hoodie and sweatpants. She was beautiful. She looked almost exactly like she did that night of Homecoming, standing on the stairs as he passed her with her towel wrapped on her head. He thought he was dreaming. Before he could rub the sleep out of his eyes, Jasmine fell into his arms and began to sob. At first, her tears scared him. Matt was used to tragedy and bad news. But the way that Jasmine wrapped her arms around his neck and pulled him closer as she sobbed, he realized her tears were tears of relief. She was finally where she needed to be.

After Francesca died, Matt moved back to Italy from San Diego and taught English and Creative Writing at a local high school while he worked on getting his master's degree in Education. He dreamed of one day being a full-time writer and finishing his book one day, but he loved teaching, and it paid the bills. Matt had a dog and a small house with a porch swing where he sat most nights looking at the lights of the city below through the olive trees while he graded papers. On a crisp September night, many years earlier, he was reading a paper one of his students had turned in for his Creative Writing Class. The topic had been to describe a theory about life you hoped was true. Most of the students wrote about hoping their cats had nine lives, or hoped that if they hung upside down they would grow taller. One student—the student with the lowest grade in the class, in fact—wrote that he hoped if he swallowed watermelon seeds that he would grow a melon in his stomach. Matt wanted to give this student an A for humor but settled on a C.

Matt laughed to himself as he flipped through the stack of papers—some typed neatly while most of them were barely legible. He stopped flipping to come to a page titled "The Three Loves of Your Lifetime". It was his favorite student, Pietro. In typical Pietro fashion, the paper was typed, double-spaced, and one of the only papers that looked to be over the minimum 500-word requirement.

Matt read the paper twice with a smile on his face as the sun went down over Florence that night. Pietro wrote that his mother had told him that he would have three loves in his lifetime. He wrote that each love would teach him a different lesson. The first of the three loves would teach him what to expect from love as first loves often do. This love would challenge him, but it wouldn't be real love, just young love. At the time, this first love would feel all-consuming with extreme highs and lows. But this love would be one that he would look back on later in life and realize the purpose of this love, to teach him about caring for someone other than himself. It was so simple that it was complicated—first love that is. Matt wondered if Pietro had found his first love yet. He was around the age Matt was when he thought he was in love with Zoey.

The paper continued. Pietro wrote that the second love would teach him about himself and who he really was. It would be the intense love that often ends in heartbreak. This love would come when he wasn't expecting it and it would challenge him and force him to grow in ways he might not have ever admitted he had to grow in. Matt looked away from the page and imagined Pietro in his twenties. He would be a lady's man with his way with words and his dark hair and good looks. Maybe he would meet his second love in a bar or in school. Matt laughed out loud at the thought of Pietro in a bar as a 20-year-old as he continued to read.

The third and final love, Pietro wrote, would be unconditional love. This love would be healing and safe. This love would be his forever love. There was still a possibility to meet this third and final love at a bar or a party, but this is usually the type of love that grows over time. Perhaps someone that starts as a friend and turns into a lover. Matt laughed at the fact that if he was teaching in America, he doubted that any of the kids would use the word "lover". Italy was so full of love and that was one of the things that drew him there. Pietro's paper ended with him answering Matt's probing questions and with him proclaiming that he had yet to ever be in love.

Matt felt a lump form in his throat when he read the last line of Pietro's paper. He said that, although he didn't think he had been in love, he felt like his mother could be one of the three loves of his life. He knew exactly what the young boy meant when he added that last line to his paper.

Matt admired how in touch Pietro was with his emotions and he reminded him of himself when he was that age. Although, growing up in touch with your emotions in a small country town in Idaho had been difficult, it made him the man he was today.

Matt dropped the paper on top of the stack and wrote a large 'A' in the top corner. He noticed the date typed in Italian on the top corner of Pietro's paper and realized it was Jasmine and Zoey's birthday that day. Later that night, after the scooters stopped buzzing in the city below and Matt had finally come in from the porch, he sat at his small dining room table and wrote two letters. One to Zoey and one to Jasmine. The first and third loves of his life. The next day, Matt only dropped one of the letters in the mail. He needed to hear from Zoey before he reached out to Jasmine. He folded and put the letter he wrote to Jasmine in an envelope and closed it inside his favorite book of poems by Robert Frost. When he was ready, and after he heard back from Zoey, he would send Jasmine her letter.

Years later, as Matt watched Jasmine sleep on the morning of her 26th birthday, he felt a calmness he hadn't felt since he was young… since before his mom died when he still felt like he had his whole life ahead of him to figure it all out. His mind wandered back to his trip to Europe the summer before his senior year. Matt remembered the feeling he had watching his mom and dad dancing in the living room of the apartment they rented during their trip to Italy. Those days before his mother told him she had cancer on the hike overlooking the sea were the last days he had felt so calm. He still had his childhood left and he was also experiencing the fact that his parents were absolutely still in love with each other. Although he didn't realize it then as a teenage boy, he realized now that it was beautiful. It was in that moment Matt knew Jasmine was the love his mother was telling him about so many years before. The unconditional love of his life was laying right next to him with her long hair sprawled across his pillow. Matt also knew that a part of his calm was that Zoey had responded to his letter. She must have replied right after she received it because he had a letter addressed to him from Portland within a few days after grading Pietro's paper and deciding to write the two letters that night in September. Zoey's reply was simple, but it was all he needed to hear.

Matt,

Please just make her happy and stop wasting time. If anyone knows that life is short, it's you. Good luck. She needs a man like you...

Love,
Zoey

The day after Matt received Zoey's reply, he pulled Jasmine's letter from the book of poems by Robert Frost that sat on his coffee table. He put more than enough stamps on the envelope and dropped it in his mailbox. Matt was devastated to have never heard back and thought that maybe he was just imagining their chemistry so many years ago. He had no idea if she was single or even where exactly she lived. He sent the letter to her old address in Idaho but knew that her parents wouldn't ask questions, they would just forward the letter and then make sure she received it.

Matt poured his heart out to her in that letter. For months, he thought he had made a terrible mistake by sending the letter and felt like maybe she didn't love him the way he had just proclaimed to love her. Maybe he was imagining it all. Matt was more than shocked to see her in person months later with tears streaming down her cheeks when he answered the door. Now, two years later, there they were, waking up together in Florence on the morning of her birthday.

Matt rented a car for the day and planned to take Jasmine to the very spot his father proposed to his mother. He would take her to the same spot his mother told him that one day he would have a family of his own. Matt didn't have an elaborate plan for the day outside of bringing Jasmine to that spot to feel if she truly was the one. He couldn't mess this chance up with her, so he wanted to be sure. He knew bringing her there would give him every answer he needed. This was the one place in the world where Matt knew he would feel guidance.

"Good morning, handsome," Jasmine said as she slowly opened her eyes and noticed Matt watching her sleep. She brushed her long hair out of her eyes and sat up to stretch her arms above her head. It was a beautiful fall morning in Florence. Matt had bought eggs and bagels to make Jasmine breakfast before he picked up the rental car. He wanted to spoil her on her birthday. It had been hard to get her to open up and trust him over the past two years because of all she had gone through with James. He also knew that him being her sister's first love also was a lot for them both to accept. Still, he knew she loved him, and their love felt healthy and real.

"Happy Birthday, beautiful. I can't believe I get to wake up each day to you," Matt said as he sat up beside her in the bed that they had shared for the past two years. The last woman he shared a bed with was Francesca so many years before.

Matt cooked a breakfast of scrambled eggs with bagels and cream cheese. He picked up some prosecco from the local market and fresh orange juice.

"Do you have some good shoes? We are going for a hike," Matt said to Jasmine as he handed her a champagne glass and kissed her on the forehead.

"Where are we going?" she asked after taking a long, slow drink.

"To the place where I realized life is too short to not send the letter," Matt said as he smiled at Jasmine and held up his glass.

CHAPTER 19

FALL — 2006

Kofi

Kofi couldn't believe his ears. The call came just a few minutes after Zoey had left for her run and he was barely awake enough to comprehend what was being said.

"Kofi Dean?" the voice asked softly as he picked up the phone that laid on the bedside table. Kofi sat up, acknowledging the seriousness on the other end of the line as the soft voice became louder, asking again if he was, in fact, Kofi Dean.

"Yes. That's me. Um, who is this?" Kofi pulled himself out of bed and was now zipping up a hoodie he had found near the bed on the ground.

"This is The Connection Adoption Center of Seattle. Is this a good time?" Kofi's mind raced as the woman's voice on the phone again repeated itself. He sat stiffly on the edge of the bed for the next 30 minutes and barely uttered a word as the woman's voice told him the news that would change his entire life.

An hour later, Kofi was sitting at the kitchen table with a lukewarm cup of coffee, staring at Zoey. She had just walked through the door from a run and was dripping wet. It had been raining for what felt like a month straight and it was only September. He watched her strip her raincoat off and fumble as she tried to pull her hair out of a ponytail as the water dripped down her back. He was relieved to be giving her this shocking news after, rather than before, her run. Kofi still hadn't fully processed the news of the last hour.

"Zoey, I have a daughter." The words came out of his mouth before he realized what he was saying. She stared back at him with wide eyes. He waited for her to question him but then he remembered Zoey was different… she would let him explain and not jump to conclusions. His daughter was born before he met Zoey, the love of his life. His daughter. Kofi had a daughter.

"What? Who was that? What are you talking about, Kofi?" He could almost see her imagination racing as he grabbed her hand. She stumbled, kicking her soggy shoes off while she balanced against the door but never took her eyes off of him.

"It's not what you think," Kofi said as he grabbed her cold hand and pulled Zoey across their small apartment to the kitchen to sit down. He knew she needed to sit down for this. He barely had all the information but knew he needed to tell Zoey everything he knew at that point before her mind started to wander even further. They sat staring at each other in silence for a moment that felt longer than it actually was.

Finally, Kofi broke the silence and spoke, staring through the window as words fell out of his mouth as though he was tracing his steps that led to this day.

"Cassidy never got the abortion before she left Portland. She had the baby. She put her up for adoption. It's a girl. Zoey, I have a daughter."

"Jasmine's Cassidy?" Zoey said more as a statement than a question. She was Jasmine's Cassidy. Zoey needed him to agree as if to make sure he didn't think of her as his Cassidy. It had been years since the day Cassidy and Kofi faced each other in Denver on New Year's Eve but it felt like yesterday. It took Zoey and Kofi so long to get on the same page after that night and for him to open up to her. He knew she felt a certain competition with Cassidy after learning how much he went through with her and realizing he had kept that all from her. Still, he loved Zoey. He was in love with Zoey. He was never in love with Cassidy, but they shared a lot. They shared more than Zoey could understand and Kofi was not naive to this as he held her hand across the table to try to make sure she was secure in this news.

"Yes. Jasmine's Cassidy." Suddenly, the reality of this morning's phone call was filling the room. Zoey sat in shock in their small kitchen, staring at him as he continued to look through the window that was blurry from the falling rain. The sound of the raindrops was cutting through the silence in the room. It seemed ironic that the small plant on the windowsill was so badly in need of water while the rain poured down outside. Kofi could see Zoey's eyes fixed on the dying plant as if to take her mind off what was really happening in that moment. He held her hand tighter to keep her from standing up to water it. He needed her to just sit and listen, if he could only find the words.

Kofi hadn't seen or spoken with Cassidy since the night in Denver. It seemed like Jasmine didn't really talk about her that much to Zoey lately either, which Kofi felt was on purpose. He wondered if Jasmine knew about the daughter they shared, and he was sure Zoey was wondering the same thing. Kofi hadn't really gotten that close to Zoey's twin sister over the years, and it honestly felt like Zoey and Jasmine were sort of growing apart. He couldn't help but blame himself and his past. It was Cassidy and Kofi that put Zoey and Jasmine in this awkward position.

Zoey leaned back in the black chair at their small dining room table they had just picked up from the thrift store around the corner on 21st Street. Kofi sat in the green chair and stared down at his hands. Not much in their apartment matched but it was home, and they loved the home they had made together after all these years. Zoey pulled her hand from his and stood to finally water the plant he saw her fixating on.

"Kofi. Where is the baby? Wait… she isn't a baby. She must be seven or eight years old by now. Where is she and why are you just now finding out about her?" Zoey turned around from where she stood near the kitchen sink and her green eyes were locked on Kofi as he continued to stare down at his hands in shock.

"She lives in Seattle. I have had a daughter for years who lives just three hours away from me and I had no idea. It wasn't even Cassidy who told me about her. I got a call today from the adoption agency." Kofi felt anger welling in his chest as he thought of this notion.

Kofi shook his head and closed his eyes. He thought back to his little sister sitting on his lap. He heard her laugh and could see her toss her head back with the biggest smile as though it was yesterday. She had been the biggest part of his life when he was young. He practically raised Naya and now he was learning about the fact that he had a daughter that didn't even know her biological father. Tears started to fall down his cheeks as he closed his eyes tight. He thought of his own father who never even bothered to meet his son. Suddenly, Kofi questioned if his mom had done what Cassidy had and never even told his dad about him. Kofi was overwhelmed with emotions. Zoey rushed to him and sat back down in the mismatched chair at their kitchen table. He felt Zoey's hand over his and suddenly he felt a slight sense of calmness fall over him. Kofi felt so many different emotions running through him as he took a long, exaggerated breath in. He closed his eyes as he held his breath and slowly opened them as he exhaled. He was angry, excited, sad, and happy all at once. He couldn't process what this news meant to him yet.

"Ok. Just breathe in and breathe out. Take your time, babe." Zoey managed to smile lightly as Kofi finally looked up from his hands and opened his eyes. Through the blurs of tears, he could see her nodding her head slowly as if to say everything would be alright. Not even realizing he was doing it; he nodded his head with her.

It felt as though hours had passed while they sat in silence at the table and listened to the rain. Zoey made coffee while Kofi mentally sifted through his feelings. There were more details to his story he had yet to tell her but needed the shock of him even having a daughter to settle before he dropped the rest of the news. After their second cup of coffee, Kofi finally told Zoey about the reason he received the phone call today about his daughter.

"They said that she needs a kidney transplant, Zoey. The agency only told me about her because the adoptive parents are hoping one of us is a match and would be willing to be a donor." Kofi felt his eyes fill again with tears the moment the words left his mouth. He noticed Zoey's eyes were doing the same.

"Wait, what? That's horrible, Kofi. Oh my god, this is a lot right now."

"Yeah. They said apparently Cassidy arranged an open adoption, but they haven't heard from her in a while, and she listed me as the father. In an emergency, they are allowed to contact me. Apparently, she..." Kofi trailed off.

"Zoey, I don't even know her name..." Kofi stopped and shook his head as he realized he didn't know the name of the girl who had half his DNA. He suddenly wondered what she looked like.

"Kofi. It's ok. It was the best idea. Cassidy didn't want an abortion and that was her right. She should have told you, but it was ultimately her decision and there is nothing we can do about it now." Zoey knew that Kofi didn't disagree with her, but he knew that Zoey had to be wondering how Cassidy held this in for so many years. He was also sure she was wondering if Jasmine knew.

"I know. And you are right. It was her choice. But why the fuck didn't she tell me? This was something we could have discussed." Kofi was staring into Zoey's eyes as though she had an answer.

"She had some infection it sounds like. She has been sick for a long time and wasn't getting better. Thank God this wasn't something hereditary that I gave to her. That was my first thought… that not only did I kill my sister but…" Kofi's voice trailed off as he left the kitchen and rushed to their bedroom.

"Slow down, babe," Zoey yelled from the kitchen as she heard him drop the laundry basket full of clean clothes yet to be folded on the floor. The day had flown by, but it felt like that phone call had come in just minutes before. Kofi was frantic as he sifted through the laundry basket.

"Please. Slow down. And you did not kill your sister!" Zoey followed Kofi into their bedroom and found him putting on a jacket with his keys in hand.

"I am going to the library. I need to look up where to get tested to be a match." Kofi rushed past Zoey and grabbed his bike helmet that lay on the couch in their small living room. He closed the door behind him harder than he expected and heard the phone ring on the other side of the door inside their apartment. He didn't have time to turn around to see who was calling but heard Zoey's voice answer the phone.

Kofi fumbled to unlock his bike from the railing just past the front steps. Tears were still coming down his cheeks as he felt a tap on his shoulder. Kofi didn't have time for small talk. He turned slowly as he heard his familiar voice.

"Kofi. What's up, man? I finally made it. Surprise!" It was Reggie. Kofi remembered that he had sent him a plane ticket for today months ago for his birthday just as Reggie had done for him years before.

"Oh, shit. Are you ok? What is going on, man?" Reggie put his hand on Kofi's shoulder as he noticed his best friend seemed hysterical.

"Reg. It's so good to see you but I am not ok. Did you rent a car?"

"Uh. Yeah. It's right there," Reggie said with confusion.

"We gotta drive to Seattle. It's three hours. Sorry. I will tell you what's going on in the car." Kofi gave his childhood best friend a quick hug and dropped his bike in the grass.

In the car, Kofi caught Reggie up on everything that had happened in the past eight hours. He was shocked. Reggie barely said a word until they were one hour outside of Seattle.

"Hey, did you tell your girl where you were going? That was kind of abrupt and I know it's her birthday today, right? I was excited to meet her tonight to be honest," Reggie said loudly through the sound of the radio and windshield wipers.

"Oh, shit. I forgot it was her birthday today." Kofi lowered his head as Reggie turned down the volume on the radio as if knowing that Kofi needed the silence to process this huge mistake.

"You gotta just call her when we get to Seattle. Just admit you made a mistake and ask for her forgiveness." Reggie smiled at his best friend, calming him down immediately. Reggie had been more of a father figure to Kofi than anyone had ever been.

Kofi smiled back at Reggie and turned the radio up when he noticed it was his favorite song.

"See… everything's gonna be alright." Reggie sang along to The Fugees and winked at his best friend.

CHAPTER 20

FALL – 2006

Zoey

I was still in shock when I picked up the phone on what had to have been its last ring. I figured Kofi hadn't meant to slam the door on his way out but couldn't help but feel like that was an exclamation point on him forgetting what today was—not to mention the bomb he just dropped on me.

"Hello." I pulled the receiver away from my wet ear and tried to dry it on my shoulder. I couldn't wait to shower and felt a chill run through my body. Sitting around for hours after a rainy long run to listen to how your boyfriend has a child you both never knew about was not a great idea, both mentally and physically.

"Happy Birthday, sis!" I was so happy to hear the sound of Jasmine's voice. I couldn't believe we had gone so long not talking but understood she was now living in an entirely different country. We had so much to catch up about and I was also happy to be distracted from the fact that Kofi had actually forgotten my birthday.

"Oh my god, it's so good to hear your voice, Jas. How are you? Tell me everything. Feels weird to always ask... but how is Matt?" We both chuckled quietly.

I didn't know if it would ever feel normal to ask my twin sister how her boyfriend, who was my first love, was doing. Still, I couldn't be happier for them both. I was actually elated when I received that letter from Matt so many years earlier explaining how he never wanted to hurt me, but we were grown now, and it was time for him to finally come clean.

His letter was just as I had expected from a great writer like Matt. He told me all about his fiancé, Francesca, in Italy that died in the September 11th attacks. In his letter, Matt reminisced about his mom and how she taught him to always go for what he wanted and to not waste time because life was precious and short. He apologized to me for hurting me in high school and told me that he couldn't have gone through his mother's death without me. Matt also acknowledged that he wished he could have helped me more to get through my anorexia. He just didn't understand. I understood but I needed to hear him say he was sorry for leaving me during a time I felt so alone. It took me years to realize that he actually did help me in that time.

Finally, in his letter sent from Italy all the way to Portland so many years ago, Matt asked me to give him a very basic yes or no answer. *Would I be ok with him asking my twin sister to give them a chance?* He was in love with her, and he had no idea if she felt the same. I waited for any amount of jealousy, sadness, or anger to take over as I folded up his letter. After all, he was my first love. Matt was also the first boy to ever break my heart. I couldn't help but think back to the night of our Homecoming Dance in our senior year. The worst heartache I ever felt was that night, being left alone in that gym by the boy who had proclaimed to love me. I was at possibly the worst phase of my disease during that time and that was the night everything changed for me and Matt. Or, maybe that was just the night that I realized it had changed. That was also the night he decided to live and that was the night he told me that he couldn't be the one deciding if I wanted to live as well. He was tired after his mother's death. Not just tired of the stares from our classmates and friends, or tired of having to bail his brother out of detention every week because his dad had basically given up parenting after his wife died. Matt was tired of worrying about other people.

Finally, I understood. After all these years, when I read the letter that I knew was not easy for him to write, I finally understood that we were not meant to be each other's final love, just each other's first love. Matt explained in his letter that he learned a lot from me and his second love, Francesca. He explained that everything he learned so far was what would make him the man that deserved my sister. All he wanted was for me to say I understood and that I did want them to both be happy.

As I wrote a reply to his letter so many years ago, I wondered if I would have had a different reply if I wasn't in love with Kofi. I wondered if I would have been bitter or angry that Matt didn't ultimately come back to me after learning all these lessons that were apparently helping him become the version of himself that he knew was finally fit for my sister. The answer was no. I wanted Matt and Jasmine to be happy. They both deserved it. They deserved each other. I didn't write a long, eloquent reply to Matt's letter so many years before. It was simple, but I knew that he understood I didn't need to explain myself. He didn't need to either. We both knew our paths were meant to intersect in the exact way that they had.

Jasmine cleared her throat and said loudly, "Matt is great! It's actually pretty late here. We just went to dinner at this great cafe downtown and he is apparently taking me somewhere secret tomorrow. I am packing a bag now! How many outfits for two days… 10, right? Maybe 15 pairs of shoes?"

Jasmine laughed loud at her own joke. She sounded happier than I had ever heard her. I thought back to the times I spoke with her when she was dating James a few years earlier and how my heart always sank when I hung up the phone following those conversations. I never knew the full extent of how he treated her, but I put together the pieces just based on the sound of her voice over the phone. She was miserable with that man! It really was true, twins could always tell what was going on, no matter how far away they were from each other! I did, however, hope I could hide what I was going through that night from her. I could hear Matt in the background seemingly yelling at a TV in Italian.

"Sorry. Matt is watching a soccer game. He is obsessed," Jasmine said loudly.

"It's football here, Jas! Remember?" I heard Matt yell.

I wondered if he knew who she was talking to. Matt and I hadn't talked since I sent the letter to him giving him my blessing to pursue my sister. Just in hearing those five words, I could tell that Matt was also as happy as he had been. I smiled into the phone as I heard a door close on the other line. I tried to imagine the house in Florence that Jasmine and Matt lived in. All I knew about Florence was it had a lot of olive trees and a lot of scooters! Jasmine told me that they each had a scooter and didn't need a car because they lived close enough to walk to work and the store. I had never been to Italy but was planning to visit her in the next year. I was proud of her for following her heart and starting a new life in another country.

"How are you? What has Kofi planned for your big day today? He is usually good at birthdays, right?" Jasmine spoke loudly to drown out the sound of the scooters in the background on her end of the phone.

I thought back to the year before and how romantic it was. Kofi booked a house right on the beach on the Oregon Coast and just the two of us spent the entire weekend eating, drinking, talking, and making love. Listening to the waves crash at night with a full moon over the ocean was how I wanted to spend all my birthdays. But this year looked like it was turning out to be not so romantic. My pride, and the fact that I still really had no idea how much Jasmine knew about Kofi from Cassidy, urged me to not let her know that my boyfriend of seven years seemed to have completely forgotten my birthday.

"I am not sure yet. It's apparently a surprise," I said quietly as though if I was quiet enough, I wouldn't technically be lying to my sister.

I sat down at the kitchen table and glanced at the plant on the windowsill that I just finally watered after who knows how many days. It already seemed to be perking up and I made a mental note to do a better job of watering it. After all, it was the only living thing I needed to take care of outside of myself.

"Nice. Well, I hope he does something special. You know you deserve the best, sis." I imagined Jasmine rocking back and forth on a porch swing overlooking the lights of Florence as she spoke. Maybe they had a few olive trees in their front yard that were framing the view of the busy city below them.

"I do, right!? I will let you know what he ends up surprising me with. How is life in Italy? I can't believe it's been two years since you have been there."

"I can't believe you haven't come to visit me yet. It's amazing here. You would love it. There is some great running too I would imagine here. I love the food and the people are so nice. But mostly, I am just so happy to be here with Matt. He really is wonderful. But you know that." Jasmine laughed and the sounds of the scooters seemed to subside.

"I really am so happy for you guys, Jas. It's funny how life turns out, right? Speaking of which, have you talked to Cassidy in a while? Are you guys still friends or what?" I asked, hoping to find out how much Jasmine knew about my boyfriend's daughter in need of a kidney in Seattle.

There was a long pause on the other end before I heard Jasmine exhale slowly.

"No. We sort of lost touch. I honestly haven't spoken to her since I left Denver. I miss her but I really think she was going through something that I couldn't help her with. She pushed me away to be honest. I don't have many friends here besides Matt. I mean, does he even count as my friend?" Jasmine laughed again at her own joke. She really was happy.

"I don't have many friends here either. I have been working so much. And running is not exactly a social activity."

"Yeah. Weirdo." I was shocked she didn't laugh at herself again.

"Well, I love you, sis. Happy Birthday. Maybe next year we can celebrate together in Italy! I guess, tell Matt hello and have fun on your secret birthday getaway tomorrow."

"I love you, Zoey."

"I love you too. I miss you, Jas." I heard a click and my heart dropped. I missed her more than I realized. I missed Erin and Sophie too. Frustration came roaring back as I remembered that Kofi had put me in a situation to lie to my sister about what I was doing for my birthday.

The rain started to fall again as I washed my coffee mug in the sink. It was starting to get dark earlier, and I couldn't help but wonder where Kofi was. His chances to redeem himself and surprise me with a fancy dinner were dwindling as the day turned into night.

I decided not to wait around for him anymore and took a long, hot shower and poured myself a big glass of red wine. Finally, a blanket of darkness took over the sky and I decided to get dressed and find somewhere nice to order takeout from for the night. The phone rang just as I closed the door to the apartment behind me, but I didn't have the energy to talk to anyone else that day. I was pissed. I had already lied to Jasmine, and I didn't have it in me to lie to whomever else was calling me asking me what my amazing boyfriend had planned for me for my birthday. I would listen to the message when I got home.

As I wandered up my street and turned onto NW 23rd, I realized just how much I loved living in this part of Portland. It was so charming with its tree-lined streets and cozy coffee shops. Sure, most nights it rained too hard to even think of going for a walk, but on this September night, my little piece of Portland was perfect. I tried hard to not let the events of the day ruin my birthday. Tonight, I would have to celebrate alone.

I walked past the Thai restaurant that Kofi and I went to on the first day we met—his birthday and the anniversary of his sister's death. It had rained that day too almost all day so many years before. I couldn't help but be sad realizing that there was so much about him that night that I didn't know. There was so much he was hiding and so much he ended up keeping from me far after that first night that we shared our first kiss. I had been sure since the day we met that Kofi was the man I wanted to grow old with, but today felt different. I was upset that he didn't tell me about Naya, but we worked through it together. We hadn't had many fights or arguments, and overall, I felt happy. I felt calm and content with Kofi… until today. Something changed.

Memories flooded my mind as I turned around and decided to go back to order takeout from the Thai place from our first date.

"Hey, Zoey." I looked up and was surprised to see Cole, my favorite barista from the coffee shop near PSU that I had spent most of my nights studying at in college. It had been years since I last saw him.

"Hi, Cole. Wow, it's so great to see you. I have tried to catch you at the coffee shop and just never went when you were there apparently. Do you work here now?" I said to Cole who was standing behind the bar holding a bottle of red wine. He raised the bottle with a smirk as if to emphasize how obvious it was that he worked there.

"I do. I quit the coffee shop last year and have been working here since then. I can't believe I haven't seen you."

Cole raised his eyebrows and grabbed a large red wine glass.

"First one is on me. Do you drink red?" Cole asked after he had already poured a glass and pushed it toward me across the bar top.

"Thanks, Cole," I said and finally sat down and took a deep breath before taking a sip from the glass.

I ordered Tofu Pad Thai takeout and finished a second glass of wine while I waited for my order to be done. It had to have been close to closing time when Cole appeared from the kitchen with my order in a plastic bag.

"It was great seeing you, Cole. This has always been a favorite restaurant of mine but now I will need to come in and have a drink instead of just order delivery!"

I grabbed the food and hugged Cole tighter than either of us were ready for. I was sad that he was the only person I was really spending my birthday with. I barely knew Cole and he actually didn't even know it was my birthday. Regardless, I needed a hug.

"Sounds good, sweetie. See you next time," Cole said as he smiled and closed the door behind me as I stepped onto the sidewalk with my Tofu Pad Thai and a red wine buzz. He pulled a small white string and the red lights of the *Open* sign turned off abruptly. Cole disappeared into darkness.

I was alone. I wanted desperately to call Jasmine again and knew I would probably sob the minute I heard her voice. It was also technically still our birthday in Italy.

It was warmer than normal for late September in Portland. I turned off of NW 23rd onto a residential street with small houses and apartment buildings. Through the window of a one-story white house, I could see a family sitting on the couch with the TV softly flickering in front of them. I couldn't tell if this made me long for a family of my own or if it made me long for my parents and sisters. I missed them, especially on my birthday, but probably noticed so much more this year with Kofi being so distant.

The news of today crept back into my mind as I stopped and watched the family through the window of the small white house. As of tonight, I was 27 years old. When I was young, daydreaming in my bedroom after a bike ride with Matt, I always thought that I would have been married by now. I wanted to be a mom. I had fought back from anorexia knowing that for sure the one part of me that would die if I didn't beat that disease was going to be the ability to become a mom. Hearing that Kofi had a child with Cassidy was affecting me more than I realized as I watched the family through the window in the white home. I loved Kofi and I wanted a family. I was finally realizing he had a lot to work through before we would get to our happily ever after. I wanted a family, but I wanted it with someone who was ready and who had worked through his past enough to focus on his future. I wanted to be his future.

It was after midnight when I finally walked up the steps to our apartment. Kofi's bike laid on the grass and I strained to remember if I actually saw it laying there when I left for the night. There was no way he would leave his precious bike unlocked. I grabbed it and pulled it up the steps and into our apartment, scraping my shin on the brakes as I drunkenly tried to balance my takeout on the seat of the bike.

I dropped my takeout on the kitchen table and poured a glass of water from the faucet. The place was empty, just as I had left it. The red light was blinking on the answering machine, and I suddenly remembered the phone call I ignored on my way out the door.

"Zoey. I am sorry. It's me. I can't believe I forgot your birthday. I promise I will make it up to you. Um. We are in Seattle. I should have talked to you about this before I left but… I was just in shock. Call me back. The number here is 206-227-4157. I love you."

I listened to the message three times and finally wrote down the number after the third time. My head was spinning slightly from the many glasses of wine I had at the restaurant when I dialed the number. I asked the receptionist for Kofi Dean when she answered the call on the first ring. It was a hotel.

"Hello. Hey, babe. I am so sorry," Kofi said anxiously.

"I have been about as patient as I can be, Kofi. Are you with her? Who is 'we'?" I asked through tears.

"Who are you talking about? I am with Reggie. He came here to meet you. I sent him a ticket months ago for his birthday because I want the only two people that I love to meet each other. It was a surprise and I completely forgot I did that with everything happening today. I am sorry, Zoey."

"Kofi. There was a lot happening today and not for one second did you think of me. Call me tomorrow. I can't do this tonight. I am drunk and tired and upset." Before I knew what I was doing, I slammed the phone down. This was it—our first real fight—and I had no control at all over how I was feeling. Because of the many glasses of wine I had consumed, I also seemed to have no control over what I was saying. My hand was still on the receiver when it rang again.

"I told you. I can't do this tonight!" I yelled into the phone, suddenly feeling overrun with emotions. There was a long pause.

"What? Hey, Zoey. It's me, Jasmine. What did you just say? I couldn't hear you. I needed you to be the first to hear. Matt proposed!" Jasmine's voice was hard to make out on the other line.

I fell into my bed with the phone on my ear. I took a deep breath and felt the tightness in my chest like it had felt so many years ago when I was in the hospital on New Year's Eve.

"Hey. Zoey. Are you there? Hello?" Jasmine's voice trailed off as I dropped the phone and ran to the bathroom. I was sick and I was alone. Suddenly, it was clear to me what I was longing for when I watched the family in the white house earlier in the night. I wanted a family of my own and I had never felt further away from it than right now.

I heard Jasmine's voice trail off and the sound of the dial tone as she hung up. I looked in the mirror, wiping my mouth after throwing up in the toilet. I needed change.

Tears rolled down my cheeks as I reached for the silver pair of scissors on the edge of the sink. I closed my eyes and was shocked to realize how sharp the scissors were as they cut through my thick hair.

I opened my eyes to see my long, brown hair lying limp in my hand. In the mirror, I watched as the freshly cut hair on my head curled quickly as it was freed from the tight grip of my braid. I needed change, and this was a start.

CHAPTER 21

WINTER — 2006

Kofi

It was New Year's Eve and Kofi watched as Zoey flipped the page of her book and pushed her reading glasses up on the bridge of her nose. She always squished her face when she did that and he couldn't help but smile as he watched her from across the room. He needed to smile. It had been stressful since Zoey's birthday three months earlier when Kofi and Reggie arrived in Seattle. They had been in the hospital since the day before and were waiting for the nurse to bring Reggie back into room 340. Kofi was a wreck.

"You should get some rest. I don't remember you sleeping at all since yesterday." Zoey watched Kofi as he straightened his back and massaged his neck. Zoey was right. Kofi hadn't slept or eaten since the nurse wheeled his best friend out of room 340 and into the operating room. Kofi tried to close his eyes as he stretched out as much as he could on the small couch across from where Zoey sat in the chair.

Moments later, Kofi heard Zoey's soft snores as he finally forced himself to just close his eyes and tried to will himself to sleep.

A lot had happened since the day Kofi learned of his daughter who needed a kidney transplant in Seattle. As he closed his eyes, his mind raced. Kofi thought back to the night of Zoey's birthday and the days that followed. He had never expected her to hang up on him when he called to tell her they had gone to Seattle to the hospital where his daughter was. When Kofi picked up the phone and heard her voice, he knew she was more upset than she had ever been. She was hurt and he was three hours away. After Zoey hung up on Kofi, Reggie had spent most of the night trying to console his best friend in the hotel room they rented for the night near Rainier Beach in Seattle by the hospital. Kofi and Zoey had never really been in an argument, and there he was, making mistake after mistake, and on her birthday no less.

Kofi was lucky to have his best friend there that night. Thoughts ran through his mind like they had the day he stood at the top of the Hawthorne Bridge the day he met Cassidy. He had hurt the only woman that he ever truly loved, and she had just hung up on him. As Kofi paced the room, Reggie reminded him that everything was going to be alright. He had seen his best friend feeling hopeless and knew that he needed to help him get back on track. Reggie wasn't going to lose Kofi again like he had when Naya died. He noticed that his best friend seemed happier than he had ever been before in the last few months whenever he caught him on the phone. He was thrilled when Kofi sent him the plane ticket months earlier to come and visit. Reggie didn't expect this for his first night outside of Kentucky, but he was happy to be there for his friend.

"Hey, man. It might not be an accident that I am here for this, Kof. You need to lean on me right now, ok. You gotta stop walking away. This is a lot. Zoey will understand, I can tell by the way she talks to you, even when she is yelling at you, that she loves you. Get some sleep and we will go to the hospital tomorrow to see what we need to do for your daughter," Reggie said to Kofi as he sat next to him at the end of one of the double beds in the Hampton Inn. Reggie had given Kofi some time to decompress and walked across the street to pick up some Maker's Mark. Minutes later, he returned and poured Kofi a glass and sat in the small chair across from him.

Kofi took the drink out of Reggie's hand and nodded at him. He was right. He needed to start to slow down before he acted. If he had stopped to think before he rushed out of the house, he and Zoey wouldn't have gotten into the fight. He also should have taken the time to come up with a plan before he rushed Reggie to Seattle. They showed up at the hospital that the adoption agency said his daughter was at but weren't allowed to see her or get any information without the adoptive parents there. Kofi didn't even know her name.

"Let's just get some sleep. Come up with a plan for the reason we even came here, and you need to figure out how to make it up to Zoey." Reggie finished his drink and was asleep within minutes. Kofi listened to his best friend snore as he laid on top of the covers in his clothes that he had greeted Reggie in earlier in the day outside of his and Zoey's apartment. As Reggie's snores got louder, Kofi realized that Reggie had probably been awake for hours longer than he was used to and was exhausted from the day of travel. He suddenly felt selfish realizing that as he laid back on his own bed. He was lucky to have Reggie.

The next morning, Kofi and Reggie drove from their hotel back to the hospital near Rainier Beach. Kofi tried calling Zoey again, but she didn't answer. The same receptionist sat behind the desk as the night before and smiled at them as they looked at each other.

"Well, good morning. Nice to see you two again. I have some good news. The adoptive parents are here, and they want to see you." The receptionist nodded her head toward a long hallway behind Kofi and Reggie. At the end of the hallway, Kofi saw a couple holding hands. He knew that was them.

Reggie put his hand on Kofi's shoulder as they walked toward the parents of Kofi's daughter. Many emotions ran through his mind as he got closer and could see the pain in the eyes of his daughter's adoptive parents. The father was tall and held onto his wife's hand tight. She had to have been a foot shorter than her husband and looked like she had been crying for weeks. They both began to smile slightly as Kofi and Reggie approached. Reggie took a step in front of Kofi and put out his hand to the wife first after seeming to get a nod of approval from the husband.

"Ma'am, my name is Reggie. This here is Kofi. He is... um... the dad." Reggie hesitated and looked at Kofi as though he said something wrong. There was no right way to handle this situation. Luckily, they were all aware of that and the wife put out her hand and smiled gently at Reggie.

"Nice to meet you both. We weren't expecting you in person, but we are happy you are here."

The husband dropped his wife's hand and put it out in front of Kofi.

"Kofi. I am Adrian. Nice to meet you. Naya looks just like you."

Kofi froze and felt Reggie's hand again on his shoulder.

"Naya?" Reggie said with his eyes locked on his friend.

"Yes. Cassidy named her. She insisted on that name. She told us everything, Kofi." Adrian's eyes were locked on his wife as he spoke. The couple caught eyes with each other, realizing that they should have sat Kofi down before they told him that they named their daughter after his sister who died. The wife put her hand on Reggie's hand to comfort him.

"Let's sit down and catch up. There is a coffee shop on this floor. Follow me." Adrian put his hand out again and shook Kofi and then Reggie's hands quickly. He was direct but nice and Kofi could tell he was a dedicated husband and father just by the way he presented himself to these two strangers in an extremely awkward situation.

Kofi, his best friend, and the adoptive parents to his only child sat in a coffee shop for two hours that day. Adrian and his wife, Sara, told Kofi that they had met in college at The University of Washington and had been trying for six years to have a baby of their own before they decided on adoption. Kofi could tell they were in love. They were a happy and healthy couple, and they were giving his and Cassidy's daughter a better life than they could have. It was the right decision.

"Kofi, we didn't realize that Cassidy kept this from you until a few weeks ago," Sara said as she put her hand on Kofi's across the small coffee shop table. The sound of a steamer filled the air and Sara waited a beat until it was quiet again. Kofi looked around and wondered what everyone was there for. He wondered if everyone was just passing the time while they waited to hear if their loved one was going to be alright. Suddenly, the room felt completely silent.

"She told us that you didn't want to be involved but that you knew all about the adoption. We really wish you didn't find out like this." Kofi looked into Sara's eyes and felt more comfort than he had his entire life from his mom. She was a loving woman.

"We contacted her about Naya's kidney disease and haven't heard back from her after we told her we needed to reach out to you. Have you heard from her?" Adrian asked Kofi as he finished his latte.

"No. I haven't spoken to her in years. So, she isn't getting tested to see if she is a match? What if I am not a match? Isn't it best to get a donation from a living relative? I can't believe she wouldn't call you back. I don't have any other relatives. It's just me." Kofi felt Reggie's hand on his shoulder again, urging him to slow down and take a deep breath.

"We have both been tested. Neither of us are a good match for Naya. And yes, it is best to get a donation from a relative but that's not the only way." Adrian was nodding his head as his wife continued.

"You can get tested today here and we can go from there, Kofi. They will tell you everything you need to know," Adrian said as he stood up and tossed his empty cup in the garbage next to them. He took his wife's hand and helped her up. Kofi and Reggie stood quickly and followed the couple back down the long hallway to the reception desk, the sound of the coffee shop fading behind them.

"They can help you get scheduled, Kofi," Adrian said as he motioned toward the front desk. There was a new person sitting where the familiar receptionist from earlier sat. She smiled and typed fast on her keyboard before looking up at Kofi and asking him his full name. It was obvious she thought Kofi was handsome. She tried to lock eyes with him as she smacked her gum and smiled dramatically.

"Hey, can you get me in too for testing?" Reggie said just as Kofi dug out his wallet for his ID.

"Are you brothers?" the receptionist asked as she scanned Kofi's ID for his date of birth, still smiling.

"Not by blood. But yes," Reggie said as he smiled at Adrian and Sara before they turned to leave. The couple began walking back down the hall that they came from, and the receptionist continued to smack her gum.

"Oh. Wait. Can I meet her?" Kofi said as he put his wallet back in his pocket.

Adrian and Sara turned back toward Kofi and looked at each other as if to agree on an answer without exchanging words.

"Well. She is pretty sick right now, Kofi. She was asking to meet you before she got sick and I just think this might be too much for her right now, ya know? How about we wait until after the transplant?" Adrian said with his arm wrapped around his wife's shoulders. She looked up at him and nodded.

"Um. Ok. That's fair." Kofi had no other answer to give. After all, they were her parents.

"Ok. Nice meeting you both. We will be in touch. Thank you again for coming, Kofi. You too, Reggie." Adrian smiled and looked back at his wife.

"She really does look just like you. Thanks again," Sara said as she reached for her husband's hand.

Kofi and Reggie watched as the parents of Kofi's daughter, Naya, walked away. It seemed like hours passed as they stood in silence, but just a minute later, the receptionist asked Reggie for his date of birth and they both turned quickly.

"Man, you really want to get tested? I appreciate it but I have been doing research and these donations aren't so simple. Just think about it," Kofi said to Reggie as he watched him hand over his ID to the receptionist.

"We are family. You know I do everything in my power to make sure my people are good." Reggie smiled at the receptionist as she handed him back his card and asked them both to have a seat in the waiting room. They could test them both in a few minutes, she said, although they wouldn't know if they are a match for a few weeks.

Kofi and Reggie drove back to Portland that night after finishing their testing at the hospital near Rainier Beach in Seattle. The two friends walked up to the front door of Kofi and Zoey's apartment building after three hours on the road and Kofi turned to his best friend. It had been an eventful and scary 24 hours.

"You really are my brother, man. I don't say enough how much it means to me that you have always been here, Reg. I love you," Kofi said, realizing how lucky he was to have Reggie by his side.

"Love you too, Kof. This is going to work out. It's a blessing I was able to be here for you. I know you would do the same thing for me. Now, let me meet this girl you've been hiding from me all this time." Reggie pushed Kofi lightly toward the door and laughed just as the door opened from the inside and Zoey appeared. Kofi was shocked to see she had cut her long, brown hair and stood before him with a pixie cut. She blushed and looked down as if questioning if he liked her new look. He loved it.

"Well, there she is. Nice to meet you finally. I am Reggie," Reggie said as he held out his hand to Zoey. She stepped past Kofi and pulled Reggie into a hug.

"Nice to meet you, Reggie. Thank you for everything," Zoey said as she released her hug and kissed Kofi on the cheek. Kofi pulled Zoey in close and whispered in her ear, reminding her how beautiful she was to him.

"Yeah, you are a lucky man, my friend," Reggie whispered to Kofi as they followed Zoey inside the apartment.

"The luckiest," Kofi said as he looked back at his best friend.

That first trip to Seattle with Reggie was almost three months earlier. Reggie went home to Kentucky after a few days in Portland with Kofi and Zoey. Two weeks later, he got a phone call from the hospital telling him that he was a match for a kidney for Naya. Kofi also got a call from the hospital. He was not a match. Kofi was devastated that he could not help the sick girl in the hospital that had half of his DNA. He was also worried about Reggie. His best friend wasn't in the best shape and Kofi knew that this surgery was not a simple procedure. Still, maybe it was fate, and Reggie was insisting that Kofi let him do this. They were family and this little girl was sick.

Months later, Reggie arrived in Seattle on a Sunday night. It was the day before New Year's Eve and Kofi and Zoey drove up from Portland and picked Reggie up and stopped for dinner on the way back to the hotel. They stayed in the same hotel that Reggie and Kofi stayed in three months earlier when they first came to Seattle after hearing the news about Naya. The next morning, Reggie went into surgery to donate his kidney to his best friend's daughter.

Kofi paced the same hallway where he met Adrian and Sara three weeks earlier as he waited for the surgery to finish. Zoey put her book down and walked over to her boyfriend, pacing endlessly in the hallway.

"Come and sit. You need to relax. Everything will be fine," she said as she grabbed his hand and led him into the waiting room.

"It's taking too long. They said it would only be an hour. It's been like three." Kofi sat and twisted his hair nervously as Zoey rubbed his back gently.

A short male doctor appeared where Kofi had just been pacing and called his name.

"Kofi? Reggie is out of surgery. You can go to his room. We had a few complications, but he will be ok. He needs to stay here to recover for a few days. You are welcome to stay with him."

Kofi glanced at Zoey, and she nodded.

"Whatever you want to do, we'll do," Zoey said, still rubbing Kofi's back gently with her book in her lap.

The next day, Reggie opened his eyes and smiled when he saw his best friend sleeping on the small couch in his hospital room.

Three hours later, Reggie grabbed his chest and told Kofi to call the doctor to his room. By the time the same doctor from the day before arrived in room 340 to check on his patient, Reggie was coughing up blood and Kofi was hysterical.

"I need to take him for observation. We will check in shortly," the doctor said to Kofi as he pushed multiple buttons on a portable computer. He motioned for the nurse to wheel Reggie out of the room and down the hallway. Before Kofi and Zoey could even realize what was happening, Reggie was being wheeled down the dark hallway.

"It's a new year, babe. Everything will be fine. I love you." Zoey dropped her book in the chair she had been sitting in for hours and climbed onto the small couch where Kofi sat, trying to close his eyes still.

Kofi lifted his arm and Zoey laid her head on his shoulder. Outside of room 340, they heard music in the hallway and the sound of fireworks outside.

"I love this song. Happy New Year. I love you." Zoey kissed Kofi passionately for the first time since they had arrived in Seattle as the first few notes of "Auld Lang Syne" filled room 340.

"I love you too, babe. Happy New Year. He is going to be ok, right?" Kofi asked as he brushed Zoey's hair off her face.

"He will make it, Kofi. It's going to be fine," Zoey said as she kissed his forehead.

The hallway grew silent as the night turned into the early morning. Kofi did finally end up getting a few hours of sleep and woke up when the nurse tapped him on the shoulder. He woke quickly and Zoey rolled closer to him on the small couch but was still asleep. She dug her head softly into his chest and took a deep, sleepy breath.

"Any news?" Kofi whispered to the nurse as she collected two empty water bottles from the bedside table and leaned over to check the trash can under the window.

"I will have the doctor come and talk to you when he is ready. Do you need anything?" she said as though she had said that exact line millions of times in her career.

"A miracle?" Kofi said under his breath with his eyes locked on the window.

"Looks like you have everything you need, honey," the nurse said, glancing at Zoey and smiling.

"Your friend is going to be just fine."

CHAPTER 22

SUMMER – 2007

Matt

Matt couldn't believe his eyes as he watched Jasmine walk down the aisle toward him on the day they would make vows to love each other through sickness and through health. He couldn't believe that, after all these years, Jasmine Jordan had said yes to marrying him. Matt glanced over his shoulder to his brother standing behind him and to his father sitting in the row of white chairs spread on the lawn in the small park on Lake Como. Matt looked across from him and saw Zoey holding a small bouquet of white roses, watching as her mom and dad walked with her twin sister between them. Zoey had a smile on her face, and he noticed her winking at her older sister, Erin, sitting just a few feet away near Matt's dad. Erin was holding her newborn baby and was rapidly tapping her feet to soothe her. Matt could hear the soft baby sounds coming from the bundle in Erin's arms and also couldn't help but smile. As he looked closer at Zoey, he noticed she was glowing. Matt was happy that he and Zoey ended up becoming such good friends. In moments, she would be his sister-in-law.

Jasmine had chosen a light peach dress with lace sleeves and a long veil that she found in a small shop in Florence a few months earlier. Jasmine's hair was pulled into a low ponytail, and she wore a dark shade of red lipstick on her plush lips. She was beautiful. As she walked toward him, Matt thought back to the day he knew she was the one he wanted to marry. He had thought about proposing the first time he brought her to the spot overlooking the water in the Cinque Terre where his dad asked his mom to be his wife. Matt knew he had to do something different. Jasmine deserved her own romantic proposal and not the same one his dad had done for his mom so many decades earlier. He waited a year after that visit to the Cinque Terre. Matt proposed to her on her birthday the year before. He had brought her to this very spot to ask her to be his wife. They drove four hours from Florence on the morning of her birthday. Matt drove right to this spot before checking into the hotel after deciding that he couldn't wait any longer to ask her to be his wife. His dad had sent him his mother's ring and Matt took the diamond out and picked out a new setting that he was sure Jasmine would love. He was right. Ten months later, everything he had envisioned for his life was right there, walking toward him with tears in her eyes and a handful of vibrant pink and red roses.

As he stood, watching his future wife walk slowly toward him with the sound of the violin playing behind her, Matt tried hard to be in the moment. He blinked back tears as so many memories flooded his thoughts.

Matt couldn't help but think of all the moments that brought him to that one. He thought of all the heartbreak, all the tough decisions he had to make in his young life. Everything that had brought him so much pain and worry had ultimately been what brought him there.

The pink roses in Jasmine's bouquet reminded Matt of the dress that Zoey wore to their Homecoming Dance, the night Matt realized she seemed like she was losing her battle with anorexia. That was the night he finally understood how serious the disease was and the same night that he realized there was nothing he could do to help her. His first love had taught him a lot. The red roses reminded him of the woman in the red scarf at his mother's funeral. That day had always been so clear in his mind, but he always wished that woman in the red scarf would fade from his memories of that day. Matt heard a plane fly overhead in the distance and thought of Francesca. He also often thought of the second love of his life, the hard one, as Pietro explained it. Francesca was the love that hurt. She was the one who reminded him what he deserved and also how it felt to lose something so quickly.

Matt had been through a lot to get to this spot, waiting for Jasmine to reach out her hand and take his. She would say yes to loving him through sickness and through health. *We made it,* he thought as she stood in front of him, smiling and holding out her hand for him to pull her toward him. Her mom and dad each hugged him and took a seat next to his dad and Erin in the white chairs lined up on the lawn. There was just one row of chairs on the lawn in the park for Matt and Jasmine's wedding in Lake Como, Italy. Matt and Jasmine didn't need a lot of people that day to witness them become husband and wife.

Matt had tried to find Cassidy, but every time he called her, it went straight to voicemail. He wrote her letters and even found where her husband worked and reached out to him. After a few months of trying, he finally gave up. He knew that Jasmine was upset about not hearing from her anymore, but he also knew how complicated the situation was. He never got the chance to meet her, but Jasmine had told him all about the baby and Kofi and the New Year's Eve in Denver so many years ago. Matt was sad to have not found Cassidy, but there was a part of him that understood more than anyone how hard it is to deal with pain. Sometimes, a situation is so painful that the only way to heal is to start over. That was what he had done when he moved to Italy after his mom died. He did it again after Francesca died when he left San Diego. That, Matt assumed, was what Cassidy was doing in not returning his calls to try to get his fiancé's friend there to witness this day. Matt looked around at the people he loved and realized that he and Jasmine had all the support they needed that day.

The day that Matt and Jasmine became husband and wife was a perfect day. There was not a cloud in the sky in Lake Como, Italy. The breeze off the water blew Jasmine's hair out of her face almost on cue as she read her vows to Matt. When it was his turn, Matt pulled a folded piece of paper out of his pocket, just as he had at his mother's funeral so many years before. He thought long and hard to find the perfect words to say to Jasmine that day. He was, after all, a writer.

Matt looked down at the words on the paper as he stood in front of Jasmine in her peach dress and long veil that now blew softly in the breeze. He thought back to Pietro's paper about the theory that he had hoped was true. It was true. Matt thought back to the poem he read at his mom's funeral and how the words felt so perfect for that moment. He felt like he was reading those words to her instead of a room full of people that included the woman with the red scarf in the front row. Matt felt his mom's presence standing in front of Jasmine in the park in Lake Como. He knew she was smiling and happy he had found what she wanted him to find the day of their hike when she told him she was dying. Suddenly, as he gazed at the paper in his hands, Matt's vows didn't feel like they were right. He folded the paper and handed it to his little brother standing behind him and turned back to Jasmine. Matt had spent the last few months trying to write the perfect vows to say to the love of his life on their wedding day. He caught eyes with Zoey standing just behind Jasmine and she smiled at him as though urging him to speak with his heart. She also knew that, for Matt, it had always been Jasmine.

Matt looked back at Jasmine and let the words flow from his mouth. He told her, and everyone they both loved, that he knew he was in love with her that day in Idaho in high school when she had the towel on her head and they caught eyes as she walked down the stairs. Matt talked about their first kiss and how he thought about that kiss for years. He had to wait to kiss her again until the morning she showed up in Italy with tears streaming down her face. He told Jasmine and their families sitting in the white chairs about Pietro and his paper and how everything he had been through led him to her—his third and final love. Matt peeked around Jasmine and mentioned Zoey. He thanked her for understanding. He thanked her for teaching him at such an early age what it meant to support someone. He thanked Zoey for now being his friend. Matt looked into the first row and saw his dad. His dad never remarried. As far as Matt knew, he never even tried to find a love like what he had with Matt's mom. He thought of how broken his dad was for so many years after his wife's death. Matt realized that his dad knew he wouldn't ever be able to replace the love of his life. He hoped that one day, he could find a new type of love. Matt realized that not everyone was the love of your life. That didn't mean you couldn't have a new love. Matt told the story of his mom telling him, on the day she told him she was going to die, that he would have a family of his own one day. He talked about the little boy in the boat in the Cinque Terre on the day his mother told him she was going to die. Matt's dad looked up into the sky as Matt mentioned his mom and he saw Jasmine's dad put his hand on his shoulder for support.

"Today is the day I have been working toward, Jasmine. You are my future. And I will love you until the last sunset of our time together here on Earth," Matt said as he looked deep into Jasmine's green eyes. She smiled at him, noticing that the sky behind them was turning from blue to pink as the sun was setting over the lake.

A few minutes of silence filled the air and Matt's friend from his teaching job—who also happened to be an ordained minister—told Matt that he could now kiss his bride.

Matt took in how beautiful Jasmine looked before putting his hand on the side of her face and pulling her toward him. The sound of the violin filled the air. Their first kiss as husband and wife was met with cheers from everyone that loved them who traveled so many miles to witness the beginning of this chapter in their lives. Sure, a few people were missing, but all Matt could think about was the fact that he was now married to the love of his life.

Matt and Jasmine had a small reception with their families after the ceremony in the park on Lake Como. The small Italian restaurant that was just a short walk from the park only had five tables but agreed to let Matt and Jasmine rent the entire place for the night. Before the ceremony, Zoey and Erin had decorated each table with white tablecloths and small white candles. They strung thousands of fairy lights from the ceiling that made the room feel as though they were in a scene from a movie. As Matt stepped in with Jasmine right behind him, he squeezed her hand as he looked around the room. It looked like a dream. Each table had large plates of pasta and red wine glasses full of Montepulciano. Their families had been there already waiting for the couple to arrive when Matt and Jasmine finally sat down at the small table with the best view of Lake Como. He couldn't believe he was there, with his wife.

After hours of eating and drinking, a short, Italian woman approached Matt's dad and they shook hands gently. She was the owner of the restaurant. Matt's dad had insisted on paying for the reception and it looked like it was time to settle up.

"Dad. Thank you again for everything. I really don't know how we can thank you, but it was really amazing of you to get this," Matt interrupted his dad as he put his reading glasses on and went over the check with the owner.

"Son. Um… it was my pleasure. I would like you to meet someone. This is Camilla." Matt's dad grabbed the woman's hand and took off his glasses.

"Camilla is my girlfriend." Matt watched as his dad dropped her hand and put his arm around her shoulders. They looked at each other and smiled. The woman then turned to Matt and smiled softly. In the moments after Matt's dad had introduced him to his new girlfriend, it felt as though time turned back and Matt could see his mother clearer than he had seen her since the day she died.

Suddenly, Matt was back in his house in Idaho, watching his mother wash the dishes as she sang her favorite Celine Dion song off-key. He was watching her cheer from the stands during his soccer games in middle school. Sitting next to a bowl full of sliced oranges and a pan of brownies she had brought for the team each Saturday morning during their long season. Matt blinked and he was watching her lay on the ground in their living room playing with their golden retriever before bed. She loved that dog and some days Matt thought they had a secret language between them. He blinked again and was back on their trip in Italy, watching his mom and dad dance in the living room of the rented apartment. The song that night sounded almost exactly like the song playing just then in the restaurant in Lake Como on his wedding day. Finally, Matt remembered the look on his father's face at his mother's funeral. He had lost his best friend and his lover. He had lost the mother of his children and the woman that he asked to spend the rest of their lives together when he was only 45 years old. That day had broken his dad and he hadn't been the same since. Matt tried to think of the last time he saw his father really happy. Not happy for someone else like him and his little brother… Matt tried to think of a time when Matt's dad was happy for himself.

"Son. Let's talk." Matt's dad nodded his head to Camilla, and she slowly turned and headed back to the kitchen after nodding back.

The door of the small restaurant closed behind them as Matt followed his dad outside. Lake Como was beautiful at that time of night. The moon was full, and stars filled the sky. Matt and Jasmine would spend their honeymoon at the resort just a few blocks away.

"I met Camilla a few years ago, Matt. We have been friends and kept in touch. You know I come here often for work, and we just sort of hit it off. Sort of felt like how you met Francesca. She has been helping me with my Italian. We just started dating a few months ago but I didn't want to tell you until you had a chance to meet her in person." Matt's dad almost sounded as though he was apologizing to his son for moving on after his wife died. Matt wondered what he needed to say to make sure his dad knew that it was ok for him to be happy again. He thought again of the pain in his father's eyes on the day of his wife's funeral so many years before.

"Your vows. Matt, I really believe in that. I think Camilla is the third love of my life. No one will ever take your mother's place in my heart, but I don't want to be alone anymore." Matt's dad was shaking his head as he spoke to his oldest son.

"Dad. You were never alone."

In the distance, a shooting star lit up the sky over Lake Como.

"See… there is Mom. She is happy for both of us," Matt said as he looked over at his dad, expecting to see tears where instead he saw a smile. After all the years, Matt finally saw a glimpse of the man that sang Dean Martin's "Volare" to his wife as he danced in the kitchen on vacation with his family. For the first time since that night, Matt's dad was truly happy.

CHAPTER 23

FALL – 2008

Jasmine

Jasmine woke up on the morning of her 29th birthday to the sound of the phone ringing in the kitchen. Jasmine and Matt had been living in Lake Como for the past year. They moved from Florence after Matt quit his teaching job to work full-time on writing a novel. Lake Como was, they agreed, their favorite place on Earth.

Matt's dad and his partner, Camilla, lived a few blocks away with their golden retriever, Felix. Almost every morning, Jasmine took Felix for a long walk before she started her job at the local newspaper. Jasmine and Felix had a three-mile loop that was beautiful this time of year. She was contemplating skipping her walk to sleep in longer on her birthday but decided that her daily walk was a small part of the reason why she woke up so happy in her new life. It was a life so far away from the small town in Idaho that Jasmine and Matt were both thankful for every day. She missed her family, but they always seemed to find a way to stay connected, especially Jasmine and Zoey. Still, there was nothing that Jasmine missed more than just spending time with her sister in person.

As Jasmine sat up in bed, mustering the energy to put on her walking shoes and leave their comfortable king-sized bed, Matt wandered into the bedroom with the cordless phone in one hand and a cup of coffee for Jasmine in the other. He kissed her on the forehead and put his hand over the receiver as he mouthed "Happy Birthday" to her and stepped outside into the small front porch of their one-bedroom first-level apartment on the lake. Jasmine could see Matt through the window rocking on the rocking chair that he had insisted they bring with them from Florence. She laughed as she thought of their argument over that rocking chair. It had cost them way more than what the chair was actually worth to move it from Florence to Lake Como. But Matt loved it. Jasmine hoped to watch her husband rocking in that chair in front of Lake Como until they were old and gray.

The orange and red leaves fell from the trees just past their porch and Jasmine saw a young girl on a red bike pedal past Matt on the road in front of him. He waved and smiled at the girl. *He is going to be the best dad one day,* Jasmine thought to herself as she tied her shoes and pulled her long hair into a ponytail.

A few minutes later, Jasmine closed the screen door behind her as she felt the crisp fall air hit her cheeks. Matt was still on the phone rocking slowly in the chair on the porch when she turned to wave at him with the leash in her hand on the way to pick up Felix for their walk.

The past year since their July wedding had been a whirlwind. After two weeks of relaxing on their honeymoon, Jasmine and Matt went back to Florence for a month before deciding that they wanted to wake up every morning in Lake Como. Matt had started writing a novel during their honeymoon and they agreed he should quit his teaching job and focus full-time on making a career out of writing. Jasmine loved their new life on the lake. The only thing missing was her family and some friends. It had been difficult to make friends in another country. She missed Zoey and longed for her walks with Cassidy in Washington Park in Denver. As Felix jumped up to lick Jasmine on the cheek, she remembered the first time that she met Cassidy and her dog on the path in the park in Denver. It felt like a lifetime ago that the two new friends began their daily walks where they would tell each other everything. At least, Jasmine thought at the time that they were telling each other everything.

During their honeymoon, Matt told Jasmine that he tried to find Cassidy to get in touch with her and tell her about the wedding. He knew it was a long shot, but he knew that Jasmine's wedding day would have been perfect if he could get Cassidy to come. Jasmine didn't realize that she missed her that much until Matt told her he had tried to find her with no success. It was almost as if the girl that she thought of as her best friend for all those years in Denver had vanished. After everything Jasmine learned about what Cassidy was going through in silence, all she wanted to do was to be there for her friend, she just couldn't find her. Apparently, no one could.

It was two years almost to the day that Jasmine called Zoey to give her the news of her engagement. That was the same phone call where she learned much more about Cassidy and the secrets she had been keeping from what she thought was her best friend. As Jasmine led Felix to the path that they walked on almost every day in Lake Como on the day of her 29th birthday, she thought back to that phone call two years earlier she made to Zoey in Portland. Jasmine's heart sank as she remembered it. At first, Zoey sat quietly on the other line while Jasmine gushed about each and every detail of Matt's romantic proposal. Zoey's silence on the other line warned Jasmine that something was wrong. Within minutes, Jasmine knew Zoey needed to talk. Jasmine stopped talking in the middle of her sentence and sat silently, hoping for Zoey to open up.

"Are you ok? Zoey?" Jasmine waited a beat while her twin sister, oceans away, sounded to be fighting off tears. Jasmine and Zoey had talked enough about Matt that Jasmine knew the shakiness in her sister's voice had nothing to do with him proposing to her that day. Something else was going on.

Finally, Zoey burst into tears and told Jasmine what was happening. Kofi left, not before forgetting her birthday, and drove with his best friend, Reggie, to Seattle. He had a daughter. Cassidy had a daughter. Kofi and Cassidy had a daughter. She didn't get the abortion. Zoey was crying uncontrollably as she told Jasmine everything that day two years earlier. Jasmine sat silently on the other line while Zoey continued. She wanted desperately to be there for her sister, who was alone and seemingly drunk on their birthday in Portland. Jasmine sat on the phone with Zoey for as long as she could and urged her sister to just get some rest. She urged her to also understand what Kofi was going through. Sure, she was tired of being told to be the understanding one, but love doesn't just come around like this. Men like Kofi are complicated, and Jasmine knew that Zoey loved him. She also knew that Zoey's emotions were on the verge of being out of control and that if she said or did the wrong thing in Kofi's moment of need, neither of them knew what his response would be. Jasmine was thankful she had the words that day to calm her twin sister.

Every single day following that phone call two years earlier, Jasmine had thought about Cassidy. Sure, she thought about her before that day after they grew apart when Jasmine moved to Italy, but this was different. She had always assumed that Cassidy was just busy with her new life. Maybe she was in love, just like Jasmine was with Matt, and was just spending all her time and energy on something other than friendships. After hearing about the shocking news that Kofi had delivered to Zoey, Jasmine worried about Cassidy more than she had ever worried about a friend, outside of Zoey during her battle with anorexia, of course. She worried about the birth parents not being able to find her after realizing that their adopted child needed a kidney transplant. Jasmine worried about the friend she met almost a decade earlier in Denver in Washington Park that seemed to just always be the one listening and not the one to talk.

After learning about Kofi and Cassidy's relationship, it was clear that she was always the one supporting others. She talked him out of jumping off a bridge and then he basically abandoned her. Jasmine knew she would never be able to fully understand the hurt Cassidy must have gone through in her past. Jasmine felt guilty knowing that Cassidy must have felt like she couldn't tell her about her past and what she had gone through after meeting Kofi on that bridge in Portland. When she looked back, Jasmine was always the one leaning on Cassidy for everything. And Cassidy was always there for her. Jasmine had been so exhausted supporting Zoey during her battle with anorexia that she wasn't the friend that Cassidy needed. She was the same way when she was in an abusive relationship with James—always needing a shoulder to lean on and a friend to talk strength into her when she was the weakest. It broke Jasmine's heart that she must have missed the opportunity to be there for Cassidy. It was too late.

Felix darted toward a squirrel and Jasmine shook her head, bringing her back to the present on her walk. From where she stood, almost half a mile up the trail on her walk, she could see her and Matt's small first-story apartment in the distance. It was a small building with four one-bedroom apartments. Each had a small front porch and a bright red awning that hung over the front door. It felt more like home than anywhere ever had for Jasmine. She squinted to see if she could see Matt on the front porch rocking chair but couldn't see clearly through the trees that were blowing in the wind. Jasmine looked down at Felix and smiled. His big eyes were fixated on hers and she could swear he was smiling back at her. Camilla, who rescued Felix when he was just a puppy years before she met Matt's dad, called her "Aunt Jas" when she arrived to take Felix for his daily walk. Felix loved Jasmine and she loved him back.

Jasmine felt a lump in her throat as she watched Felix smiling back at her. It was then that she realized she might only ever be "Aunt Jas". Jasmine and Matt had been trying to have a baby for over a year with no success. She longed to be a mother and knew that Matt would make the best dad. But it just wasn't happening for them. Over the past year, Jasmine had taken countless pregnancy tests and had one miscarriage. It was the most painful thing she had ever experienced to lose a baby she had carried for four months. Just then, with Felix finally taking his eyes off Jasmine to watch a bird fly overhead, Jasmine realized what Cassidy must have felt like. Jasmine had lost a baby, but so did Cassidy. She knew she could never understand what Cassidy went through to carry a baby for nine months, deliver the baby, and then give the baby up for adoption because she knew the baby deserved a better life than what she could have provided.

Jasmine had Matt during the darkest time of her life when she suffered her miscarriage. He was there the moment she realized what was happening, when blood began to soak through her white shorts as she stood in the kitchen slicing mushrooms for their pasta sauce on a cold February night. Her stomach cramped and she knew exactly what was happening. She was losing her baby. She was losing the baby that she had already pictured being the best part of the rest of their lives. And for months after that cold night in February, Matt knew when Jasmine was thinking about that night, and he would rub her back and take care of her. And each time Jasmine would see the pregnancy test was negative when they finally decided to start trying again, Matt was there to comfort her.

Cassidy had no one. Jasmine imagined Cassidy in the hospital bed, after bringing her baby into the world. She imagined Cassidy in the hospital room, bright with harsh lighting full of nurses and doctors. Jasmine imagined the nurse pulling the baby away as she entered the world and took her first breath. She envisioned Cassidy watching as the baby that she brought into the world left her world for possibly forever. Jasmine thought of how Cassidy must have felt when the adoption agency called her and told her that the baby that she gave up for a better life was sick. It was too much to handle on her own. Jasmine should have been there for her friend. She should have read the signs like she did when Zoey first started to battle the disease that almost took her life. Jasmine was there for Zoey, but she failed Cassidy. Everyone failed Cassidy.

Felix pulled hard on her leash and Jasmine jumped. Another dog's tail was brushing back and forth on Jasmine's leg, and she gasped when the woman who seemed to have appeared out of nowhere brought her out of her daydream.

"Hi. Beautiful day, right?" the woman said with the same American accent that Jasmine had. Jasmine looked up from where she crouched near Felix and saw a woman about her age with dark brown hair and a big smile on her face. The woman had scooped up her small Shiba Inu into her arms and started laughing as it licked her face.

"Yes, it's really pretty today. Sorry about my dog. I never usually see anyone on this hike," Jasmine said, still trying to control Felix and his excitement.

"My name is Cherie. Nice to meet you." The woman held out her hand as her Shiba Inu tried to wiggle free.

"I am Jasmine. Are you heading back this way?" Jasmine said as she pointed in the direction she was heading to get back to her apartment.

"I am!"

The two women finished their first of many hikes together in Lake Como with Felix and the Shiba Inu. Jasmine didn't know it then, but she had just met the woman who would be one of her best friends throughout her entire life.

"Well, this is my place. Nice to meet you, Cherie. Let's definitely get together again soon." Jasmine smiled at her new friend and walked past the empty rocking chair on their patio, looking for Matt.

Cherie waved and turned to walk back down the paved path that the two women had just come from leading back toward the lake.

"Hey. I am glad you are home. I just got off the phone. Um… you should sit down, Jas. I have some bad news." Matt pushed his glasses to the top of his head and took his wife's hand and led her to the red chair in the kitchen.

"It's Cassidy. I found her," Matt said as Jasmine stared at Lake Como through the small window above the kitchen sink. A strong wind blew, and her view of the clear water was covered by red and orange leaves.

CHAPTER 24

WINTER — 2008

Kofi

Kofi sat in the waiting room of his therapist's office two days before Christmas. Soft music played as he picked up the candle on the table in front of him to read the label. He loved the smell of the waiting room and made a mental note to look for this same candle next time he was at the store. The smell calmed him down as he took a deep breath, closed his eyes, and slowly exhaled.

"Hi, Kofi. I am ready for you," Dr. Lewis, a tall, slender man in his late 40s said as he opened the creaky door and smiled at Kofi. Kofi stood and followed Dr. Lewis into his first of many therapy appointments.

Kofi never thought he was the type of person that would end up going to therapy, but there he was, sitting across from a doctor with a pen and a notepad, ready to deal with everything that had happened in his life. Kofi had hit rock bottom and felt like he was losing everything. First, Naya, then his mom, he almost lost Reggie, and now Zoey was on the brink of leaving him too. Kofi hadn't willingly sought out Dr. Lewis, but as he pulled a pillow from behind his back and looked around the room at the multiple degrees in dark frames on the wall, he was relieved to be there. He needed professional help. If he was honest with himself, he should have done this the year that Naya died. If this was the first day of his road to getting the love of his life back, he was ready. He was ready to fix what had all felt so broken.

It had been two months since the day Kofi had asked Zoey to be his wife. It was also two months to the day that she said no. She wouldn't agree to spend the rest of her life with him until he went to therapy. Zoey couldn't be there for him until he agreed to be there for himself. It was that day, two months earlier, that Zoey had packed her bags and boarded a plane to Italy to visit Jasmine. She told him that if she learned anything from fighting back from the brink of death herself, it was that she had to be the one to decide to live. If Zoey could fight depression as a high school kid, Kofi could do it as a man. He needed to show up for her, and by showing up today at Dr. Lewis' office, it felt as though today was the first day of the rest of his life.

Kofi knew he had to fix himself and that Zoey was right. He was depressed, blaming himself for what had happened to Naya, and now, what had happened to Cassidy. As Kofi glanced from degree to degree in Dr. Lewis' office, he thought of that day two months earlier he watched Zoey walk out of their apartment, wondering if she would ever come back. His mind flooded with memories of his mother turning her back on her only son on the day he needed her the most. He thought of Jasmine and Matt's wedding a year and a half before in Lake Como, and how Zoey had gone alone because Kofi couldn't get himself together enough to be by her side. He was selfish. And he was losing the only woman to ever love him.

Dr. Lewis sat quietly across from Kofi for what felt like an hour. Perhaps he didn't know where to start.

"Kofi. Tell me what brought you here today?" Dr. Lewis said, his degrees seemed to throb behind him in their frames. The dark-haired doctor pushed his glasses up on his nose and flicked his pen on the empty pad of paper in his hand. A wedding ring that was too tight on his finger caught Kofi's eye and he cleared his throat.

Kofi noticed that the same candle that sat in the waiting room sat on the coffee table between them. The flame flickered and he pulled in a deep breath and let the smell relax him as it had moments earlier.

"Well, Dr. Lewis, my girlfriend said I should get therapy. I have had a lot happen in my life. Been through a lot. I just don't think I have gotten past it… any of it really." Kofi stopped, thinking of the most recent tragedy he had gone through and wondered what kind of loss Dr. Lewis had gone through in his life.

Kofi noticed a picture of a family on the side table facing him. Dr. Lewis, his wife, and a little boy were all smiling under a big tree with matching black shirts on. Kofi wondered what kept Dr. Lewis up at night, if anything, as he thought of all the guilt he held in his heart. Suddenly, he felt his eyes well up with tears.

"Kofi," Dr. Lewis said as he handed him a tissue already in his hand as though the onset of tears was a first therapy appointment rite of passage.

"I am sure you are here for more reasons than your girlfriend saying you *should* get therapy." Dr. Lewis sat back, noticing Kofi looking at the picture in the frame.

"Can you tell me what is causing this emotion right now?" Dr. Lewis said, looking back at Kofi from the picture of his family.

Kofi felt a lump in his throat as he inhaled the calm smell of the candle deeply. He thought back to his birthday in Kentucky, the night Naya died. He could hear the dog barking almost as though he was in the same room with him and Dr. Lewis in the small brick building in Northwest Portland. Kofi thought of his mother, her voice screaming at him, but he couldn't hear anything but sirens and the same dog barking over and over again. Kofi told Dr. Lewis about the day that Naya died. He told him that he felt like he killed her. It was all his fault.

"Kofi, that was an accident. It was not your fault." Dr. Lewis scribbled on his paper and glanced back up at Kofi. He grew silent again, urging Kofi to continue.

Kofi told Dr. Lewis about his bike ride to the Hawthorne Bridge the year after Naya died. As he recounted that rainy day so many years before, he saw Cassidy, standing next to him on that bridge. He shook his head hard as he tried to erase the thought of her on that bridge. Tears streamed down his cheeks and Dr. Lewis handed him a short water bottle and told him to take a breath.

"We will come back to that. Just try to breathe." Dr. Lewis nodded his head to Kofi, letting him know he didn't need to keep talking. All the framed degrees had taught this man that he had gotten to the point with his patient that they needed to unpack. They sat in silence.

Finally, Kofi looked up.

"I pretty much killed her too. It was my fault. Naya, Cassidy…" Kofi trailed off and his shoulders began to shake.

"I have four lives on my hands, Dr. Lewis." Kofi trembled as he struggled to catch his breath. Dr. Lewis sat silently taking notes in his notebook without moving his eyes off of Kofi.

"Four?" Dr. Lewis stared at Kofi.

Adrian and Sara—Kofi couldn't say their names since that horrible night three months earlier. The couple who had adopted his and Cassidy's daughter and given her the life they knew they couldn't were dead.

As Kofi sat in silence in Dr. Lewis' office, he thought back to that night. It was the night before Zoey's birthday, and they had been on their second glass of wine at the Thai place on Northwest 23rd they had gone to on their first date. As Kofi found out later, it was also the place Zoey went to two years before when he forgot about her birthday on the night he and Reggie drove to Seattle. They were celebrating a day early because Kofi was scheduled to fly out to Kentucky the next day to visit Reggie. Once Reggie fully recovered from the complications of donating his kidney to Naya, Kofi vowed to keep in touch with his best friend and tried to see him a few times a year. The cheapest flight to Kentucky happened to fall on Zoey's birthday so they agreed to push up the celebration to the day before so Kofi could go and visit Reggie the next day.

Kofi and Zoey had become regulars at the Thai place on NW 23rd and Cole, the bartender and one of Zoey's closest friends now, always hooked them up with free drinks. They sat at the bar and held hands as they watched Cole clear their plates and fill their water. The restaurant was almost empty, and it was late. Behind them, the TV flickered, and Zoey noticed Cole's eyes grow large.

"Holy shit. This looks wild. I think this is Seattle," Cole said as he laid the plates back down on the counter. He rummaged around behind him looking for the remote amongst bottles of half-drunken wine.

"What is going on, Cole?" Zoey asked as she turned her head quickly while Cole turned the volume up on the TV.

Kofi turned just as a large picture appeared on the top of the screen while a newscaster reported live from what looked like a horrible car wreck. Kofi's jaw dropped as he saw the woman with two dark braids on the screen with a fiery scene behind her. It was Cassidy.

Words coming out of the reporter's mouth seemed to all blend together and Kofi and Zoey watched in horror as the news unfolded. There were words flying by on the bottom of the screen that were jumbling together in Kofi's brain.

"Hit and Run."

"Wanted."

"Both deceased."

"Attempted kidnapping."

"10-year-old daughter left behind."

Zoey grabbed Kofi's hand tightly as he finally heard the words coming out of the reporter's mouth.

"We are live from Seattle's Pike Place Market where hours earlier witnesses reported a hit and run. This looks to be a targeted attack and the driver is yet to be detained… a man and a woman were walking with their daughter and were hit by an oncoming vehicle. The driver then got out of the car, which had appeared to have caught on fire, and tried to grab the young girl who was able to escape unharmed with the help of witnesses…" The woman's voice trailed off as Kofi's mind raced. *Naya?*

Kofi felt Zoey's hand squeeze his and she repeated the words of the reporter.

"Ten-year-old daughter… unharmed… Naya is ok. What the fuck, Kofi?" Zoey stared at Kofi in shock.

Cole looked at Zoey and reached across the counter to grab her hand as he turned up the volume on the TV.

The reporter grabbed her ear and looked down at the ground as if to try hard to hear the words coming through her earbuds.

"Oh my god. Cassidy. What have you done?" Kofi said as the reporter continued.

"We have an update coming to us from Portland." The reporter disappeared from the screen and a tall man holding an umbrella appeared in her place. Cassidy's picture stayed on the top of the screen.

"We are live from Portland's Hawthorne Bridge. Witnesses reported an abandoned vehicle that matches the description of the vehicle used in the deadly hit and run earlier this evening in downtown Seattle. Divers are working to recover what is expected to be the body of the driver in that attack. It appears the driver jumped to her death from this area on the bridge. We will share updates as they come in." The man stood in silence as Kofi realized that the reporter stood at the exact spot that Kofi had met Cassidy on the top of the Hawthorne Bridge.

"Kofi. Take your time but I do hope you will find the courage to tell me what you are thinking," Dr. Lewis said as Kofi looked up. He had been staring at the candle as his mind took him back to that horrible night three months before the day he sat across from Dr. Lewis.

"I just… I just feel like this is all my fault. I told Cassidy to have an abortion. Then I just left. She killed them. Then she killed herself. I don't know if I can ever forgive myself for all this, Dr. Lewis. I took away all my daughter knows as family."

Kofi looked up as tears continued to stream down his face.

"I am going to leave you with a few words to think about in between sessions, Kofi. First, forgiveness is a part of happiness. If you can't forgive yourself, you won't ever be happy. If you aren't happy, then you can never make anyone in your life happy that you care about. Lastly, your daughter has family. Sometimes with loss comes unexpected love."

Dr. Lewis closed his notebook and removed his glasses. Kofi noticed that darkness had fallen outside, and he thought of Zoey in Italy with her sister. He didn't know what time it was there, but he knew, no matter how much time it took him to heal, she was worth it.

"This is for you." Dr. Lewis ripped a page from inside his notebook and handed it to Kofi. He stood and opened the door. Kofi grabbed the note and read the last words that Dr. Lewis had said to him on the piece of paper.

"Sometimes with loss comes unexpected love." He folded the piece of paper and put it in his pocket.

"See you in two weeks," Dr. Lewis said as Kofi smiled and walked past him, entering the lobby. He took a deep breath and exhaled.

"Can we do this every week?" Kofi said, glancing at Dr. Lewis with his hands in his pockets.

"Sure. Same time next week."

Kofi began to walk back to the apartment that felt so empty without Zoey. He stopped in front of a one-story white house to watch a family through the large window. *I want a family,* he thought as he watched the little boy sitting on his father's lap at the kitchen table while the mother carried a pan of food toward them with a smile. He wondered if this was the same family that Zoey had told him about a few years earlier. She had brought up to Kofi that she wanted a family when they were waiting for Reggie to get out of the hospital after donating his kidney in Seattle. She wanted a future with him. That was the first time they spoke about him really getting help, after Zoey saw the family that she longed for so badly.

Kofi looked up, and for the first time since he had been living in Portland, he saw snow falling from the sky. He watched as the little boy jumped off his dad's lap and ran to the window, looking up into the sky just as Kofi had. Kofi didn't really believe in much after all he had been through. It was hard to believe that everything happened for a reason, or that fate had a way of guiding you to where you were supposed to be. He had seen and been through too many hard times to believe. But the snow falling from the sky that day felt like a sign for him. It was a sign from his little sister. Kofi felt the snow fall onto his face as he looked up into the sky and decided that it was time for him to forgive himself and to finally believe he could be happy.

As Kofi opened the door to their apartment, he noticed the flashing red light on the answering machine. He smiled as he listened to Reggie's voice on the other line. His best friend was happy and healthy, and Kofi appreciated him checking in on him so often as nobody had ever done that before. As he went to pick up the phone to call Reggie back, it began to ring. He dropped his keys and answered.

"Hello?"

"Kofi. It's me, Zoey. I have something to tell you."

CHAPTER 25

WINTER – 2014

Zoey

Jasmine laughed as I pulled the pink and purple blanket over my feet. I sniffed it and raised my eyebrows, and she glared back at me. I felt a rush of nostalgia as I realized that the blanket was almost as old as we were—35 years old.

"Auntie Jasmine. Will you help me?"

I watched as my twin sister knelt to tie my son's shoelace and smiled as he put his hand on top of her head to balance himself on one foot. He looked over at me and smiled back, anxious to run outside in the freshly fallen snow to play catch with his dad. It didn't snow that often in Italy in December. Jasmine's dog, Jasper, licked his cheek and he wrapped his small arms around the dog's neck and laughed. Jasper wiggled to release his grip and rolled onto his back.

It was the day before Christmas and we were in Lake Como, at Matt and Jasmine's house. My son, Taye, had just turned five. He had big, brown eyes and soft, curly dark hair. It was the first time I had been back to Italy since before I became a mom. It was the first time we were in Italy together as a family.

As I watched Taye run through the kitchen and out the front door, Jasper following right behind him, I thought back to my life before him. Those days before him, I thought I knew what love was, but I was wrong. I thought back to the day, exactly six years before, when I found out I was going to be a mom.

That day, six years earlier, I sat in the kitchen with Jasmine, looking at the lake through the window. The water grew still as the day turned into night. I had known for just a few hours that I was two months pregnant. I hadn't ever really gotten back to regular periods since being anorexic and finally took a test after waking up sick the morning before.

"You have to tell him, Zoey. He knows what he has to do to stay in your life and this news is not going to change that. You love him. He just has to love himself and that is what he is trying to do right now. Give him the time he needs."

Jasmine handed me the phone and left the room. She returned just moments later and wrapped a blanket around my shoulders. I laughed, realizing it was the same blanket that she had brought for me in the hospital in high school on New Year's Eve when I was fighting to beat anorexia. I could almost hear "Auld Lang Syne" playing over and over again as it had during my senior year in the hospital on New Year's Eve. Maybe it was a sign that my memory brought up that moment, I thought as I looked at the phone in my hand. The first words of that song ask if old acquaintances should be forgotten. I knew Kofi was trying to work through all that he had been through. He was trying to forget. I hoped one day, we could move past all of that.

Jasmine smiled and nodded at my hand, grasping the phone. I watched as she disappeared through the front door to join Matt on the porch. Jasper was a puppy then and followed her closely through the front door. I laughed as he ran into the back of her legs when she stopped in front of Matt. I caught eyes with Matt and smiled. I wondered if he loved that Jasmine loved dogs just like his mom had. I thought of her laying on the floor with their golden retriever in high school. Jasmine would make an amazing mother one day, hopefully.

I dialed the number to the apartment I shared with Kofi in Portland, and he picked up quickly. I hadn't spoken to him since I turned down his proposal and told him that I could not be with this broken Kofi. He needed to heal and forgive himself if he wanted a future with me. He needed professional help. He needed to do this if he wanted a future at all. I knew I couldn't do anything more for him when I left that day, but it was still the hardest thing I had ever done.

That day I left Kofi in Portland, I remembered how I felt when Matt had left me alone on the dancefloor in high school. Suddenly, that day felt like yesterday that I was standing, watching the man I thought loved me walk away. That was the day Matt made me realize that I had to learn to live. I needed to love myself before I could ever expect anyone to love me. I knew I had hit rock bottom that day. It was the first day of the rest of my life because I had finally understood that I was the only one who could save myself. When I left Kofi alone in our apartment in Portland two months earlier, I needed Kofi to understand that too.

"Kofi. It's me, Zoey. I have something to tell you."

Kofi sat silently on the other line after I told him I was pregnant. I wondered if he was thinking about his sister. I wondered if he was thinking about the little girl in Seattle who shared his DNA and just lost her parents and her birth mother on the same day. She was once again looking for parents to give her the life she deserved. The two girls shared more than just the same name. Finally, he told me what I needed to hear.

"I can do this. We can do this. You know, maybe I do believe in fate. This is fate," Kofi said confidently on the other line.

He sounded much closer than the oceans away from me that he was. Kofi told me about his appointment with Dr. Lewis and that he decided to go weekly and already felt a weight lifted off his shoulders after just one session. He told me how he stopped on the way home and saw a family through the window of a white house off NW 23rd. It was the same white house I had stopped in front of when I realized I wanted a family of my own. He told me about the snow falling in Portland for the first time since he had lived there and about the little boy running to the window to watch the snow fall.

"Zoey, sometimes with unexpected loss comes unexpected love."

Kofi was right six years ago when he said those words to me over the phone. *And I have found the third and final love of my life,* I thought as I watched Kofi through the window throwing a ball to Taye in the front yard of Jasmine and Matt's house in Lake Como.

"Aunt Zoey. Did you see my gift? Mom and Dad said now that I am 17, I can finally read Dad's book." I turned to see Naya with her head bowed, staring at the cover of Matt's book. I caught eyes with Matt who was sitting across from his adopted daughter in the same kitchen chair I sat on six years earlier when I called Kofi to tell him I was having his child. Matt glanced at Naya, the girl who made him a dad by complete chance and came into his life because of tragedy. She had found the parents to give her the life that she deserved. Dr. Lewis was right, Naya did have a family.

Matt looked up and sipped his coffee, recognizing the irony of the fact that his daughter was also technically my stepdaughter. I smiled back, recognizing the irony of how our entire lives had played out.

"Do you think 17 is old enough for her to read it?" Matt asked with another slow sip of coffee.

"Well, it's the story of a couple of 17-year-olds anyway, isn't it?" Naya said as she flipped the book over to look at the picture of her dad on the back of his best-selling novel. It was a black and white picture of Matt, sitting on the porch swing of his and Jasmine's old house in Florence. Jasmine wandered into the kitchen with a cup of water and dumped it into the plant on the windowsill. She stood over Naya and smiled at the picture of her husband on the back of the book. She bent down and kissed Naya on the cheek. Tragedy and fate had finally made Jasmine a mom.

"It's not technically a story of 17-year-olds. It's our story. All of it," Matt said, his heart full of pride as he watched his adopted daughter read every word under his picture on the back of the book.

I thought back to Matt at his mother's funeral. The poem he read as her favorite song played that day was the first page of his book. He and Naya had both lost their mothers. In Naya's case, she had lost two mothers. I caught eyes with him again as we both waited for Naya to flip back to the first page of this book in her hands. Just as she opened it to the first page, I heard Kofi open the front door. I opened my arms as Taye ran to me, Jasper following behind him. Kofi brushed snow off of his black jacket and pulled his hood down. I mouthed "I love you" to him across the room and he smiled.

Matt stood and turned the radio up that sat on the mantel above the fireplace. A combination of piano, guitar, and strings filled the air as he grabbed Jasmine's hand and pulled her close to dance with him in the kitchen. Kofi smiled at me and winked at Naya as she rolled her eyes at Matt and Jasmine.

Dean Martin's voice filled the room as his words changed from Italian to English.

"We can sing in the glow of a star that I know of
Where lovers enjoy peace of mind.
Let us leave the confusion and all this disillusion behind
Just like birds of a feather, a rainbow together we'll find
  Volare..."

"Will you read it to me?" Taye asked me as he watched his cousin, who was also technically his half-sister, grab the purple and pink blanket and lay down on the couch in front of the fireplace, book in hand.

One day, I would tell my son the story of our lives. I would tell him about the sleepy town in Idaho where it all began. One day, I would tell Taye about the rainy day in Portland when I met his dad. Eventually, he would understand all the ways that fate had brought us all to this house in Italy on Christmas Eve. He would hear the story of the phone call that Jasmine made to the Adoption Center of Seattle on the day of the fiery crash that killed Naya's parents.

Kofi sat next to me and pulled Taye onto his lap.

"I can tell you a story about the first time I saw snow in Portland. It was the same day we found out about you," Kofi said as Taye's eyes grew sleepy and his head fell onto my shoulder.

"It's bedtime," I said, noticing that Jasmine and Matt had turned off the radio on the mantel and retired for the night.

"I wanna sleep with Naya," Taye said as he wiggled from Kofi's lap and stood in front of Naya, waiting for her to make room for him on the skinny couch.

Naya smiled at Kofi and motioned to Taye to join her on the couch. As the moon took over the sky on that Christmas Eve night, she opened the book and began to read the story of two 17-year-olds and all the losses and all the loves of their lives.

Made in United States
Troutdale, OR
09/10/2024

22721636R00130